TALLEYMAN

Victorian Maritime Series
Book One

John James

SAPERE
BOOKS

TALLEYMAN

Published by Sapere Books.

20 Windermere Drive, Leeds, England, LS17 7UZ,
United Kingdom

saperebooks.com

ISBN: 978-1-80055-437-5

For Mary, who came with me to Eyories.

NOTE

There is no Martello Tower at Eyories, nor any jetty. But the welcoming Hutsman's House at Cashel existed till recently, and that efficient policeman, Superintendent Trant, was real enough. So too were Mr William Smith Bronterre O'Brien, and the members of his Committee; and the Man in the White Coat certainly was present at the Rebellion in the Cabbage Patch, but no one ever found out who *he* was. The Bay concerned is the Coulagh Bay on the Kenmare River.

PART I: WINTER

1

Santorin came to her anchor in the long bay. The open sea was ten miles behind. To port, to the north, the hills rose straight from the salt water's edge, two thousand feet into the blue sky, flecked with the driven clouds coming in fast on the front from the open ocean. Cricklade sat miserably in the sternsheets of the launch, under the ship's quarter. He felt frightened, frightened of the seamen in the boat, frightened of the shore to which they were bound, most of all frightened of Talleyman. If there were anything to do wrong, he would do it in front of Talleyman, he was sure of it. And he *liked* Talleyman, that was the worst of it. Therefore, he waited in silent terror till he saw the lieutenant's gaunt length come swinging down the ship's side, out of the mizzen chains into the launch.

'Push off,' Talleyman ordered. He sat beside Cricklade, took the tiller from him, stared over the seamen's shoulders at the southern shore. Cricklade had been looking at that shore since daybreak, wondering what it would be like going there, getting out on to that beach. He had been at sea for six weeks now, six weeks in his first ship and not yet once out of it. He could scarcely remember what it was like to sit in comfort, to eat a meal off a real table which stayed still, to eat more than a few inches from where he slept, to eat out of the stench of stagnant water. A Cadet was not fit even for the gunroom, but lived and ate where he could, slinging his hammock, once he had learnt to sling it and stow it, far down inside the ship in the cockpit. He knew better than to address a lieutenant without an invitation.

He remembered the first time he had spoken to Talleyman. It was the most important night of the past weeks. Cricklade had first seen him sitting over the remains of a dinner in the Keppel's Head at Portsmouth, a tall bony man in a blue uniform, drawing on the tablecloth with a stub of pastel which he had taken from his pocket, and had left stains of chalk dust on the dark cloth. Cricklade clung close to the waiter's elbow. He felt miserable and lost. He had been twelve hours by coach and train and cab in the cold of December, and he had not the slightest idea of what to do next or how to do it.

'If you please, sir,' asked the waiter, when Tom Talleyman looked up from his sketching to gaze out into the harbour, 'Are you going out to *Santorin*, sir?'

'I am. As soon as I have finished getting warm. Why? Do you want to go to sea? I could get you a berth. Always berths for healthy men. Queen's ships always short.'

'Oh, bless you, no sir. But there's a gentleman here as wants to go out to her, too, sir.'

Cricklade felt that the slight hanging of breath over the word gentleman was as good as quotation marks. He watched the tall man's stony brown eyes as they travelled down the waiter's arm in search of this doubtful quantity. Cricklade hoped he was dressed properly. He had read his Peter Simple and was terrified of making some dreadful error which would blight all the rest of his life.

'I'll look after him.' Cricklade felt that his own expression was lightening and wondered why, since he did not feel any real relief.

The tall man asked, 'You're going to sea, then?'

'Oh, yes, sir. I'm to be a cadet, sir.'

'Why?'

'I've got a nomination, sir. From the Admiralty — my mother's sister knew the First Lord's wife.'

'No. Why go to sea? I can see what you are. But why?'

Cricklade now really felt a load off his mind. At least his uniform must be correct enough to be recognizable. But the question was one he had heard asked a hundred boring times in the weeks before. He still had no real answer. To say that it was a quick way of leaving school, that it was better than going into the Church like his father, he had learnt by experience were not acceptable answers in the adult world. And this was certainly an adult, much older than Cricklade was, and he was twelve: years later he found out that Talleyman had been twenty-two that December of 1847, but at the time, Cricklade was not able to make fine distinctions. He was a boy, this was a man. He weighed up this opposition as best he could, and answered in what he thought was a tactful manner, 'I want to be a captain, like you, sir.'

Talleyman did not seem flattered, or amused, or even offended. He simply said, 'Don't know much, do you. I'm not a captain.'

Cricklade did know that much, but little more. So he asked, 'What are you then, sir? A mate?'

Talleyman gazed down on him with a wary expression. It told Cricklade that here was a man who had been gulled in his time by smaller morsels than this, and Cricklade quailed. But then Talleyman seemed to decide that this was indeed an innocent, and protected by whatever gods there were.

'I'm a lieutenant. Look, one gold ring on my cuff, and two epaulettes. A captain has three rings. A mate has one, and one epaulette. They altered it all a fortnight ago. Again. They alter it all twice a year. First Lord married a tailor's daughter. Good for trade.'

An older and wiser Cricklade would have guessed how Talleyman could sound so confident. One epaulette was worn and tarnished on the sea-stained frock coat; the other was bright, sewn on, it was clear, a day or two before. Talleyman went on, 'You'll learn the difference in time. Anything with an epaulette, you call "sir". Nobody else. Don't dress like that at sea. Pea jacket. Old trousers will do. Don't suppose you've got any *old* trousers in that chest. You got undress?'

Cricklade was doubtful whether he was meant to take his clothes off, so he said, 'I think so, sir. The outfitter told me I'd got everything.'

'If he said you'd got everything, you've got more than everything. And twice as much again. You'll find out on board. Don't buy anything more. Not without asking. Don't ask me. Ask a mate. How old are you?'

'Thirteen, sir. Nearly.' The short sentences were catching, Cricklade felt. Was this the way sailors really talked?

'You look older. That age — I was in Mr Inman's Academy. In Portsmouth. One of the last. Year after I left, they closed it down. Probably my fault. Packed the lads straight off to sea. Like you. Been doing it ever since. I learned a lot there: how to draw, how to play chess and win money. I didn't go to the gunroom green. Don't suppose you'd like to play chess? No? You'll learn. You ever been in a ship?'

'Not in a ship, sir. We live near Windermere, and I've had a little sailing boat on the lake for years. That's what I like, sailing, it's all so clean and quiet, and you feel — you feel like a god, just free and controlling yourself on the water.'

'Join the navy and be free? Remarkable. Won't do you much harm. Only mark you for life, like me. What's your name?'

'Cricklade, sir.'

'Right, Mister Cricklade. Have a glass of rum. Warm you up to go out.'

'Oh, no sir, thank you sir, but I couldn't touch drink, sir, not strong drink. There's nobody in my family would drink, sir, and my father's very keen on it—'

'Your father's keen on drinking?'

'Oh, no sir, not *on*—' and then Cricklade caught Talleyman's eye, it wasn't hard and stony after all but rather moist, soft like a spaniel's. He began almost to laugh.

Talleyman grunted, 'Mind your language at sea. No quarter asked nor given. Waiter! Hot coffee for this gentleman. Very hot. You'll need it in that weather out there.'

Cricklade scalded his throat with the coffee. He felt a glow of virtue at standing true to his ... well, to his father's principles. Everyone at home had told him he would be tempted in all kinds of unnamed ways, and here he was resisting temptation already before he even got into a ship. But even he could see, now, that Talleyman had been in the Keppel's Head for some time already, busily not resisting temptation and getting ready for the driving rain out there. He was not old enough to suspect that this big grown-up lieutenant might be as nervous about joining this new ship as he was.

'Right! Are you ready? Have you a boat cloak or something? Wrap that top coat well around you. Now follow that porter with our chests in the barrow, and we'll get ourselves out to *Santorin*.'

'Which is she, sir?' Cricklade peered about him in the early dusk. 'Is she that one?'

'No. That's *Victory*. Firm aground on her own boiled beef bones. A good thing too. Rotten to the keel. Looks like a Chinese herring net. I don't know where *Santorin* is.'

'Will the waterman know, sir?'

'The *Santorin*'s round by the vittling yard,' the waterman told them. 'She's loading Indian corn in sacks. Going out East, they say.'

'Indian corn? I suppose there's some reason for sending corn to the Indies. Their Lordships will have some reason. Usually it's because they've gone mad. Again.'

'Will the captain tell us, sir?'

'Captains never tell. Especially they never tell why they're captains.'

Cricklade was not sure whether that was meant to be funny or not. Instead of risking a laugh, he asked, 'Who is the captain, sir?'

'I don't know. Who's the captain, my man?'

It appeared that the waterman did not take kindly to being called Tom Talleyman's man. After the question had been asked twice more, he grumbled, 'I dunno, only the first captain they 'ad, 'e was in 'er a week, and then 'e got out of 'er and they puts another captain in 'er. And 'e only come four days ago, and 'e turfs one of the lieutenants out what was in 'er already straight away and nobody don't say why. And getting 'er out in a 'urry they are, but for what nobody's not saying either.'

'They called me in a hurry,' Talleyman salved his dignity by addressing, ostensibly, the cadet: Cricklade had enough perception to realize that, to know that he did not in himself count for such confidences. 'Got my commission as her fourth lieutenant yesterday. Orders to join, all in the same post. No captain's name. But it *is* a captain, I know that. Not a commander.'

'How do you know, sir?'

'Looked her up in Steele's list. My orders said Frigate *Santorin*. In the list, she's a sloop. Sixth-rate — about two hundred and fifty men. Sometimes that's a commander, sometimes it's a junior captain. Can't have a captain in a sloop. Alter the name to a Frigate to make her fit for a captain. So it must be a captain new promoted.'

'There she is, now,' put in the waterman. 'Over there she is, close in to the observatory.'

Cricklade peered into the rain, driving into his face, filling his eyes. Then, in a voice of heartbreak, 'But — she's got a funnel. She's a steamer!'

'Of course she's a steamer.' Talleyman was laughing at him, rubbing it in.

'Did you know she was a steamer, sir?'

'Yes. She's got our boilers.'

'Your boilers? What do you mean, sir.'

'Can't you see my name on my chest?'

'It's Tal… Talleyman. Oh.'

'Yes. My father made her boilers. Or his men did. Our first navy contract. I was a mid then. In the old *Argyle*. They built her as a steamer. Then she was laid up as soon as finished. Been in reserve ever since. This is my day, youngster. I've had ten years in the navy. I came into it the day the old King died. I grew up in a boiler works. This is my first steamer. Don't you like the idea?'

'No!' The boy was near to tears. 'I don't want to go to sea in an old tea-kettle.'

'There's no other way to go,' Talleyman assured him. 'Not if you've got any sense.' The waterman snorted.

'There ought to be a law agin steam. They're going to 'ave a steam ferry 'ere one day, they says, to take the bread out of our mouths.'

'Then you can take a turn nearer honesty,' snapped Talleyman. 'Become a pusser.'

The waterman broke off social relations altogether at this titanic insult. Cricklade stored it up against future emergencies. He examined his neighbour closely, to see what kind of criminal wanted to have steam in the navy. Seated in the boat he did not seem so terrifyingly tall. But his nose was hooked, broken some time, and with the brown eyes which now flashed, now looked soft and placid, he alternated between the spaniel and the hawk. Now it was a limpid, cow-eyed look of absolute worship which he directed at *Santorin*. Cricklade followed the look.

To his land eyes, the ship looked lopsided. The paddle boxes bulged out from the sides. With the two funnels, they filled the midships' third of the ship, forcing the main mast aft till there was scarcely room to step the mizzen beyond it. The black hull rose twenty feet above the water, flush over all. Six feet from the water line there was a white strake, broken by gun ports, three forward of the paddle boxes on this exposed starboard side, three aft. There were ports on the upper deck too, but they were black, merged into the side, and hard to count. Boats hung from davits beside the mizzen mast, and one was tied to a boom. It was clear, even in the dark, that on the hidden port side there was a lighter from which sacks were being swung up into the frigate by a derrick.

The waterman brought the boat into the side under the boom, close in to the foot of a companion ladder leading up to an entry port abaft the paddle box. A seaman caught at the wherry with a boat hook to hold it in place, and others waiting on the base of the paddle box came to heave the chests inboard. Talleyman pushed the boy in front of him up the companion way.

'When you get to the top, lad, turn aft — to your left. And touch your hat.'

Talleyman himself, at the top of the companion way, turned to the quarterdeck and raised his hat, instead of touching it. The master-at-arms noted this bit of old-fashioned punctilio, and drew at once a host of conclusions, more or less correct, about what he might or might not get away with. This would be a straight-laced one, all right. And then Talleyman started, and Cricklade jumped out of his skin at a bellow from aft.

'You're late, Mr Talleyman, you're late, you're a day late! Get your working clothes on! I can't stand your watch for you for ever.'

To Cricklade's surprise, Talleyman turned to the speaker with a beam of pleasure. Cricklade had not seen him smile before. The face was neither hawk nor dog, now, but pure man. He called, 'Aye, aye sir.' Then, to Cricklade, 'Go aft, and report yourself to Captain Pentstemon. The gangway messenger will take your chest down to the cockpit.'

Pentstemon disposed of the cadet in a few well-chosen words, a speech calculated to combine terror, obscenity, economy and a wave of warm and brotherly welcome, and looked for his first lieutenant. *At least,* he thought, *I'll have one man in this ship I can rely on. I've put the third son of a viscount out of her on to the beach to get you this berth, young Tal, and you'll have to work to keep it.* Not that the young lordling had wanted much to stay when he found that his first protector was, after all, refusing this command. Dirty work, perhaps, well … so what else was a navy for but to do Government's dirty work. With commands for not one captain in three, Vallins must have been mad to turn it down merely because he did not like the sound of the commission. Pentstemon would never have turned it down — well, of course, he hadn't. Once Vallins had said no, it had to go to a commander beneath him in the list, to be made up into it. And this, if only Vallins had seen it, was *the* command. There could be nothing better for a captain who wanted to have his name in the newspapers, and have a claim to another commission after this, and perhaps then a seat in the House or some such sinecure. And Pentstemon wanted desperately to be employed again, to have a ship, ships, to see his name move up the list, to have his flag, his own flag, at last.

Yes, that had been a good day when Vallins had not liked what he had read, and told their Lordships that they could do what they liked with their ship, so only he were not required to sail in her. Not that anyone who actually *saw Santorin* could really fail to sympathize. So Pentstemon had been taken off the top of the Commander's list, where he had expected to spend another five years, and made captain in an instant. This was a make-or-break appointment, made with malicious intent, he knew that: but Pentstemon was sure that he was made.

The first lieutenant appeared from the main hatch. He looked desperately ill and tired, Pentstemon thought. Would he survive through this commission? Or did someone hope him dead? He was as tall and thin as the captain was short and — not stout, but with too much flesh hanging on a slight frame. The skin had a pallor which meant that something was not right with the captain, that somehow what he ate was being turned into a burden, not a joy. Paxton Only was sere and grey, grey of face and of thinning hair. He peered down at Pentstemon in the gathering dusk.

'The cornmeal is all aboard and stowed, sir.'

'Would it not have been done earlier if we had thought to move the main deck armament into the hold before we had filled the main deck with the sacks?'

Only swallowed and said nothing. That Pentstemon, his junior, should have got all these appointments and was now a captain, while he himself was still a lieutenant, and suddenly, senselessly, in a ship after seven years on the beach, showed that someone at the Admiralty had it in for Paxton Only. This captain, however — at least he had been at Navarino: it was something. There weren't many left at these low ranks today who had any idea of what action was like. When the time came to fight the French again, it was men like this, not baby-faced youths, who would do the bloody business. It meant something, still, to have smelt powder. What use would this baby-faced fourth lieutenant be, that Pentstemon had been so keen to get, telegraphing to somewhere deep in the Fens the moment he got into the ship, hardly waiting till he had made at least one of the lieutenants so miserable he just went. But nobody was going to taunt and irritate Paxton Only out of a berth. So he said nothing, only waited till Pentstemon should speak again.

After a long minute, he heard, 'We ought to be ready now to sail at any minute.'

Only debated whether this were an order or a question. There was no knowing what style a captain would adopt. There were those who never gossiped, never spoke except to give their orders: there were those who gossiped and explained what they were about, often hiding it successfully in a stream of personalities: and among these were captains who left all decisions to their juniors: and there were captains who never spoke at all except to blame their officers for the actions they had taken in the face of their leader's silence. He made therefore an indecisive contribution, 'The wind's in the west, sir.'

'Then will getting out not require some preparation and skill?'

'Shall I ask for a steam tug, sir?'

'This is a steam *ship*, Mr Only. Why keep a dog and bite yourself?'

'But sir, have you considered the position in the engine room? We are at least spared the possibility of using that filthy machinery.'

'The position in the engine room will soon be remedied. Here comes our dog.'

So this, thought Only, *is our new fourth lieutenant.* Another tall man. Only despised short men: it showed a lack of determination to grow. Tall men he regarded as rivals. This one was taller than he was.

Pentstemon looked up at him, and spoke sternly, 'Be respectful to your first lieutenant, Mr Talleyman. At least, be more respectful than you were to your own first first lieutenant when you were in *Argyle*.'

'Aye, aye sir.'

Only felt a little mollified. He must curb his feelings and regard this cuckoo introduced into what had been a well-behaved and properly brought up wardroom. The man had changed into a pea jacket, already. But the thought of the open sea was already flooding into the first lieutenant's mind. He had not been near it for five years, and then it had been in a bathing machine. He could feel sick already.

Pentstemon was going on, 'Now, young Tal, I see that you did put your working rig on. Since you are the fourth and last lieutenant of this mighty ship, I give into your charge the engineer and all his works, although if he does any work, I will be much obliged if you would bring it to my notice, since I have not been able to discover up to now what he does do. In addition to all the other lowly duties that befit your station, you will be responsible to me for the steam engine.'

'Is the engineer … indisposed, sir?'

'I suppose you mean drunk. It may surprise you, as it did me, that this engineer is the very pattern of sobriety. There are other things wrong with him — incompetence for one, and stupidity for another, and I suppose that he must be obnoxious in some way I have not been able to discover, because he has no Mates where he ought to have two, no juniors in all Pompey being willing to sail with him. But I intend that with him or without him we shall clear this harbour as soon as we can which ever way the wind may blow, so we will have to do it under steam. I well remember how you used to lecture me on the virtues of steam when you were a mid: pray will you demonstrate them to me? How soon can we cast off?'

Talleyman looked from Pentstemon earnestly requesting information, to Only, who tried to dissociate himself from the whole bad business. *He must be tempted*, thought the first lieutenant, *to make some quick and definite response to impress me. But if he is wrong, then he risks ... well a life of hell at best from the first lieutenant, and if he seems to deceive the Captain* — Only reflected that he himself had spent seven years on the beach for less than that. There was little chance that this lad would have a peer as neighbour to bring on a little political pressure and get him into a ship.

He heard Talleyman ask, 'Have you steam up, sir?'

'Now, lad,' asked the captain. 'How should I know?'

'Are the furnaces alight, sir?'

The question brought a look of horror to Only's face. He had not yet spoken a word. He did not trust himself to say anything in reply to such lunacy.

Pentstemon asked, 'Does it make any difference to you whether the kettle is on the fire already or not?'

'If the fires are drawn, sir, it does. It will take us at least four hours to raise steam.'

'Then we will sail in four hours. Mr Only, I am sure that you will be well able to navigate this channel in the dark, but should you find yourself in any difficulty, be sure to tell me about it — in the morning.'

Only knew that he would have little but difficulty. Before he could say anything, Talleyman coughed.

'I beg your pardon, sir...'

'Now, what strange paths of thought has your mind gone down this time, young Tal?' Only felt a hint of exclusion, a sense that he was only a witness to a conversation that had begun long ago, in *Argyle*, a language with its own constructions, its own lunatic vocabulary.

'First, we raise steam, sir. But then we must warm the engine.'

'Warm the engine? Now, I do believe, young Tal, that you have mistaken this machinery for some old and rare red wine, but I can assure you that it is nothing but a load of scrap iron, especially the boilers.'

'Wine's the same all the way through, sir. But even *old* iron— '

'I am used to hearing your obscene language, but although I am full of admiration for the recondite and subtly obscene terms I have heard you use, I really will not tolerate blasphemy.'

'An engine's a lot of different parts, sir. We can't start just as soon as we have steam up. Some parts will be cold then. Others will get hot very quickly. You get differential expansion.'

'I admit I get gout, but I do not know if that is the same as differential ... what do you call it? Digestion? You young lads get so scientific nowadays, there's no keeping up with you, and we may as well all go to *Excellent* and become gunners.'

'Some parts will expand quicker than others, sir. Then they will break. Like wood warping, sir.'

'Oh, warping, why didn't you say so in the first place? We all know about warping, being warped ourselves in various places. I suppose we must have all this machinery, though I have lived long enough without it and done reasonably well so far, although I have more experience of steam than most captains — I once travelled on a steam packet between London and Greenwich. What about you, Only?'

'I have never been in a steamer in my life, sir. It's quite unnecessary for there is enough motive power in the ship already to move it against any wind, as I have already set out in a hundred pamphlets to the Admiralty, although their Lordships—'

'Yes, yes, quite unnecessary. But their Lordships say we must have steam, and we may as well use it. So! My orders say that we must sail as soon as we have finished loading and have aboard a reasonable proportion of the ship's company, which I have always taken to mean every man that she is rated to carry, which is why we had to wait for young Tal here. So since we have done loading that very peaceful cargo into a man-of-war, and since the orders make no mention of the state of the tide or wind, we must start as soon as we have steam. When will the engines — your engines — be ready, Mr Talleyman?'

'It will take eight hours, sir, at the least. If the machinery is in good order.'

'We will allow for that. We will cast off at first light, Mr Only, which will give us about twelve hours to wait on the differential expansion in hourly expectation of the explosion which the engineer is bound to provoke. Off to your tinkering, Mr Talleyman, and God give you a good deliverance.'

Only watched Talleyman move cautiously forward on the greasy deck, till he found the engine room companion way. He unhooked a lighted lantern, and went down into the darkness of what Only knew was a cramped and dirty space, large but crowded with machinery. Forward of the engine room, in the forward stokehold, drowned in a general smell of dead coke and cold oil, and a sense of huge unused … things, a man sat by a furnace door, scrabbling among the ashes with his bare hands. He looked up at the thump of a flat hand on the bulkhead. He did not bother to stand up, he only snarled, 'What do you want?'

The answer was simply, 'Who are you?'

He was cold and miserable, he had no desire to go to sea, especially in a new ship when nobody seemed willing or able to tell him where they were going, or for how long. He was tired of the long procession of officers of the Military Branch who had no idea of what he could do if he were given the chance or of what he ought to do, and simply asked him stupid questions. He answered grudgingly, 'I'm Pellick. I'm the engineer. And who are you?'

'I'm the fourth lieutenant, just joined. The Captain wants steam.'

'Well, he can want. There's no way of getting it without fire.'

Talleyman pushed him aside, and looked into the furnace door.

'Of course you can't light that. It's all clinkered up. Get the ash cleared. Call a couple of matelots.'

'That's easy said, ain't it? If the Captain wants me to have any matelots for cleaning a furnace, he can let me have them. He ain't rated me no stokers, either. I'm an engineer, I am, I got no executive rank. I can't order nobody about, I can't, not like some people.'

That settles him, thought Pellick. He watched Talleyman go back into the engine room and climb towards the deck. Pellick sat in his despair, scrabbling anew in the ashes. The officer of the watch, huddled under the lee of a boat against the rain, saw the tall figure come to him.

'I'm Talleyman, fourth, just joined.'

'I'm Mallow, third. I hope you last longer than your predecessor.'

'I had a predecessor?'

'This captain's a Tartar. He didn't like poor Charles, not at all, and got him moved into a liner. But I think it suited Charles, too. I'm glad you got here — we've been very short-handed.'

'Where are we going?'

'Nobody seems to know. I think it's Saint Helena, myself, from things I heard in the Keppel's Head.'

'I want six men out of the part below of the watch on deck. Now. And another six in an hour.'

'All right, they need exercise. What do you want them for?'

'To start the engines.'

'Oh, the engineer can do that, when he feels like it.'

'Not by himself. And he doesn't feel like it. And the Captain told *me* to get it done. I've sailed with him before. If you can't let me have men, tell him why. I'm not telling him why. I did once.'

'Is that how you got your nose broken? I'll send them. Do you know you're on first watch?'

Talleyman swore, and Mallow admired the choice of language. Pellick still sitting by the dead furnace looked up vaguely as Talleyman clattered down to him again.

'How long have you been in this ship?'

'Three year, since she were built. She been laid up in ordinary all that time.'

'Haven't you cleaned her up at all?'

'It's clean enough, ain't it? Anyways, you don't need to, not when she's in ordinary. Admirals don't look at much what matters when they inspects. And what's your name, then, and what do you know about engines? None of you commission officers knows anything about engines. It's all sail with you.'

'You'll address me as "sir"! And my name's on the boiler. That answers all your points.'

Pellick stared at the officer, and then in the lantern light at the maker's name-plate on the furnace door. He read it letter by letter, under his breath, his lips moving. He opened his mouth wide to speak again, but he was interrupted by the entry of half a dozen seamen.

Talleyman asked the leader, 'Have you been rated yet?'

'No, sir. We only came aboard today. I been a commission in a liner once, six years ago, but the others never been to sea at all. And I never been in a steamer before today.'

'Then you're stokers. All of you. I'll see you're rated tomorrow. Give your names to Mr Pellick.'

One of the new men muttered behind his hand that he wasn't big enough to be a stoker. Talleyman turned on him.

'Big men can't move in this stokehold. It's stoker or coal trimmer. Take your choice. Stoke. Or spend the commission *in* the bunkers. A landsman, a trimmer, gets twenty-three shillings a month. A stoker gets two guineas. Three when we get to the tropics. And plenty to drink.'

The men heard this last with interest, even with greed. That the plenty to drink might only mean extra rations of water never entered their minds. Talleyman gave them a moment to repent, then went on.

'First, you, what's your name? Walker? You've been at sea enough. Ever thought you could be a first-class petty officer? Do well tonight, and we'll have you leading stoker in the morning. Mess with the nobs. But work for it. Rig a line. Take those baskets by the bunker. Get the ash cleared out of this furnace. Hoist it up and over the side. Make your men do it. Take it in turns to get inside. Mr Pellick will tell you how.'

Cricklade peered through the line of sailors, listened to Talleyman, and then as the men went towards the door of the first furnace, he walked up to the lieutenant.

'If you please, sir—'

'Holy Christ!' Cricklade winced at the blasphemy. 'What do you want?'

'There was a Mr Mallow, sir, and he said I was to come to you.'

From Talleyman's expression, Cricklade knew that he wasn't wanted. He waited for the lieutenant to say so. But he heard, 'You can be a doggy. Run messages. Learn your way about the ship. Stay with me. Here, take that coat off. You can wash a shirt. You can't clean a wool uniform. From now on, those are your *old* trousers. Any time you're sent down here, wear 'em. Let's inspect the machinery.'

Cricklade followed Talleyman into the dark engine room, watching the grotesque shadows the lantern threw. Talleyman probed and pulled things and poked things. His hands grew filthy with grease. Cricklade had noticed already that Talleyman had big hands, square, with short stubby fingers. He had not realized that they were *so* big, so strong, huge, gigantic in the flickering contrasty light. From then to the end of his life, whenever he thought of Talleyman he thought of a pair of enormous hands to which a tiny six-foot man had somehow become incongruously attached. He watched the hands and provided an audience for a stream of muttered comments.

'It's *been* greased, once. Probably when we built her. Thick with tallow and dirt. No, more tallow than dirt. Seems all here, though. See this? Climb up here. Look at this oil box. Keep it filled up with oil — it trickles down the thread on to the journal. Yes, that's a journal. There is *some* oil. This one here, harder to get at … well, well, this box is topped up too. Pellick has done some work. All the moving parts are well oiled. And clean. There's dirt, but only where it doesn't matter. Dismal job, keeping a laid-up hulk in trim.

'Now, let's see the boiler. Look at this glass. Show's there is some water in it. Enough. How are they doing with that furnace?'

The first furnace was clear of ash. The fire bars were back in place, and the stokers were working on the second. Talleyman turned to the newly made petty officer.

'Send a man to the lamp-keeper. We want waste rags and turpentine. Get all he'll give and then steal some more. We want all we can get. Now, you … Dunne? Straight to the carpenter. My compliments. I need firewood. Any firewood.'

'I seed the carpenter a bit ago,' said Walker, taking up his superior position with relish. 'He were just going to turn in. If Dunne goes to him now and wakes him, Mr Parsons will kill him.'

'If he doesn't bring wood, I'll kill him.'

It was obvious to the conscripted stokers that Talleyman, his face black with grease and sweat, was not a man to press points with, was perfectly capable of killing them all. They began to wonder if the tales they had heard of brutal naval life were true. Cricklade was sure they were.

Talleyman looked into the furnace, then turned on Walker: 'What are you sitting about for? Make them work. Start breaking out coal from that bunker. Smash the lumps up — size of a walnut. Throw the smaller pieces on the fire bars — not like that, handfuls, shovelfuls. Not too deep though: a couple of inches. Here, Dunne, you weren't killed, were you.'

'No sir, but I will be in the morning when the carpenter finds what I took. I didn't wake him.'

'That's a grand man. Pile the wood here. Close to the furnace door. Rags and turpentine — here. Pile some big pieces of coal over it. Open the grate, there. Now, a lucifer, somebody — thank you, Mr Cricklade, light this piece of tow ... then the rags ... now, close the furnace door. Hear her draw?'

'And that's all, sir?'

'No Walker, you've another seven fires to do. Light the others from this one when the coals are well alight. Mr Cricklade, my compliments to the bo'sun. Will he please step down here. Repeat that. Off with you. Now, Walker, if any of these furnaces goes out before I tell you, you'll clean the lot yourself. Make your men work.'

The bosun came, distastefully looking at the greasy machinery. 'We'll need more stokers, Mr...'

'Senescall, sir.'

'We'll need another dozen now for lighting, Mr Senescall, and for steaming in the morning, we'll have ten more out of each part of each watch. Four hours on, four off.'

'Aye, aye sir.'

'Now, Mr Pellick, you carry on here for a while. Get all the furnaces cleaned and lit. Make Walker take his share. Have you had a meal, youngster?'

'Yes — aye, aye sir.'

'That was a question, not an order. Yes will do. Stay here. If Mr Pellick wants me, he'll send you. Keep the men working.'

Under the wardroom lamp, four officers were playing whist. Only looked up from his hand, and observed,

'You need be in no hurry, Mr Talleyman. The Captain has instructed that a mate shall stand your watch while you are needed in the engine room. Pray do not be too long, since I feel nervous when the ship is in the hands of these young men.'

Only could see that Talleyman was wet, cold, dirty and sweaty. But he answered, calmly, 'Thank you, sir. As soon as I have washed and had dinner I shall return to the stokehold.'

The Marine Captain offered, 'I've told off Private Rowe to be your servant. If you don't like him, you can change him later, but he's got your chest into your cabin and unpacked it. This is Doctor Hampson, and Mr Moss, the purser.'

'I'm mess caterer, too,' Moss told Talleyman. 'Three pounds a month, and three months' subscription to start off, not returnable. I hope it suits you. We used poor Charles' three months to pay for the port.'

'It suits me very well. I'll have a glass when the steam blows off.'

Talleyman disappeared into the cubicle which had the courtesy title of cabin, with just room for a bunk against the side of the ship, a wash-stand, a tiny table and a shelf. The wash water would be cold, but, Only noted with approval when he reappeared, he had done his best. He had sleeked back his curly brown hair, tied his cravat over a clean shirt, scrubbed the worst of the oil out of his nails. Mallow was by now in the wardroom.

'Have I missed dinner then?' Talleyman asked the company at large. 'Can the steward find me something hot?' Only looked up from his cards.

'You will find nothing hot at this time of night.'

Moss made a grimace at Talleyman over the first lieutenant's head, wondered if it had been seen. 'Mr Talleyman, I cannot think what you expect, since galley fires were drawn two hours after noon.'

'The galley fires drawn, sir?'

'Galley fires have been drawn after dinner in every ship I have had the honour to serve in, because of the danger of burning the ship to an ash.'

'Sir, I have been the last three hours trying to *light* eight fires.'

'Indeed so, Mr Talleyman, but that is not our department as military officers, and the less we meddle with it the better.'

Only saw Talleyman swallow.

'Sir, it is by the Captain's express order—'

'I know, Mr Talleyman, I know.' *Pentstemon must have it in for this boy*, thought Only. *In that case, I can't do much to spare him, but what I can do...* 'I am sorry to see a commission officer so humiliated and made to go into the engine room. All that machinery is quite unnecessary and we did not need it to beat the Turks at Navarino. I trust that your engines are now quite warm and comfortable, and can be left in peace for the night. Since you have stood a whole watch already—'

'The engine is by no means ready. I will return to it.'

'But do not go without your grog. It will warm you a little. And if you will look into that locker of mine, you will find some fresh bread and cheese. If I were you, I would take it back to your post and refresh yourself there.'

And he has the grace, thought Only, *to take it without an argument.* The new officer of the watch saw Talleyman come on deck.

The forward fires were well alight. A red glare from the fore funnel lit up a stream of smoke and white steam and smuts which were carried by the wind across the water towards Whale Island.

'Talleyman? I'm Collins. Second, and guns. I met you once, in Lagos. You were out on the town with somebody called Partridge, but I shouldn't think you'd remember me, not the state you were in that night.'

'Partridge is dead. That Commission.'

'And there was someone else … oh, yes, that idiot whose father had just come into an Irish peerage and the fool said he was going to leave the service. What was his name? Supple, Stipple?'

'Suttle, Philip Suttle. His father became Lord Denain.'

'That's the one. Did he leave? He did? He'll be another Only in seventeen years. You have met the first lieutenant?'

Talleyman recounted, with some restraint, the substance of his conversation in the wardroom. He made, nevertheless, his attitude clear.

Collins laughed. 'Yes, he is a bit odd. But I don't think he meant to be insulting.'

'I don't think so. He *is* sorry I have to see to the engines. In another ten years, where will he be? There'll be no sail then. All finished.'

'Did you get the Navarino story again?'

'Once.'

'Sixth today. That must have been the only event of his life. Funny thing, though — he hasn't been very consistent about what ship he was in. I say — do you think he was never there at all?'

Talleyman laughed. It broke his face up, the eyes turned into starlings. 'I've heard tales before. We'll soon know. Pentstemon *was* there. Now come and see what I've done.'

Collins looked around the stokehold in wonder.

'I've never been in a steamer before. D'ye realize, Tal my boy, that you've got a fire down here?'

'If you knew the effort that goes into one, let alone seven.'

'Then why are you worrying about missing dinner?'

Talleyman reached into the pocket of his pea jacket.

'I've got some bread and cheese. Gift of Only, Esquire.'

'I know for some bacon and potatoes. I haven't had a hot meal since midday, either. Where's your doggy? Here, lad, go and get — no, why should you work, go and turn out my steward. I wonder if we could make some coffee?'

'There's a tap behind you,' Talleyman told him, 'and the water isn't rusty, either.'

Collins and Talleyman, Pellick and Cricklade stood in the glare of the after stokehold. The steam was moving in the pipes. The engine made rumbling, gurgling noises. They ate and drank hot. Seamen bargained with stokers for hot coffee and a chance to cook themselves, but, in the forward stokehold; the social niceties were being preserved.

'Better than my last commission,' said Collins. 'I was in *Dragon*. We ended up in the Liffey, with guns cleared and charges and projectiles ready, for a week. No going ashore in Dublin, either, in case of a riot. Anywhere's better than that.'

'But where are we for?' grumbled Pellick. 'I wants to know, and how long, 'cause I left my missus and six kids and a tidy house in Portsmouth.'

'I got my orders,' Collins countered. 'When I was at my own wedding breakfast. Read out with the other messages of love and affection. I've got a fur coat and a pair of tropical duck trousers in my cabin. My Patty learned to pack a sea chest in no time, and it's not the last day she'll do it. No married comforts till I get back.'

'Madras?' Talleyman asked. 'Or Hong Kong? I've had enough of the Coast.'

'I asked Number One,' Collins told them, 'and he hummed and hawed, and pretended he was being discreet, but he couldn't carry it off. He came clean in the end, and said he had orders to work out a course for the Lizard, and to ask when he got there.'

'And there,' said a smooth, unctuous voice, 'I will tell him.' The four men got to their feet. Guilt hung around them, tangible as a fog. Pentstemon came among them delicately upon his feet. 'A first lieutenant may sleep sometimes, gentleman, but a captain, never. I know only one thing about a steamer, and I act upon it. See, I have brought my own mug.'

2

That was seven weeks ago. Cricklade knew Talleyman better now, and yet he was still frightened of Talleyman. If there were anything he could do wrong, and he felt that there was very little he could do right, he was bound to do it in front of Talleyman, hear those clipped sentences, that precise voice, set him right. Yet he *liked* Talleyman, that was the worst of it. Talleyman never bullied him, was willing to explain again and again the lessons on steam which Admiralty Orders now said must be given to all cadets, told tall tales about the Coast and had described seventeen different occasions on which his nose had been broken, all of them ludicrous and some of them indecent. And it was always Talleyman who could produce the sausages, the potatoes, for hungry boys to toast in the furnace door in the small hours of the morning. Yet Talleyman still frightened him. There had been a moment, alone in his hammock in the gloomy cockpit, below the waterline, when Cricklade had wondered if the fear and love he had been told to feel for God were anything like the mixture of his feelings for Talleyman. He had dismissed the idea as blasphemous. And yet, was it not true that he worshipped Talleyman?

The shore to the south of them was backed by a long line of low hills, cleft by a pass folded into them. Closer, there were stretches of flatter ground: all green, no ploughed land, nothing ready for sowing. And that green country came down at last to the edge of the sea, to little cliffs perhaps twenty feet high. There were rocky crags half under the water, and patches of surf between them and the shore which picked out the reefs which kept *Santorin* at a distance. She was out of sound of the shore, out of shot. There was no way to get to land except by boat, and that would be run up the one small beach of yellow sand.

Elsewhere, the seas broke against the land directly. Here and there, where the rocks were broken and the cliffs low, a single man might come ashore, but not dry, not from a boat. He would have to swim the last twenty yards, wade if he were lucky, and come in the last few paces over slippery rocks, covered with mussels and seaweed. Only there by the stream mouth could troops come ashore.

The seamen strained in silence. The two marines sat in the bow; the sun shone on scarlet coats, on white pipeclay, on well-browned musket barrels, on bayonets already fixed. Talleyman held the boat's head straight for the beach. Suddenly, he spoke:

'There it is. Look there. Along my arm. Three fingers left of the river mouth. Then a little inland. See it?'

It might have been a rock among the other crags, an outcrop of the stone the country was made of. It was built of that stone, grey and barren, not a good home for lichen even. But if you knew where to look, it was plain, alien, a sign of something foreign, that was not of the country, however it might use the stuff of the land.

'That tower, sir?'

'That Martello. That's where we're going. It's what we're inspecting, boy. See how well it's placed?'

'Well placed, sir?'

'Yes. Look through my glass. Only one embrasure this side. Covers the beach. Probably one embrasure on the other side. Covers the road. Must be a road through that pass. Can't land on that beach till it's reduced. Can't bring a ship in near enough to fire at it, for the rocks. Clever. Three men can do it. Hold that tower, hold every useful inch you can see.'

'I see, sir.'

Cricklade could not quite see, literally; he found it difficult to hold the long telescope steady, keep the Tower in the centre of his view. In fact he could only catch an occasional glimpse as the boat rose on a wave. He could not make out an embrasure at all. He knew better than to say so. He had once said 'No, sir' to Only when he had been meant by all rational nature to say 'Yes, sir,' and he would not risk that again, no matter what the damage to the truth. And he felt still a little frightened, but now that perhaps there *were* three men to hold that tower, that when they grounded there would be a flash and a cloud of smoke, and broken boat planks and bloody fragments on the beach. He had heard enough tales already in *Santorin*. It was better not to look. He let his glance wander along the beach, to his left.

He looked at it three times, debating to himself whether he dared speak. Perhaps Talleyman wouldn't bully him too much if he asked, 'What are they doing over there, sir?'

'What's that? Where?'

'Along there, sir. Is it a jetty, sir?'

Talleyman trained the telescope on the shore as the boat heaved up again.

'Very smart, boy, very smart. They're building something.'

Now Cricklade could make it all out clearly, men on the shore, moving dots and bigger shapes that must be horses and carts coming to it from along the shore, and from inland.

'It's going to be a jetty. When they finish it.'

Talleyman had delivered himself of a judgement at last. Cricklade accepted it. He watched again for the place, a low ridge of stone pushing out into the sea, looking like a natural outcrop except for the men on it. And when you saw them you noticed the hard edge of the blocks straight against the water, straight against the rolling cliff top.

'Nothing to do with us,' said Talleyman. Cricklade grasped eagerly at this hint of the right attitude. He found it hard, sometimes, to catch the hints he was sure he was being thrown about how to think and behave.

'No, sir.'

'Take no notice of it.'

'No, sir.'

This was fine, this was definite, this was real unambiguous instruction.

'Then we'll be in trouble. Sooner or later.'

Cricklade felt confused, hurt. First Talleyman had told him how to think, and then he had contradicted himself. It was very confusing for a thirteen-year-old. So he stayed silent. They were close in to the beach, and this couldn't be very different from coming to the shore on Windermere. But he watched Talleyman. His big hand on the tiller, the lieutenant watched the run of the waves, turned his head to feel the wind on his cheek, watched for a roller, took his chance. He spoke to the seamen, now sharply, now in a slow drawl. Cricklade had been taught that the tone of the voice shows the manner in which the order is to be carried out. He watched for the changes in Talleyman's tone.

'Steady … steady … steady… NOW! PULL! PULL!'

The big hand beat the stroke on the gunnel. The boat leapt forward at the last minute, on the oar stroke and on the wave, and flung herself far up the beach. The seamen leapt from her, pushed her even further up on the sand.

Cricklade felt his feet on dry land again, and was surprised to find it so steady. He went to Talleyman who was standing on the green turf, above the tide mark.

'I want one seaman here, as a sentry. Challenge anyone who comes close to the boat. You two sodgers — over there under the lee of the rocks, with a clear field of fire. The rest of you, stay by the boat. Mitchell, you're in charge. Keep one man awake by the boat, and change this sentry as soon as he seems to be nodding. You can smoke. Now, don't sleep. This is bad country. Check your pistol primings. Men have been killed all along the Coast because they forgot to keep watch. I'm going inland. Don't follow me. Don't come farther than the sand. If there seems trouble, two pistol shots will bring the rest of the Marines ashore.'

This was more warlike than anything Cricklade had yet seen or heard. Even the upper deck guns in *Santorin* had remained covered in canvas since he had been in her. Talleyman turned to him.

'You come with me. Mitchell can look after the boat.'

Cricklade gulped. *He might as well have called me useless,* the boy thought, *he can't even trust me to look after the boat.* Talleyman looked down at him, and then, as if he could read the thoughts in the boy's eyes, told him, 'You're learning to be an officer. It takes time. I'm going to inspect a shore station. If you stay here with the boat you'll learn nothing. Come with me. See what you have to do. Won't be long before you do it on your own. Come on.'

Cricklade cheered up a little. Nobody else had ever hinted that some day he might be good enough to be an officer, except for the cockpit steward, and the schoolie, Mr Hargitt, for whose opinion he had little respect since this was a person who was not and could never be a wardroom officer himself. It emboldened him to ask, as Talleyman strode confidently along a footpath, yellow and hard-packed in the green grass, 'Do you know the way, sir?'

'Never been ashore in this country in my life.'

Cricklade was about to ask how Talleyman knew this would be the way to the Tower, but he suddenly bit the words off his tongue. He must be mad, questioning an officer like this. It must be the shore air going to his head. But then Talleyman looked down and said to him, as if it were an ordinary conversation, not of course between equals but between any young man and any small boy, 'There's only one path. Men have gone from the beach to the Tower. We know that. So there must be a path from the beach to the Tower. And this is the only path from the beach.'

It was simple, after all. Cricklade could see that. He followed in silence through a silent country, in silent air. There were the sounds of a few birds, the soughing of the wind but nothing else. There were no voices. No one had come down to the beach to see them land, to look at the ship. There was nobody to take any notice of them. Even though the dots were still moving on the jetty a mile away, there were no voices here.

The path did lead to the Tower. It wound through a green lush country, even in February. There were green trees, green reeds, a seasonless green with never a flower, never a touch of red or yellow, only the green of fertile, plentiful, over-brimming growth. Surely this was land where whatever was planted would grow. The path forked, and one way it went into a gully. But their way was clear, and they took the right fork, which climbed the mound of rock on which the Tower was built. Steps were cut into the rock, wide enough for three men to climb abreast.

Now, seen close to, the Tower was not merely an isolated block. It was the seaward end of a complete fort. From the base, along the top of the mound, ran a wall, thirty yards long and fifteen feet high, against the thirty-five feet of the tower. Near the top was a row of loop-holes, as if there were a platform inside. The steps led to a gateway, twelve feet wide under an arch, closed with double doors of oak. By the left-hand leaf of the gate was a postern. Talleyman knocked on it, beating at it with the flat of his hand. Cricklade knew that beat of the great flat palm, that thumped on bulwarks or bunker walls or the side of a boat, that timed hauling and pulling and shovelling and the movement of a musket to the shoulder. It echoed like a musket shot in that empty place, came back off the walls of the Tower, sent a cloud of birds into the air.

Talleyman shouted, 'Ahoy!'

There was no answer, only the birds and the echoes again. Talleyman grumbled, 'They sleep late here.'

'Yes, sir.'

Cricklade felt some further comment was called for, 'Nine o'clock, sir.'

He wondered if his phrasing were correct, after all they were on shore, they needn't talk about bells now, surely. He tried to recalculate, fell into confusion and silence once more. Talleyman lifted the latch and pushed at the postern. It opened. They waited a little, and Cricklade found himself sweating, counting the seconds under his breath. When he reached twenty, he saw Talleyman step forward: had he been counting, too? The lieutenant went gingerly through the archway. Cricklade followed.

The wall, he noticed as he came through the arch, was about ten feet thick. In the courtyard he could see that it was not solid, because doors opened into it, and windows. Not just a wall, a building all around the yard, which was twenty yards wide. Before them were three wooden huts, long and narrow, in good repair, not at all derelict. One was obviously a cookhouse, with a long iron stove pipe sticking through the roof, and a stack of coal convenient near the door. Talleyman opened the doors of one hut, and then another. None were locked. All were empty. The kitchen still had the range in it, and pots lined on top, all shining clean but with a little dust on them as if they had been left untouched a few days since they were last scoured. It was all clean. It was all cold. Dead cold.

'There ought to be three men here,' Talleyman observed.

'Perhaps they're in the Tower, sir.'

'Then they'll be damned hungry.'

Cricklade winced at the word, he could not yet bear the sound of everyone swearing. He stood while Talleyman climbed the steps that led to the door of the Tower itself. Cricklade suddenly asked, 'Where are they, sir? Do you think they're dead?'

For he had a sudden vision, frightening and vivid, of dead men, dead and rotting in the Tower, horrible bubbling masses of liquescent corruption, like the dead lambs he had seen up on the Fells, dead of last winter's snows and touched by the spring wet and the heat of May. He felt that if Talleyman opened that door anything might be in there, anything might come out, a devil, a wild dog, a dozen men with muskets … anything.

'Yellowed bosuns don't die,' Talleyman told him, shortly. 'They've gone away. Somewhere safer. Deserted their posts. What else d'ye expect. These are the conditions for it. There's been enough men killed elsewhere.'

'Perhaps the rebels have shot them, sir.'

'If there are any rebels. And they'd have looted the place. Anyway these were sensible men. They'd run too fast for a bullet. Come and see.'

Talleyman pushed at the Tower door. Nothing came out. Cricklade followed Talleyman in. Whatever might be inside, it was better than being out in the courtyard, alone. These walls were eight feet thick, but obviously solid stone this time. There was a stone-flagged floor, with a grating in the middle: this would have led to the magazine when there was a gun mounted to be fired through either of the two embrasures, wide here but narrowing to eighteen inches at the outer end. One covered the arc of the beach. The other did face the gap in the hills and the road that came through it.

'See it,' said Talleyman. 'Three men and a boy could hold it.'

Cricklade felt he must speak. He almost shouted, 'It doesn't cover where they're building the jetty.'

Talleyman looked at him, surprise on his face. Then, 'No. You're right. Good lad. It doesn't. Now we know why the jetty is where it is. I'll make a note of it.'

Pad and blacklead came out of his pocket, the pad that came out again and again to show points on Talleyman's lessons on steam to the four cadets and the mids … that came out when there was an unfamiliar coast, a strange run of sea over rocks, in any idle moment when the look on a face or the shadows on a sail caught his eye. He sat in an embrasure and worked away, frowning and sticking out his tongue occasionally as he found, it seemed, accuracy difficult and important. To Cricklade it made him look younger, a boy at school again. He finished, tucked the pad away, and then touched the lead to the wall.

At last he announced, 'So much for the empty Tower. Is anyone outside? Let's see.'

Before he left, Cricklade looked at the wall by the embrasure. There Talleyman had caught them both, in a dozen strokes apiece, a crueller caricature than anyone could have done of them, the tall gawky figure in its usual strut, the little round one at his heels, holding his shoulders back the same way. Cricklade wondered, was it true, was he beginning to walk like Talleyman now? There was hope yet.

They want back to the fork in the path, and now turned left into the gully, the road sunken between high earth banks. The path was soggy with mud, the water in the ditches was stagnant. They were out of sight or sound of the sea, in a green wet land. There was still the same silence. No one moved in the green fields. There was no one to watch them, greet them, ask them their business. Cricklade felt uneasy. He kept close to Talleyman, and noted with unease that the lieutenant himself was moving close to the side of the gully, as if to shelter at least one side from the hidden marksman, if there were one. The cadet wished he had a weapon, of any kind, a shotgun, a stick, even the absurd dirk he was not yet of rank enough to wear. He knew that Talleyman owned a pistol, a big and complicated weapon, and he wondered if it were in one of the pockets of the heavy pea jacket. They came to a bend in the way. Round it, Talleyman stopped, said, 'There's a house.'

'Where, sir?' Cricklade could not think what Talleyman was talking about.

'There, look, right ahead. And to the right.'

Cricklade peered into the all-surrounding green. It was like a child's puzzle. If there was a house there, then it wasn't one that anyone could see, it was —

'Oh, yes sir, there is a house, I can see it now. I thought it was part of the bank.'

'So it is, in a way. Or the bank is part of the house.'

Cricklade could see what he meant. The house was set deep into the wall of earth and rock. The walls were of sods, cut from the fields, piled in courses still green at the edges. The roof had been thatched with reeds originally: now it too was green with growing weeds. There was no chimney that Cricklade could see, only the thatch roof over a wall perhaps twenty feet or so long, set about ten feet forward from the bank.

What at a distance had been a blur against the green, so that Cricklade had taken it for a bush or a patch of moss or a piece of jutting rock, was a door, set midway in the long side. It was of rotting planks, nailed clumsily to crude stiles, divided into two leaves upper and lower, like the door of a stable at home. But this was not like a well-run stable. Besides the door was a great pile of ordure — horse dung, pig dung, man dung. It steamed and stank in the pale winter sun, oozing dark liquid into the ditches.

'That's not a house, sir. It must be a stye.'

'It's a house.'

'But people can't live in … in *that*?'

'You've seen pictures of this. In the *Illustrated*. You must have. Don't bring your cosy home ideas to this place. Wait till you've been in Africa. I have. I know, people can live in anything. That *is* a house, my lad. Let's see who's at home. Open it up.'

He motioned at the door. Cricklade hesitated. Talleyman looked at him, pointedly. The cadet gingerly came near to the doorway, grasped the edge of the upper leaf and pushed. It would not be pushed. He pulled and it came open, it almost came off in his hand, swung crazily from its lower hinge: the upper hinge had long pulled away from the crumbling wood. He let the leaf swing back against the wall of the house. He

44

looked inside, jerked his head back from the smell, then forced his head back in again: he told himself in plain words, and tried to believe it, that this was no worse than the smell in the cockpit of the messdecks in the early morning when the ship had been battened down all night for the heavy weather. He turned greenly to the lieutenant, waited to be asked, 'What's it like?'

'It's … it's…

'Now, Cricklade,' and it was the first time that day, the boy noted, that Talleyman had used his name. 'You'll be an officer — some day. You'll have to be your captain's eyes. Some day you may be a captain. You'll have to be your admiral's eyes. You must report what is. Not what you imagine. Not what you like to see. You must describe even things you cannot bear to look at. Look inside. Go round the place carefully. Tell me everything that you can see there. Exactly.'

Item by item, Cricklade told himself, *I must list it all item by item.* Talleyman had made the cadets do this before, all of them, in the engine room, reporting the condition of every piece of machinery as they saw it. Now, he must go round the cottage in the same way. And clockwise, Talleyman would always remind them, clockwise. But here, was it the best way? Cricklade gulped in fresh air, put his head inside the door again, and started.

'There's a clear space in the middle, sir, and I think it's a fireplace.'

'Why?'

'There's ash on the floor there. And a big iron pot on — no, not on, *by* the fire.'

'What's the floor made of? Boards?'

'No, sir. Earth or clay, well trodden down, and gone hard. But there's stones under the ash, so it's a real fireplace, meant for it.'

'Anything in the pot?'

'Can't see, sir. But there's another heap of stones there, and a kind of tray, a shallow flat basket. Close to the fire.'

'So that's the middle. Go on. Go around.'

'Oh, that end, sir, there's … I can't quite see, it's so dark … oh, yes, it *is* a stable, sir, or a stye. There's a pig sleeping on the floor.' Cricklade looked upward. 'And there's a rope slung across under the roof at that end, and they must have had hens there once by the marks on the floor.'

'Any hens there now?'

'None, sir.'

'Go on round.'

'The other end, there's a bit of a platform, of flat stones, and it's covered with grass or heather or something, I can't make out. And something lying on it… I can't see very well… I think it's rags… I … it doesn't look like…'

'Here, lad, let me see. Oh, that's the householder.'

'A man, sir?'

'Not a man. People. All sleeping in a heap, all the family. Seen it often on the Coast. Here, you!' And of a sudden it was the seagoing voice, bellowing into the gale, drilling the foretop men from the quarterdeck, calling the stokers. 'Show a leg there, show a leg! Up you get, all of you! Show a leg!'

There was a movement in the heap. Someone stirred, reached out, took a lump of something from a heap by the hearth, put it into the fireplace. A man leaned over, fanned the fuel with his hand, blew into it a little. Slowly came a redness, the fire revived, smouldering, not blazing, hardly burning, a fire by courtesy only. And this must be a man, all hair and dirt. He was sitting up, not moving from where he lay, talking, saying something not understood, whining, holding out his hand, begging he must be, asking for something.

The man was saying something, with effort, with feeling. Cricklade could tell that there had been a change in the language, in the pattern of the consonants and the rhythm, the tune of what was being said. The slurred vowels were still unintelligible, but might it be, indeed, English of a sort?

'If you'd ever done your time on the Coast,' Talleyman told the cadet. 'You'd understand him. And when you've done your time out here, you'll understand it anywhere. Just listen. You'll understand.' He turned his face into the room. 'Sailors in the big tower. They gone. Where they gone? They gone long time, not long time? You tell, quick!'

The man spoke. Cricklade listened, trying to pick out words.

'I know they've gone,' Talleyman slipped into a slot of silence, sideways. 'But when they go? Where they go? Tell me that. Be telling me that, you man.'

Cricklade, still, listening, thought he could distinguish sounds which might once have been English, but had suffered some sea change, been twisted to suit a different language, a different air, been naturalized in a strange soil. Words and phrases, like 'long, long ago', and 'far away', and, at last, 'to the east, far to the east.'

'They not dead? They live-live? Just walk away? Why they go walk-away? What made them go?'

'Arra, it was an unlucky place, it was always an unlucky place.' Cricklade could understand the words, now whole sentences, his ear was becoming attuned and the language fell into order. He could see, too, now he was used to the dim light within the house, what kind of man it was speaking. Gaunt, the skin of him stretched over his cheekbones and showed his ribs.

He had no shirt to his back. He was grimed in filth. He wore something that might once have been the wreck of a tail coat, high fashion before ever Cricklade was born, but made of a rough cloth, not much better than sacking. There was a bundle of something less easily identifiable between his legs and around his waist. Cricklade found himself irrelevantly remembering something he had read once about the inhabitants of Tierra del Fuego, who went naked but for the skins of otters and dogs that a few of the men carried about their shoulders and turned to face the way the wind blew. Had Talleyman ever been to Tierra del Fuego? Would he ever go himself? It was what he joined the Navy for, but he never thought to find it here.

This man was no better, no warmer dressed than the inhabitants of Tierra del Fuego. He had been sleeping in the clothes he had, on a scrap of matting over the dried grass. Now Cricklade could see that beyond him on the bed were three naked children, and beyond that something else that moved, and might be a woman, might be more children.

And there was a smell that came from the man. It was not the smell of the dung and urine only, although that was bad enough, or of the smoke that now filled the hut and seeped out through the holes in the thatch for want of a chimney. It was a smell Cricklade remembered from home, from charitable visits to labourers' cottages in the country, and once in a town where he had strayed from his nurse and been lost for an hour, wandering, frightened, in narrow streets. The smell still frightened him. It was the smell, the bitterest smell of all, of poverty, that had eaten into this man's skin deeper than the dirt. A smell he would always carry, that would flavour every taste of food and every stitch of clothes to the end of his life. It was not dirt, not idleness or irresponsibility that brought a man to this: it was poverty, causeless, existing in its own right, that dragged every victim down.

'An unlucky place it was,' the man was saying, 'before ever they first built it, and that was in the old wars. The first night, the stones they put to mark the place to dig the foundations and the corners of the house were all cast down and tumbled about, and that was a sign that the Lovely People had a pad there, and my grandad told me so. So 'tis no wonder that your men have gone from it. For it is the Lovely People that can't forgive an anemy and they will catch a man in the dark and tear the throat out of him, that they will, the darlings.'

'But what made them go?' asked Talleyman. 'They were here a long time. Something must have happened? You say it was an unlucky place? But why did they go when they did?'

The gaunt man looked at Talleyman. Cricklade could read his face, blank, uncomprehending. These were a strange people that came out of the sea, and it might as well have been out of another world. They came out of their great ships, where there was good food and drink, in the fine blue coats and their shining brass buttons and the gold on their hats, fat and well, and rich, rich, rich. How should this man know why they did anything? Their life was strange to him, governed by different laws. Obviously, he would not have been surprised to hear them say that in their world, in England, iron floated.

The man was silent. Talleyman waited, and Cricklade wondered why he could not see what was the matter. The lieutenant asked now, 'Why are you so late abed? The day is well on. What are you about?'

'Would your honour have anything for us, then?'

'Anything? What thing?'

'Sure, and aren't we lying here because there is nothing more for us to do, not the strength to do it? And we all lay down

49

here together to die, because there is not a mouthful of food in the house, and there has been nothing left for the last five days. We have nothing left, your honour, and there is nothing left to do.'

'But it can't — it can't—' Cricklade stumbled in his breaking boy's voice, and knew, horribly, how well-fed even that was, 'Look, there's the pig, you can sell the pig, or eat him, you can, you can!'

The gaunt man looked at Cricklade, dully, without any resentment or criticism in his gaze, said, 'Arra, and how could I be eating the pig, or selling him to buy food, for 'tis selling him at midsummer I must be to pay my rent, and if I didn't pay off my rent, then I'd be put off my land entirely and the driver would come to pull my cabin down, and what would become of me then, with no land and no house, no land, no land?'

'But what's the good of land if you're dead?' asked Cricklade, with a boy's cruel logic.

The gaunt man replied, 'Why, this is my little piece of land, and my da had it before me, and his da before him, and paid their rent all the days from the pig, and ate what they grew. But this is the last of us, and dead we will surely be, unless the good God send us a miracle. But — there are no miracles left in Ireland.'

'Do not be deceived, lad,' said Talleyman. 'We are overseas. It is a different country. And a different world.'

But the man looked at them still as woodenly, muttering that it was his little piece of land, and his da had been there before him.

Then he looked direct at Talleyman, and asked, 'Wouldn't your honour have something for us, just a morsel?'

'What is your name?' Talleyman asked the man.

'And it is a king's name, I bear,' they heard the reply. 'For the O'Briens were Kings of Ireland and ruled from Cashel before ever there was an Englishman in the world, and soon there shall be an O'Brien king in Ireland again, God willing, and the Pope shall crown him here.'

'Here, Mr O'Brien.' Talleyman fumbled in the deep pocket of his pea jacket, and Cricklade wondered if after that awful flaunting of disloyalty the lieutenant were not going to shoot him out of hand. 'Here! I never go ashore without something. I was caught once myself. Nothing to eat for five days. At sea, too. D'ye know these? Ship's biscuits. They've very hard. Break your teeth, and your jaw. Soak them in water first. Then a baby can eat them. And this is salt beef. Boil it.'

He caught Cricklade's eye. The cadet waited to hear his officer excuse himself for inconsistency. But all Talleyman said to him was, 'No weevils in that. I pick and choose for myself.'

He stood in the road a moment, as if to avoid thanks, although no thanks came. Cricklade was listening, with only half his attention on Talleyman, half elsewhere. He heard the lieutenant ask, 'And to whom is it, Mr O'Brien, that you pay your rent?'

He tugged at Talleyman's sleeve, called out excitedly, 'Sir! Sir! I can hear wheels coming! A horse and wheels, sir, up the path!'

But his voice was drowned by the savage shout from inside the house, a wail of venom and bitterness such as he had never heard before.

'To Lord Denain of Ballyfine House. To Lord Denain, and the curse of Cromwell on him and all his for ever!'

3

Harriet Delauny and Jane Roding walked together on the terrace of Ballyfine House, listening for wheels on the gravel. The terrace faced east of south, sheltered between the horns of the wings, a hundred feet of paving, fifty feet wide, before the three storeys of the pillared facade. The great Hall, as Lord Denain had called it, the Gallery, as Canon Delauny and Mr Roding termed it, ran all along the ground-floor front. Through the tall windows, Harriet could see the chairs done up in dust sheets, the curtains that hung over the family portraits, the dust on the floor, the cobwebs. All the house was empty, and damp and unaired, beginning to sprout mould, all except the west wing where the Rodings lived.

Harriet glanced through the windows as they passed them, amused herself by counting the chairs, counting the pictures. She was bored. Boredom was not a chronic complaint, even, but the normality of her life, an atmosphere in which she swam like a fish. Sometimes she wondered if, supposing she were ever shown the corner, the edge, of an exciting life, she would recognize it. But sure, soon Philip would lift an edge for her.

Had life ever been exciting at Ballyfine House? Not in her memory. Perhaps once it had been, before she had come to the Vicarage, when there had been a Lord Denain living here. There had been hunt balls here, and routs, and parties, and famous people had visited. Daniel O'Connell had been there, when he was famous as the man who had presented the King a laurel crown, on bended knee at Kingstown that had been Dunleary before. Would those great days ever return? she asked, into the empty air, hardly expecting an answer,

'Oh, and a splendid place, wasn't it, when Lord Denain was here?'

Jane's reply was, as Harriet always expected, crushing and dry.

'Do you mean the old Lord Denain that built this house or his son that was Lord Denain for three months and never came near the place, or Philip's father and sure didn't he come into the estate and as soon as he had the money didn't he run off to England and never a hair or hide have we seen of either of them since?'

Harriet felt that sometimes Jane made too much of her seniority. She was three years the elder: she would be twenty-one in June. She had better be careful herself, with never an offer in sight. She had turned down that Major MacCaughlin in the Yeomanry from the south end of Armagh, for no better reason than that he was nearer fifty than forty, and smelt too much and too bad when he was close to her. *And what if he did*, Harriet thought, *so do most men, except Philip*. If there was little hope for Jane, on the shelf already, when she had, or at least her father had, that bit of land in Downshire, what hope would there be for herself if it weren't for Philip? She countered.

'Any Lord Denain. Anyone.'

'But where would the money come from?' Jane smiled her pussycat smile, not parting her lips. With her triangular face, her sleek black hair, combed under her bonnet, she always looked like a cat which had just finished washing itself. *But,* Harriet thought gleefully, *there is that down on her upper lip, and her mother has a definite moustache. What will she look like when she is old, forty or more?* And, slightly angered, she countered, 'Where does any money come from?'

'Rents,' Jane made herself sound a patient sufferer. 'And tithes, for your father. And my father's out there this moment, trying to get something out of… I think it's the MacCarthy's this time. And if he can't get something paid then he'll have to be distraining on them, because he's threatened it so often that he can't dodge it any more. But you know there's not much pleasure and less money in that, because if you turn out people that can't pay a rent the rent still doesn't get paid. So there's no rents coming in here, or precious little, and nothing at all from the land down at Eyories. And till he comes back, I suppose we will have no dinner.' She glanced sideways at Harriet. 'I suppose you will be staying here?'

'I told Mary Flannery I'd be staying.'

'Then she'll have an excuse not to think of anything. They're all alike, these Catholics, dodging work.'

Harriet said nothing. Wasn't there a rumour that the Roding great-grandfather had only kept his land up there in Ulster by turning Protestant and cheating the Penal laws that way? And now a pillar of Protestantism the whole tribe was. But the Delaunys had been supporters of Church and State since the Normans first came.

She would have liked to comment, but instead, she suggested, 'Let us walk down to the lodge gates and see if we can meet your father. If we see him, he will lift us back here in the car. If not, we can walk on to the Vicarage, and take Mary Flannery by surprise. She won't like making us tea, but what are servants for?'

'Very well.'

This, thought Jane, *was what I hoped for*. There may be something at the Vicarage. They trudged along the gravel, the half-mile to the lodge. Behind them, the hillside rose above the house to the west. Harriet glanced back at it. If you climbed the ridge you could peer between a pair of peaks in the Sheehy mountains, and see the gleam of silver waters in the long bay, going down to Eyories miles west of that again. Once, she remembered, when Philip had lived at the Vicarage, and Harriet's father had been up in Kerry, and Jane's father had already been agent here, she and Lawrence had come to stay here at the Vicarage. They had climbed the hill often, all four of them. It made her think of a different life that might have been, had she been brought up anywhere but here, at the end of the world. She mused, 'But the Suttles have other rents. Otherwise, why should they have gone off to England? They've got land in England they could have afforded to keep on living here till the bad times are over.'

'English money stays in England, Irish money goes to England, and it doesn't come back.' Jane was stubborn, so Harriet was scornful.

'It doesn't have to stay in England. And the Suttles could come back. You mark my words, in the summer, they will. In the summer, the potatoes will be all right again, like last year, and we'll all be happy again, all of us together.'

'The old Baron built this house,' Jane pointed out, 'and there was English money came in to help, because the rents here were never enough to pay for it. But that was only for practice. He started to build a bigger one in Wiltshire, and the new Baron is carrying on. That's where the Irish money will go, if there ever is any again. Philip will live in a palace, but in England and not here.'

And who will live with him? thought Harriet. *Sure, once he comes back he'll keep his promises.*

But Jane was asking, a touch of malice in her voice, 'Would your brother ever come back, then?'

'Lord Denain would ask him back. I know that what there is left of the rent money here goes to the relief work in Eyories.'

'But does Lawrence know that it's Lord Denain's money paying for the jetty he's always building, been building for two years and never the nearer to being finished it is? And if my father doesn't do better with the rents there'll be no money at all for the jetty. And I asked, *would* your brother come? If he's so hot on Young Ireland that your father turned him out of doors—'

'Oh, hush!' Harriet snapped her fingers. There was silence for a little as they walked under the bare elm branches, among the mounds of rhododendron bushes. Then she asked, 'Was there anything in the paper this morning?'

'Nothing, only foreign stuff. And Mr William Smith Bronterre O'Brien made another speech.'

'And Mr William Smith Bronterre O'Brien may speechify himself to the devil, because there's nobody else in Ireland does anything else but make speeches. And we will all die of emptiness, waiting here for the end of the world.'

A pity, thought Jane, *that this child has such wispy brown hair. The blue eyes are pleasant, but when she gets bad-tempered like this, she's quite impossible. What kind of a match will she ever make, if she can't control herself? Still, she's lived a quiet life.* Jane herself had been away to school, three years in Belfast, and she counted herself used to great events, and to towns, and political meetings and processions which brought their echoes into every house even if ladies did not mix themselves in these matters. But Harriet had never been further than Cashel, when her father spent his annual term as Canon in Residence. Any break, any visit, even if it weren't Philip, would be welcome to her.

They were at the lodge, now, where Cameron, the Scots bailiff, lived, and he had gone out with Mr Roding in the pony trap, that they called in those parts a car. Opposite the lodge gates was a pair of tall stone pillars, white-washed with iron gates hung on them. Gates like that were the ambition of every tenant farmer. But these barred the other drive that led past the Vicarage to the Church. The girls stood at the drive gates and looked each way along the road.

'I can hear it,' said Jane. 'We'll wait here and get a ride back. Father will be putting Cameron down here.'

They stood and listened, then watched as the trap came into sight around the bend in the road. They made out the figures of Jane's father, driving, and Cameron. The wind ruffled the bushes opposite the gate posts. The trap came closer, and Mr Roding lifted his whip to wave to them from afar. He shook the reins, and came up at a fair trot. Then, he leant all his weight on them to stop from speed in a yard or two. The wheels scattered grit and pebbles. Roding laughed and shouted to his daughter.

A man stepped from behind the pillars of the Vicarage gate. He shouted loud,

'Roding! That's for Ireland!'

Roding, Cameron and Harriet stood transfixed, eyes on the pistol. Only Jane moved, bending to pick up a stone, and throwing it as she came up, underhand, but fast, fairly straight. It was a good shot, she boasted afterwards, it went within ten feet of the assassin. Perhaps it did distract him, startle him. The bang, the flash, the cloud of white smoke came at once. Mr Roding's hat sailed into the air, and he sat down heavily on the floor of the car. Harriet began to scream, scream, scream. Cameron bent over the agent. Jane found another stone, a bigger one, and threw it after the man now running up the Vicarage drive. This one didn't even reach the gate posts, but Jane felt that at least she had done something.

'Catch him, catch him!' spluttered Roding, kneeling upright in the trap now. 'Go on, Cameron, run after him!'

'This is the end,' Cameron replied. 'I'll stand abuse, but I am no' paid to be shot at. If you want men to run after a murderer all reeking with blood, then send for the Constabulary.'

'Will you not even shoot at him?' asked Roding. He stood and scrabbled inside his great coat, pulled out with difficulty a long old-fashioned pistol. He held it in both hands, straight out from his body, and pointed it roughly in the direction of the church steeple. He pulled the trigger. Nothing happened. There was, by now, no target in view, anyway. Roding held the pistol close to his eyes, looked into the pan, swore. He brought out a powder flask, primed the pan, and again aimed at the church steeple. This time the weapon went off. It did not appear that the steeple was hit.

Harriet had hysterics, shrieking uncontrollably. Jane slapped her face, with some relish and more energy than might be thought necessary. Having thus got some satisfaction, she asked, 'Are you hurt, father?'

'Not at all, not at all, the villain fired too high. But he's spoilt my hat, and it was a good one. When I catch him, I'll... I'll ... oh, there's nothing for it, we shall have to have the soldiers here.'

Harriet stopped her sobbing, immediately. Soldiers! Her imagination saw the house full, the park full, of gay young officers in gold-crusted uniforms, young men with money, men looking for wives. Men who came out of that other world, England. That would settle Jane. And for herself, surely if things had come to this pass, Philip would return. And return for her.

4

Lawrence Delauny saw something fresh in the bay early in the morning. At first he took *Santorin* for some emigrant ship touting for custom around the little ports of Kerry opposite, under the blue misty mountains. There was no bringing a ship in anywhere on this side of the water without a jetty, and there was no jetty yet, because here he was building it, at Eyories.

Lawrence slept in an old peasant cabin, better than most because the walls were of rough sea-washed stones piled dry together and the gaps sealed with clay. But his heating in this cold winter night was the same as the peasants had, a turf fire in the middle of the floor and the smoke to get out where it could, the smoke that soaked into his clothes and his hair and everything that was his. He made his own coffee, boiling the crushed grains in a little saucepan when the peat was burning well. He drew water from the stream outside. He had some two-day-old wheat bread that he had brought over from Castletown, and butter in a pot. He knew there was bacon for supper, and he put the heel of his loaf into a coat pocket for the middle of the day, so that he should not seem to his labourers to eat very much better than they did. Not to their faces, at any rate.

He shaved, and combed his long fair hair. He put on his new paletot, bought that summer before in Dublin, over his waistcoat without any jacket. It was a very light grey, almost white, and was very conspicuous. The men on the works could see him coming a great way off. Thus he could always report truthfully to the Trustees that he had observed the labouring poor exerting themselves to the full extent of their powers, due regard having been had to the conditions of their daily lives.

He had no time, after breakfast, to waste looking at the ship, except for a quick glance through the glass of his theodolite. It seemed to be a big steamer, coming up under sail, her fires slack and her paddles feathered. There had been three days of rain, and nothing done on the jetty, nothing at all. It was his jetty. While he had authority and funds to build that jetty, he could keep a few men and five times as many people from starving. But in three long days of rain, when nobody could stay out and work, anything might have happened to his men. He could not even be sure that they were alive. The Hooleys down by the stream had been very far gone, when they had last been out on the works. The O'Briens up by the tower were in poor shape, and there were the Brennans out on the Castletown road.

It was not the starvation on its own. It left men so weak that they fell very quickly with the fever, or even with a pneumonia or a galloping consumption of the chest. In three days a man, or a whole family, might come to an end. Even if a man did not die, then he might be too weak to work after it, and so starve.

Delauny went into the field behind the cabin and caught the old brown horse. This was a country where horses grew fat because there was grass, of sorts, everywhere. Grass thrived on constant rain. But men could not live on grass, and those who had tried were dead. If only there was something they could do with the land so that men could live on grass or on something which used the grass as intensively as men used the potato. But the potato could grow on land too poor to bear grass even.

If the potato failed again, there would be no need to worry. There would be nobody alive to eat the grass. Last year had been good, with no blight: but because there had been no seed, or no faith to plant it, there had been few potatoes grown in Ireland. If the potatoes failed this year, he did not know what had better be done. Yet, let the potato fail or not, Delauny knew what would happen, and that it all depended on the jetty.

He backed the horse into the shafts, and set off down the track to the jetty. It was typical of Ireland, he could get money to build a jetty, but not to make a good road to it. Yet even without a road, by the summer the jetty would serve his purpose well enough. There would be fifteen feet of water at the best of times, and a wall a ship could lie alongside to unload sacks, and a track that donkey carts could manage. Yes, it would serve his purpose, if only it were ready in time.

The men were there already, as many as he could expect. They had the last of the cut stone down from the quarry, and they were filling it in between the two walls, ramming it down from the top with earth and gravel. Malachi Doyle was there, the Clerk of the Works, and brought his time sheet over to tell Lawrence Delauny, 'There's four of the Dohertys from over the bogside have come late today. Shall I be putting them down or shall I send them away?'

'Oh, put them down, man, put them down. And get the work done so that they can be paid.'

'But Mr Delauny, if we put one family of them down for a whole day when they come late, then 'tis all of them will be coming late, and there's no work at all we'll get out of them, and we'll be paying them for the kindness of looking in to say how d'ye do at the end of the day.'

'Malachi, I have said often enough that we are not paying just to have the work done, although I want it done, and so does Ireland. We have the work done to find some excuse to give the men the pay. Let me be arguing with Dublin once the money is spent, and that is why I want your time sheets, and do you be finding ways to spend it.'

'But the work *must* be done, Mr Delauny, and you know that we must have it finished before summer.'

'Anyone would think that it's your own money that was being spent, Malachi.'

'And in a way it is, seeing it's Ireland's money.'

'But it's not Ireland's money altogether, Malachi, for 'tis England's money the most of it, and the more we have to give away the better.'

'Then 'tis money that ought to have been Ireland's long ago, Mr Delauny, and careful and not wasteful we must be with it. And it is better to be using it to build a jetty than to make a ten-foot wall around Lord Denain's estates, as we might have had to.'

'But would you have the Dohertys starve, Malachi?'

'I'd have the jetty built, and the work done, Mr Delauny.' Lawrence gave up the argument. He had it nearly every day. For in the end the Dohertys would starve, and so would the Brennans and the O'Briens and the Hooleys. They would keep this cash, most of it, to pay their rents, and hold on to their useless land, and grudge a penny of it spent on food. And for food they would only take potatoes, and the money would all go back to England, to one landlord or another. Oh, now, if he ever had one of those landlords, no, if he ever had Philip Suttle, over the sights of a gun, or at the point of a pike, he'd have no mercy, he'd kill with relish.

He looked again at the ship. There were very few ships that dared come so far up the Long Bay, among the rocks that you could sometimes tell by the spray breaking over them, but were more often hidden. And never such a big ship. That would hold a good thousand of the faint hearts who would leave

Ireland when she needed them, when the tide was about to turn. She was losing way, backing her fore topsails, to swing round stern on to the shore. There was a boat already hoisted out on the davits, and it touched the water at the same instant as the anchor. That was very smart work, indeed. But none of his business. He turned back to his work. There was a stoppage again.

'There is barely enough stone,' Malachi told him, 'to last till dinner time.'

'Sufficient for the day is the evil thereof.'

'I don't know the Protestant Bible, Mr Delauny. But when we come to the end, what are we to do?'

'You can surely find something for them today? There is gravel here to fill in the ruts on the track: this part of the road is death on the donkeys.'

'But tomorrow?'

'Then we can be cutting stone in the quarry.'

'It's hard work in the quarry with no powder, sir. There's many of the men will think twice of coming till the hunger strikes them hard, and then they'll be too weak for work.'

'And slow work it will be, Malachi. But if you can think of a way of building a stone jetty without cutting stone, then let me know it.'

Delauny looked again at the ship. There was an ensign hoisted to the gaff. He looked at it again through the glass. A Queen's ship, he realized. The boat was making, not for the jetty, but for the old landing place on the beach below the Martello Tower. And there was a smudge of red in the bows. He called to Malachi.

'It's the soldiers are coming ashore. Let all the people know that the redcoats are coming ashore here, and they know as well as we do what they are to do.'

'And it's better the soldiers can do it than we can,' countered Malachi, 'because they have the powder.'

A Queen's ship ... a thought hovered half-formed on the edge of Delauny's mind, came down, perched, and then fluttered off again. Delauny snapped his fingers. A small boy led the trap forward. These little fellows couldn't do much, even at thirteen or fourteen years old, starved as they had been all these years. However, he could rate them as earth fillers or spreaders, and get them paid something. He got up on to the seat and shook out the reins. The horse trotted up the slope from the jetty, over the hill and down again into the little valley of the stream and along the sunken path that led past the Tower to the north.

It was just after he turned the corner that he came on them, standing outside the O'Briens' cabin. There was another question he would have to answer sometime: where was O'Brien this morning? He was alive, because there was peat smoke visible. And there were two sailors there: he could not tell what ranks they were, but the cloth of their coats, blue by courtesy, almost black in truth, looked expensive. One was a mere child, fourteen at most — as old as some of these lads he was paying men's wages to so that they could keep whole families alive — but well fed and smooth-looking. An Irish boy of that age looked sixty, and ill with it.

But the other man, Delauny saw, was perhaps a year or two younger than himself. He had bright brown eyes, like a mouse, or a sparrow, or some questing bird, never still, always darting from side to side, always seeking — what? And he had working hands, big and hard, the nails pared down to the quick, the flesh spotted with little scratches and scars fresh healed. Hands that could do something, Delauny thought, and now working away with a blacklead on a pad.

The younger sailor watched the trap as it came down to them, surrounded by a cloud of small boys. The older man did not raise his head, but kept his eyes on the paper till the trap came to a stop, and the horse's muzzle was almost thrust into his face. He looked up into Delauny's eyes, and said nothing: he only raised his eyebrows.

'Good morning,' and Delauny tipped his beaver hat, even while he accused himself of toadying and excused himself to himself by classing this as mere politeness. 'Are you needing anything?'

'There is no need for help.' Talleyman touched the brim of his hat with his fingers, lightly. 'Where are the coastguards?'

'Those old men? Oh, about three weeks ago I saw them off over the hill to Castletown. The oldest of them, I don't know any of their names—'

'Plackett.'

'Well, yes, it may well have been Plackett, I don't remember English names very well. He was telling me that he had had enough of service in this vile country where he might be shot at and nobody cared, so he was trying to find a ship to go back home in, and if he felt like it he would skip it in America or somewhere. And the others said that they would go with him as far as Cork if he couldn't find a ship in Castletown, or even further. But what then they didn't know.'

'They never reported in Cork. I suppose they found a ship in Castletown.'

'They were very anxious I should be witness that they were taking none of the Queen's goods with them.'

'They did not. They left the equipment. And their honour and self-respect. Pray, who are you?'

'My name is Lawrence Delauny. I was sent here a year ago by the Board of Works to provide some employment for the poor of the place. I have been here ever since.'

'But surely all relief works were suspended last year when the good state of the harvest was seen?'

'A charitable trust has provided funds for the continuation of the buildings. It pays me, also. Who, pray, are you?'

Talleyman ignored the question. He poked a moment at his pad, then asked, 'Is there no post of Constabulary in the township?'

'They were withdrawn a year ago. Sometimes when there has been a killing, the great Superintendent Trant comes here looking for the men of 'Ninety-Eight, but otherwise, the men will not stay.'

'And the resident magistrate?'

'The nearest one ceased to reside when he grew tired of being shot at and the police could provide no protection. Let me tell you... Mr... Mr... er...?'

'My name is Talleyman. And I am a lieutenant in Her Majesty's Navy.'

'I will tell you this, Lieutenant. Government has withdrawn from this part of the country and left all the people here to die. The coastguards were the last to desert us.'

'No one is deserted.'

Surely this is the coldest man I have ever met, is there no life in him, no compassion, is he a mere book of rules?

'The whole of Ireland has been deserted. We have all been left to die because it is too much trouble to the English Government to try to keep the country alive.'

Talleyman ignored the passion in the voice. He asked, still flatly, 'Is there a clergyman in the place? Or a Roman priest?'

'The Vicar died last summer of the fever. The priest here collapsed a week ago, and was taken away by his superiors. It is unlikely that either will be replaced. Who would come here? I tell you, we have been abandoned.'

'So you represent such administration as there is?'

'There was a driver, but he was shot in December, and I do not think the landlord will send one again.'

'A driver?'

'He is a man who collects rent for the landlord. If the peasants cannot pay, then he drives off their cattle and pigs to sell to pay it, and so he is called a driver.'

'If they have no pigs?'

'Then he turns them out of their houses and the land, and to make sure that they go he pulls down the house and burns the thatch. Now do you not understand why he was shot?'

Talleyman said to Cricklade, 'There is your answer.' Then, again to Delauny, 'But the Constabulary caught the man who did it?'

'The driver was shot but not here, for it was in Castletown on a market day, and since it was done in a crowded street at noonday there was no possibility at all of anyone being able to say who did it. After that, the Police advised me to leave.'

'You did not?'

'If I left, there would be no work on the jetty, and the people would starve.'

'No one has been abandoned, Mr Delauny. We are here. Would you please accompany me into my ship? My captain will wish to hear all this.'

'Will he not believe you?'

'You have the more experience. For instance,' and Talleyman jerked his head towards the door of the cabin, 'are there many like this?'

'Almost all are like this.'

'Almost? Are the others better? Or worse?'

'Can they be worse, except where there are people lying dead on the cabin floor and the others with no strength to bury them, as I have seen in some places?'

'Of that I am not sure. I have seen worse. And the people lived.'

Oh, but this is the coldest fish of an Englishman that ever was seen, Delauny thought. *There is no misery that has the slightest effect on him.* He took the reins, and said, 'If I come to your ship, there will be no work done, and the people will die.'

'Come down to the boat!'

It was curt, a direct order, there was no room for refusal. Talleyman folded his pad, slid it back into one of those huge pockets, turned his back on the engineer. He walked towards the beach without looking to see if he were followed. Delauny hesitated a moment, then turned the trap.

Cricklade, uninvited, unbidden, swung himself up into the trap as it passed. He had a vague feeling that it was what Talleyman would want him to do, and besides, he still felt more at home behind a horse than in a boat. Delauny looked down at him amused at this blond shrimp in fancy dress, loose knotted tie tucked under the opening of the white waistcoat, the big buttons on his sleeve and the front of his coat, the shining buckle of his belt and the empty sling for a sword. Delauny tried to imagine how small a sword would fit it. But sword or not, this object was guarding him, somehow he had come under military authority. Yet, it was so strange to see a boy who was clean, who wore more clothes than mere decency demanded, a boy who had had enough to eat that day, every day of his life — for the first time for weeks, Delauny laughed.

5

Cricklade had learnt a lot in six weeks in a ship. He might look a shrimp, but it was he who shepherded Delauny through the entry port, up the companion way to the upper deck. He had waved a signal to the two seamen who had seized Delauny's wrists to manhandle him on to the paddle casing from the bobbing boat, and he had nudged the civilian to touch his hat to the quarterdeck.

On the upper deck, Delauny was able to look around him. He was in a space walled by bulwarks over six feet high. It ran flush and level from end to end of the ship. Somehow, Delauny had always imagined that a ship lying so at anchor would be a place of rest, that everything in her would be as still as the vessel herself on the water. But this space was filled with men working, or at least busy. They were quiet, there was scarcely a word spoken, but everyone was in motion, cleaning brass, painting wood, scraping the deck to whiteness, silently active like a nest of ants, and all fenced in by those high wooden walls. He could not see the water, nor the mountains on shore. Except for the slight roll of the anchored ship he might have been in some factory yard ashore, with its smell of oil and hot iron, the tops of the six-foot cylinders visible through the engine-room skylight. There was a haze of hot air and a little smoke about the tops of the funnels: she had come up the Long Bay under sail, with the wind in the west, Delauny realized, so she would need steam to go back.

But Talleyman beckoned him, and he withdrew from this familiar world of polished brass and black iron, from machinery he could understand to men he could not fathom, yet. Past the base of the main mast, past two black and shining guns, past the mizzen mast and the double wheel beyond it, and to a little oasis of quiet, walled off by more great guns. And there stood a short fat man, his soft cap pulled down over his eyes, his coat buttoned up to his chin and a gold anchor on each shoulder. The hair was greying, but the blue eyes were still sharp in the smooth face.

Pentstemon listened to Delauny's story in silence. He turned to the lieutenant.

'What is it like, young Tal?'

Talleyman had been standing there with his pad in his hand and the pencil busy, *taking notes again*, thought Delauny.

'Very bad, sir.'

'I thought you said you'd seen worse,' Delauny sneered.

'I have seen worse. In Africa. It was a slaver's barracoon. I still dream of it. Bad dreams. This is nearly as bad, what I have seen. I don't want to dream again.'

He passed his pad across to the Captain. Pentstemon beckoned Delauny to look. He saw the picture of O'Brien's cabin, the turfs and the dung heap, all in a few swift strokes. In the upper corner, O'Brien himself, the features close enough to life for anyone to recognize, but an expression in those hungry eyes more general than a mere copy of the despair of one man. Pentstemon turned over. Here was the inside of the cabin, the bed of rags, the pot and the empty potato basket, the pig. In the margin more faces, each set out with a dozen strokes, the O'Brien children, the small boys who had run with the trap, and Delauny himself. Pentstemon turned the last pages, showed Delauny his own face, shadowed by the bulwark, the rigging behind him. Pentstemon grimaced. He flipped to show the Martello Tower with its courtyard of huts, the view from the seaward embrasure, the ship framed in it. He passed the pad back to Talleyman, and crooked a finger at the midshipman who waited beyond the aftermost gun.

'It has always been a marvel to me how few officers spend such a beautiful morning taking this fresh air on the quarterdeck. Even the bo'sun seems anxious to keep his own company.' The midshipman melted away. Pentstemon returned to Delauny.

'Do you say, then, that the coastguards at Eyories have deserted not only their posts but also their country?'

'So I understand the intentions they expressed.'

'Any man can understand their feelings, Mr Delauny.'

No, thought Lawrence, *if you have not seen it you can never understand it.* But in the space of those two sentences there were ten men gathered around the Captain. With a wide gesture, Pentstemon went on.

'Gentlemen, I am so pleased that you have found it convenient to join in this conversation I am having, and I am sure that you will all make the correct deductions. You see, Mr Delauny, I have been placed by the omniscient Admiralty in their wisdom at the disposal of the Captain commanding the Coastguard on this coast, to fetch and carry and to do as I think fit as has been the prerogative of every Captain since Noah went to sea. Where the Civil Government has broken down, I am empowered not only to carry meal but to see to its distribution. If there were a Board of Guardians to administer the Poor Law in this area, I could let them have cornmeal against repayment to the Admiralty, and repayment to their Lordships is always a long and difficult business. I am still corresponding with the Admiralty about a salt cellar lost from the wardroom when I was in *Argyle* four years ago, and I would be obliged if Mr Talleyman would search his chest for the object or his memory for any evidence he can adduce in my defence. But if the Board of Guardians here had failed to collect their rates, and I should imagine here that there are precious few rates left to collect, I could not let them have food under any circumstances. On that my instructions are clear.

'But luckily, the Board of Guardians here has dissolved itself, and therefore as I read the gaps in the relevant Acts and Orders, I should supervise the distribution of food through the coastguards. But if the coastguards have gone away, then as far as I can understand the spaces between the lines and the close detail in all the omissions, then I ought to distribute meal myself — not in person, of course, but I am sure what applies to me will apply to all of you, redoubled.'

Delauny could see the drift of this. He could hardly believe his ears. Surely he could not — but Pentstemon went on.

'Mr Only, it occurs to me that if the Tower is not manned, then it may well fall to us to man it, and perhaps an officer and twelve men or so would not be an outrageous allotment. Mr Delauny will surely be able to tell us about the rough shooting. The officers can take it in rotation, and later we may have a mate there instead of a lieutenant, but as a start, Captain Lidderdale—'

'*Sir!*'

'Oh, please do spare my shattered nerves your military manners. Wouldn't you like to go and be a landsman again for a short while?'

'*Sir!!*'

'At least, I will not have to hear that again for some days. Why the marines have always to be drilled over my head I cannot understand. The seamen can take it in turns too. They may have the duty as a punishment, or as a reward for good work, or perhaps they can draw lots or fight for it. I do not think the interior of a peasant cabin ashore can be as foul a place as the messdecks of a ship at sea in the Atlantic spring.'

The Captain's eyes flickered defiantly to Delauny, to Talleyman, then to the first lieutenant again. 'It might be wise if some of the big kettles were landed with the first boat, and a sack or two of coal. Then sufficient meal for a dinner for —' he looked back to Delauny '— how many people in your township?'

Delauny could still hardly believe his ears.

'Captain, I must point out that it is Government policy that all food must be issued through the authorized corn dealers, and bought from them with the money which men earn working on relief projects, such as my jetty, or in their normal daily work. I have had so much trouble over this—'

'It is hardly Government policy that poor people should starve to death for sheer want of money or of any way of spending it.' *It can do no harm*, thought Pentstemon, *to be known as the Captain who saved half a county from starvation, preferably by some spectacular disobedience to orders. The plain man entangled in verbiage always gets sympathy, and as for the man who cuts the Gordian knot … the world is his. And this is the command that Vallins turned down! There'll be support for me in Parliament, and if I should want a seat myself at any time, it must count for me on one side or another. And if ever I want a real Command and fly my own flag, it will do no harm to be known now. Besides, if the people there do look like Talleyman's drawings, and I've never found him draw inaccurately yet — then they need it, they really need it.* But Delauny was talking again. He had with difficulty repressed the urge to point out that to the best of his observation the Government *wanted* the people to starve to death: instead he tried to explain coldly and clearly, 'If you give the food away, the dealers will go bankrupt and starve.'

'Poof! Dealers never starve.'

'As a farmer,' put in Only, 'I can assure you that a corn dealer survives whatever happens.'

'These dealers are not rich merchants,' Delauny insisted. 'Even if they had been, they would be poor now after three years of hard times. They are little grocers who sell half a sack of meal by the cupful in the corner of their only room. And if you feed the men for nothing, they will not come and work on my jetty till the day before rent day, and then 'twill be too late and they will all be evicted. But I can ensure them employment for years to come.'

Oh, Lord, thought Pentstemon, *these Irish! You try to help them, and they argue you down, and yet if you listened to them everyone would starve, and then who'd get the blame?* He turned to Only.

'I think that the time is well advanced, and we may as well begin our preparations. I imagine it will be desirable to get the people fed, and we can argue afterwards. Issue free porridge to anyone who comes for it.'

But they won't come, thought Delauny in triumph. *Malachi will know what to do. The word will be around in no time, that the soldiers are offering porridge to persuade men to turn Protestant. They can boil their cornmeal till the devil comes to supper, but there's no Irish round here will be seduced. Let them play, then, if it pleases them.*

'Will you sign the issue voucher book, sir?' asked the purser.

'I will sign Domesday Book, Mr Moss, if you think it will make our lives easier, but start breaking out meal for ... how many was it?'

Delauny mentally shrugged. He might as well try to hold up the Juggernaut.

'About three thousand in this townland, as near as I could estimate. There may be many dead since I last tried to strike a reckoning, in the New Year.'

And then a thought struck him, so audacious, so incredible that it seemed foolish. Still, it was worth trying. He hesitated, obviously waiting for something, till those blue eyes caught his trailing bait, and took it, and he struck.

'Is there anything else I can do to help these poor people, Mr Delauny?'

'There is something, sir.' There was no harm now in being a little servile, showing a change of mood. 'I said that I could give these men employment for years to come. I can do that if I can finish the jetty, so that ships can come alongside and take out some of the produce of the place which we cannot at present sell easily — cheese mostly, but some wool too.' He did not say, if anybody lives to see it built, but his eyes said it, and Pentstemon was looking into his eyes.

'And so?'

'We are using stone cut in a quarry about a mile inland, the same that was opened to build the Martello. The speed at which we can build is limited by the speed at which we can cut stone with hammers and wedges.'

'Can you not blast?'

'The times are delicate, as you know. It is very difficult and time-consuming to obtain powder, and even if we could work our way through all the forms we would be paying out good money better spent on our own wages to buy the powder.'

'Well, if you will start civil commotions,' mused Pentstemon, 'you must expect a certain amount of administrative embarrassment. Young Ireland is doing little to help the Ould Sod, Mr Delauny, eh?' And the officers laughed dutifully at the joke, but Lawrence remained stony, serious. 'Have you anyone in your company who understands the use of blasting powder?'

'I have been trained as a Civil Engineer — properly. And at Trinity College in Dublin, and that is more than you could do at Oxford.'

'Oh, Oxford is very handsome, so they say, but I have never been in the town myself.' Pentstemon was thinking. *Could he go so far? If he did, his name would be made. In the county, in the country. In this county — handle it properly, and the seat would be his for the taking at the next election. The Whigs cannot hold on much longer.* He turned, calling, 'Oh, Mr Collins, are we not due for our quarter's firing?'

'Before the end of next week, sir.'

'You see, Mr Delauny, that while you and I know that a ship is made to be a ship and a thing of beauty, to sail about the sea in a lively manner and ornament the world by her sheer grace, yet their Lordships of the Admiralty are so eccentric as to insist that ships ought to be used for doing things with. And as part of this lunatic attitude, they insist that we should use lovely ships like this — don't snigger, Mr Mallow, this would be a lovely ship if only we could cut the funnels off and unscrew the paddles — should use them for shooting great guns out of. But this shooting, like steaming, is a dreadful nuisance. It makes the ship dirty. Worse, it occupies in shooting time that would be better spent in more seamanlike pursuits, like cleaning the ship. How much powder would we use, Mr Collins?'

'Including the main deck guns we've stowed below, sir?'

'Including all your toys, Mr Collins.'

'Five rounds apiece, fourteen thirty-two pounders at four pounds, two hundred and eighty, and the six main deck fifty-six pounders at seven pounds, two hundred and ten ... four hundred and eighty pounds, sir.'

'Isn't it a wonderful thing to be educated and to know arithmetic, Mr Delauny. So the main deck guns would account for about two hundredweight of powder, Mr Collins?'

'Near enough, sir.'

'We fired the main deck guns this morning, Mr Collins.'

'So we did, sir. I assume that Mr Only will enter that in the log. Would you wish to make any comment on the quality of the shooting, sir?'

'The shooting throughout was very good, Mr Collins, and you will record the large number of holes we made in the barrel.'

'Was it your intention, sir,' asked Only, 'to single out any particular gun's crew for special mention?'

'Who's that gun captain who plays the fiddle?'

'That'll be Tozer, sir.'

'Thank you, Mr Senescall. I wish specially to commend him for his high rate of fire, since I can think of no other occasion on which I could possibly make any complimentary remark about him.'

'I will go and gossip with the gunner, sir,' said Collins and went. He hated noise. His weeks at HMS *Excellent* had been the most miserable of his life. But his job was only to fire the guns, or at least order them to be fired: the guns themselves and their warlike stores were in the charge of the gunner, an old and crabby warrant officer. He had no time for anyone who wanted to fire his beautiful shining guns, and wear them out and break bits off them. Collins was sure that he would find co-operation there.

Delauny was hardly able to believe in his own sanity. He was being given, *given* two hundredweight of powder. It might not be really the best quality for blasting, but why worry? In a normal year, he might possibly have been allowed licences to buy about twenty-eight pounds. But with this, he could blast stone for another jetty and a half, and have some left over. Oh, yes, he would have some left over.

6

Pentstemon turned away. It was obvious that the interview was at an end. Delauny found himself alone. Disengagement was difficult in such a small and unfamiliar space as the quarterdeck of a ship. He looked around for Talleyman who had brought him aboard, but he was nowhere to be seen. Only touched his arm.

'We would be most honoured if you would join us for a bite of lunch in the wardroom before you go ashore. Only simple sailors' fare, you know, but…' He made a deprecatory gesture.

'That is very kind of you, but I would not want to put you to any trouble.'

'No trouble at all. Follow me.'

Only led him down a first companion way into a space filled with sacks of meal.

'We could sleep two hundred troops here for a long voyage,' he explained, 'and make it much faster than a sailing ship. For a short voyage, say from Weymouth to Cherbourg, we could carry a battalion.'

Delauny looked at the sacks. Far for'ard, past the casings around the engine-room skylights, he could see sacks being hoisted into the fresh air. Enough here to feed a battalion — or a county. No wonder the Captain could give the stuff away. Aft there was a door in the bulkhead, and Delauny turned towards it. Only stopped him.

'Not that way. The Captain lives there, on the main deck. We are down here.'

They reached the lower deck by the companion way. In a cramped space a marine stood with fixed bayonet before a

79

door. He came rigidly to attention as Only and Delauny squeezed past and levered themselves into a room about the size, Delauny estimated, of his own cabin ashore. There was a table down the middle slung from the deckhead. There were doors down the sides into what seemed to be cubicles walled off with thin planks. Surely this must be below the waterline? No, from the after end a little daylight came in to help the oil lamps.

'This is your quarters?' Delauny asked politely.

'We are quite snug in here.'

'We?'

'Four lieutenants, the master, the marine captain, the pusser, the chaplain and the surgeon.'

Delauny looked around in horror. 'Nine men in here, all at once?'

'Oh, yes,' said Talleyman, lightly, emerging from one of the cabin doorways. 'Here we hang like bats from the bulkheads. Sometimes the stewards get in to clear up. We count that foul play. Lots of room. Chaplain's having a run ashore. In Londonderry.'

'What's he doing there?' asked Mallow. They were, with some wriggling, getting seated.

'Holding a temperance mission,' Collins explained.

Mallow exploded, 'How that man has the face... But I suppose there's some kind of professional ethic, even among the cloth.'

'We learn to stay friends in a space like this,' said Only, his eyes on Talleyman. 'Hot food twice a day was a thing we never knew till Tom here lit the fire. Perhaps we ought to drink the health of this universal benefactor, but not in this hock. I'm not sure it's the right wine to drink with beef.'

'It's the best hock,' asserted the purser. 'We paid twenty-eight shillings a dozen for it, and we've got a lot more to drink yet.'

'But not with this beef,' Only grumbled on. 'You can't drink hock with hot beef. But at least the hock isn't hot — this time.'

'If we can't cool it, we may as well have it at room temperature,' argued Hampson.

'Engine-room temperature?' Only raised his eyebrows.

Delauny watched the play of banter, listened to the laughter. He had seen it before, in Dublin when a country cousin had come, or among his own workmen when a man walked across from Castletown, even in the Committee when Smith O'Brien or somebody had come across from Westminster. In front of a stranger, without meaning to, without even noticing it, the company sparkled, laughed afresh at their old familiar jokes. But they kept their own social order, teased and crosstalked in a curious quadrille of seniority. Only teased anybody. Nobody teased Only. Everybody teased Talleyman.

'The ship has no luck,' Only moaned, 'not since I lost my rabbit's foot.'

'You should not have lent it to the Captain,' the purser fed the lines.

'How was I to know he would eat it. He said the fur was the best bit.'

Delauny joined in the laughter, but he could tell that he was the only man to whom this was new, that there was a common memory among his companions of shared calamity, shared absurdity. Talleyman seemed to be a butt.

'He'd never carry a mascot,' said Only. 'He's not got the imagination. He needs somebody to wake him up. Have you got any colleens in the island will do for him, Mr Delauny?'

And that's all they think Ireland is good for, came into Lawrence's mind on a tide of irritation, *a place to look for women*. He stifled it, asked, 'And why only him?'

'Oh,' put in Mallow. 'My wife would never stand for it.'

'You are married?'

'We are all married, except Tom. Find someone to loosen him up.'

Delauny felt confused. Somehow it was difficult to imagine this group of young men — well, youngish, for Only was the oldest of them by ten years and he could be no more than an ill-looking, tired forty — crammed together in their little wardroom, as married men. Yet they all had their homes ashore, then, and children, gardens, farms even as Only had claimed, wearing ordinary clothes, riding in cabs, going to church, to theatres… And yet, as he looked around at their pathetic attempts to make the place comfortable, at the cushions and the chintz curtains at the scuttle, he could see that there were women somewhere who had wept to see their men go off to sea.

'He won't find a colleen in Eyories.'

'Oh, but Tom's got his contacts and his invitations, only he won't tell,' teased Mallow.

'There will be no welcome for him, I'm afraid, from the Irish. The Queen's coat is not so popular in this Island.'

He was not prepared for the silence that followed, the curious way they looked at him. Only seemed to recover first — *no*, Delauny realized, *it was that they waited for his reaction.*

'And why should he not be welcome? Or any of us, who wear the same coat?'

I must not quarrel with these men, who will let me have the powder. Nor show what side I am on, or might be on.

'There will be a political objection.'

'Political?' Only looked incredulous. 'Politics don't affect persons, not in Britain. Some of my best friends are Whigs. My next door neighbour, and he even had some influence or I'd never be in this ship.'

'Politics,' Delauny lectured them, 'do affect persons here. Politics are real here. This is not Britain, this is Ireland. The difference here is not between Whig and Tory, Tweedle-dum and Tweedle-dee. It is because those who want England to continue to rule Ireland, and those who want her, somehow or other, to rule herself. Those who want English rule to continue are those who are getting money out of the country. Those who want Ireland to rule herself are those who earn the money the others take out.'

'That is an over-simplification,' put in the purser, mildly, 'but let it pass. Carry on, Mr Delauny, we seldom hear the situation explained by a coherent Irishman. That is, if you *are* an Irishman, Mr Delauny.'

'I am a Protestant, if that is what you mean. But I am an Irishman born, and that is the kind of quarrel we have here where politics affects persons. My own father and I — he is black out with me over it, and I haven't spoken to him these two years.' He caught at himself, there was no call to go too far. 'But that's Ireland for you, we learn to quarrel and be passionate from our cradles. Let it be. I am an engineer and surveyor, and I am here to build a jetty. And the jetty is being built to feed men.'

'And we are here,' Only pontificated, 'to work this crank ship, that will not steam well because she was built to sail, and will not sail well because she was altered to steam, and is as top heavy as Noah's Ark, wherever we are told to go. And we have been told to sail her here and bring food to the Irish, who want it. Why then should we be unwelcome?'

'Unwelcome because of a quarrel that is not ours,' Talleyman's voice came from the bottom of the table, as harsh and grinding as his own boiler works. 'This is a dispute between the Irish. You said so. We have no part in it. But we must not let the peace be broken. Will the peace be broken? Will there be violence, Mr Delauny? Will Ireland be a country ruled by mobs and revolutions, like France?'

This man is different, thought Delauny in surprise. *This man thinks. And more, perhaps this man can be ours. Most of all, he has seen the danger.* He asked, 'What do you think of the news from France?'

There was a silence. They all looked at him. Then Only said, 'We have no news from France.'

'When did you last see a newspaper?'

'Three days ago at Fenit. And then it was a week old.'

'I had a paper the day before yesterday at Castletown. There has been a revolution in France. The King has abdicated. The red flag is flying from the Hotel de Ville. The Republic is proclaimed, and the rich are being hunted through the streets.'

There was a long pause. *They are thinking*, was Delauny's conclusion, *that soon it will be the same in Ireland, that the peasants will be on them, that they will soon be fighting here for their lives, that if the people rise in one country they will rise everywhere.*

And then Only spoke, 'Charge your glasses, gentlemen. There is an ancient toast. Gentlemen, I give you — *War, prizes and quick promotion!*

That was the toast Lawrence Delauny saw them drink, and then before his astonished eyes, this near-dozen of full-grown men began to cheer, and then to snake around the table in a crocodile. And they sang, sang,

> We're going to fight the French,
> We're going to fight the French,
> Remember Trafalgar,
> We're going to fight the French.

There was cheering outside. Delauny caught at Talleyman's sleeve, pulled him to sit down.

'How do they know about it — out there?'

'There are no secrets on a ship. The stewards took the news out. The Captain knows by now.'

'But — Why war?'

'What else will the French do? When they have civil upheaval, they will come to fight us to take their minds off their misery. Or we will fight them, to put down their rabble. We will want to restore their King. Or they will want to pull down our Queen.'

'Not that their King is very much for them to lose,' Only remarked, sitting down beside them. 'He had a chance to fight us two years ago, and then drew back.'

'But why the French?'

'What else have we been waiting for all these years? Why else do we have a navy but to fight the French with? There is no other enemy strong enough.'

'But war—'

'War is our trade.' This was Talleyman. 'That is what we are for. One day, sometime, in the mist in the Channel. Then we will earn our pay.'

PART II: SPRINGTIME

1

The ship was under sail. She had full bunkers, and a main deck full of grain. She wallowed in the sea, and rolled from side to side about an axis which appeared to Only to run through his navel. He was standing up because he knew that if he sat down, as the Captain urged him to do now and then, with malice, he would be sick. Occasionally he wondered if it would not be worth it: Pentstemon had spent a lot of effort, and some money, on having his cabin carpeted.

Only listened to the Captain reading on, reflectively, and then summing up, 'I suppose young Philip Suttle thought a great deal of you once, but now he seems to be too good for coarse company like you and me, Tom Talleyman.'

'I don't think so, sir. I saw him just before we sailed. From this letter he seems to have some trust in me. I think it is his father who objects.'

It *was* Philip's father who had objected, when he heard the suggestion, 'We can ask Talleyman to go and look.'

Lord Denain had bristled. 'I'll not have that man's son looking into our business.'

'Then why cannot I go, if you will not?'

'You know well enough they would as soon shoot you as me. That island is not safe for anyone of breeding. I've read the newspapers enough to know that.'

'And yet you think Roding is pulling the wool over our eyes. I still think we ought to invite Talleyman to go over and spend a week in the house, if his captain will let him.'

'But I will not have that — that man know all about it.'

'Tom doesn't talk to his father more than he can help. There's no danger there. And besides, you live on old Talleyman's money.'

'I do not live on his money!'

'Then what do we live on? It's the rent he pays for Fen Dilney that pays for all this.' Philip waved across the park to the Wiltshire downlands, up at the great portrait of the first Lord Denain, fresh as he came from being Quartermaster General under Marlborough, rich from the wars. 'There's no money from Ireland, else why should we bother Tom Talleyman. The farm rents here are mortgaged for the next twenty years to pay for the house. Why on earth did you have to carry on with the rebuilding?'

'I have to have somewhere to live, and this place is falling down before it is finished.'

'The Manor House at Fen Dilney was a good house enough.'

'I will not live in the fens. And you could not ask your mother to go to such a savage place, mists and reeds and drains.'

'But Josiah Talleyman is willing to live in the Fens.'

'And look what he's doing with them. He's brought in a steam engine, they tell me, and he's draining all the lower ground where your great-uncle used to take me shooting—'

'Took you once. Only the once.'

'Well, he was not to know then that the two between me and him would both die with no sons, and let me in to the Barony.'

'But they did. I'll argue with you no more. I'll write to Tom to call at Ballyfine, and I'll tell Roding to put him up. And make no conditions. But after that, I can ask him how things went.'

Lord Denain glowered at his son in defeat.

Philip Suttle went on, 'He must get some leave at home during the year. There can be no difficulty getting a few weeks' leave of absence from Ireland — it's all peaceful. I'll ask him to come here for a few days, and he can't avoid telling us without noticing—'

'It's the same in England as in Ireland. I'll not have that man's son in my house. It's bad enough having to bargain with him, face to face, have him pestering me to sell, and on top of that to have his son here doing the same — it's too much.'

'But remember, Talleyman saved my life on the Coast.'

'I did not realize,' said the Baron with a last feeble attempt at dignity, 'that that was a sufficient mode of introduction among gentlemen.'

'What do you mean, "gentlemen"?'

'It would not be fitting to have him here. You will some time be a peer of the realm. Talleyman is nothing by birth, and he would be uncomfortable here. You would be cruel to him, a mere tradesman, and it is not the society you would wish to mix in for the future. Think of Henry V and Falstaff.'

Philip turned on his father.

'What company did you send me to keep for five years at sea? Was it not good enough for you to contemplate then? I had all those years in a gunroom with Tom Talleyman. I know the company we're both used to, know it too well. Twelve-year-old midshipmen and fifty-year-old gunners all in together. Eating hard tack and biscuits with our knives, one plate between three. Stick a fork in the beam overhead and turn out the youngsters because what is going to be said and done is not fit for them to know about. That's the company Tom and I have kept at sea. If he's not fit for the company you want to keep then neither am I, neither am I!' Philip looked down at his father cowering in rusty black under the portrait. He waved his hand at the painted face.

'He would have had no scruples. Rent Fen Dilney to an engine builder? He'd have sold it, sold it all. Talleyman can afford to pour good money into the place, build a pump house, put a steam engine in, build a railway to carry his coal from Cambridge, and his corn back — when at last he has corn to carry from that soil, it'll be by the trainload, not the wagon. But look what it will cost him. If he wants to spend more, let him. We haven't got the money to think of starting it. If we sold the Fen, though — you could finish this house, and throw the farms here in together and work them sensibly. You can't do that without capital. And there's only one way to raise capital — sell Fen Dilney.'

Now Philip knew he had gone too far. What his father was about, he could not yet imagine. But the old man rose, he spoke slowly, deliberately.

'There'll be no talk of selling land, Philip. Without land a man is nothing. Hold to your land, lad, hold to your land. But … if that's the company you like…' He was silent, while Philip looked, shaken, at the face full of venom, wondered, *when I am that age will I look like him?* And he heard, hissed at him, quiet and harsh, 'There is one other way to raise money, and keep our land. One other way to raise money — marry it.'

'I must say,' said Pentstemon in his day cabin, 'I cannot understand young Suttle in the slightest. There he was, all set for a glorious career, and with luck, and interest, he might well have been a Captain in, oh, under thirty or forty years. Then just because his father comes into a peerage, he leaves the sea. I cannot understand it, at all, especially on such a pleasant day as this.'

Only could understand it well. *Santorin* was beating a little south of west going out of Cork in the teeth of a late April gale. It was sleeting.

'Now, young Tal, as I read it, he wants you to go and have some sport on his property, and let him know if all is well with the people there. Well, I admit, his father's property, but it'll all be the same in the end, and not too long, by what I hear.'

'Well, sir, he asks if I can find it convenient to go. If I can obtain leave. And then to write him, he says, interesting letters. How things stand there.'

'What you can tell Lord Denain about the state of his little farms in a distant place which you cannot make up from what we see on his land at Eyories, I cannot think, except that there is desolation compounded. I see no point in it.'

'I see a point.' This, surprisingly, was Only. 'My own land marches with Lord Denain's in Wiltshire, and he has been pleased to entertain me to wine there.' *"Marched", that was good,* thought Pentstemon, *because Only farms two hundred acres there, and Denain has three thousand acres let out.* 'I am told his Lordship's estate at Ballyfine is a great one, with a mansion and a home farm — what he calls a demesne — and a land agent to manage it all. Personally, I would have thought it more fitting that he should ask me to go, as a neighbour and a fellow-landowner of long experience. But if he prefers to do things in this way, why, it might be worth our while to oblige his lordship.'

Oh, interest, thought Pentstemon, *interest and self-interest that governs us all. Only has been all these years ashore, when a chance of interest, a right of way for his Lordship's coal cart or the chance to influence an election got him this billet as a return favour. Sick every time we hit rough weather, working always through the other lieutenants and the petty officers because he cannot control men — yet he strains for this scrap of influence, and now for another in the desperate hope of getting a ship, of being a Captain at last. And Denain is a peer, he sits in the House, he may have sufficient pull in time to give this booby a ship. If he does, I'll stay ashore. I'll feel safer.*

'Can we spare young Tal?' Pentstemon asked. Only was silent a moment. He counted up days, revolved his rosters in his mind, accounted the Tower, for watches, for the balance of Marines and soldiers. Meanwhile, Talleyman spoke, conversationally, to his Captain.

'Suttle says he is going to the other house they have. The Dower House at Fen Dilney.'

'You have a cunning look in your eyes, and I am sure that it is not there by accident, Tom. What is the attraction there, d'you think?'

'I think he is bargaining this invitation against another one. He wishes to meet my sister Arabella.'

'It is a matter,' Only brought them back to reality, 'of supervising the engineer.'

'If Mr Pellick cannot work his engines, then Mr Pellick must learn.' Pentstemon glared at Talleyman as if he defied contradiction. 'And if he must be supervised, there are four midshipmen in this ship and three cadets who have been thoroughly instructed in the principles of steam, and there are six Mates who are living in hopes of my recommendation and will certainly manage it if I order them to.'

'Then perhaps in a month, we could risk—'

'In another three days, I will put you ashore at Castletown. Ten days later, young Tal, I will pick you up at the Martello at Eyories, when I relieve it. Mind you are not late, especially since I believe the ladies in this island are in general more attractive than the ones you found so appealing on the Coast, who often detained you. I remember, you once held up *Argyle* for four days.'

'But then, sir, I was carrying Suttle. And I do it again. Thank you, sir.'

Pentstemon watched him go. He turned again to Only.

'You ride him very hard, do you not?'

'No harder than you do. Granted he is, as you will agree, lazy and will only work hard at what interests him, like the engines. Granted he is harsh, intolerant, self-righteous, and yet self-indulgent in the appetites. But he has not yet spent any time ashore in the Tower. Mallow has done that, and had a week hunting in Meath, and Collins two weekends shooting at Killarney. The sodger and the sawbones are in Cork at this moment, and if either of them can stand I will be surprised. But Talleyman has been ashore no more than you have.'

'Or you yourself.'

'You and I are different. I can pick and choose my times. I expect you to do the same. But you are grinding this lad, Paxton, you'll grind him to nothing.'

'Without grinding, sir, he'll never come to a sharp edge. He must be made to work, he must learn to handle a ship and there is no place to do that like this clumsy tub. There's no work ashore.'

'I agree, there's nothing for him to run into but trouble once he gets out of sight of the ship, in this island. But you bully him too much, Paxton. Why not pick on someone your own size?'

'But Talleyman,' said Only with relish, '*is* my own size.'

2

At Castletown, the priest looked sideways at his neighbour on the Bianconi. The young man in the green Chesterfield overcoat, and the railroad trousers, striped vertically in black and brown, turned a no less suspicious glance on the Bianconi itself. It was a long four-wheeled affair, with five seats aside, back to back. There was a canopy overhead, and a tarpaulin was pulled up over the fares' knees. A guard rode behind, and a driver in front controlled the four horses.

But this tall young man was polite, thought the priest. There seemed no harm in him at this moment, whatever his business, and even that he explained shortly, how he was going for a week's shooting, or whatever sport he could get, over to Ballyfine. He looked down from the road as it wound along the coast, looked across the roadstead to the island. He explained to Father McGuire that it could serve as an anchorage for a hundred ships, not merely as an occasional refuge, but as permanent as Portsmouth. You could have a whole fleet lie here, safe and snug, saving their coal till they were called to steam out and command the whole Atlantic and all the approaches to Cherbourg and Brest. Perhaps, one day... But then Talleyman was waving at the huge bulk of Hungry Hill, and asking what passed in the dead-looking copper mines.

'Indeed, and there would not be any men working there in a bad season like this,' the priest explained.

'But it would feed them. Do you know what copper is costing, when we buy it in for boilermaking?'

"Twould not feed them. The men work down here for some of the year, and so they get rent for their farms, and they will work no longer, because what man of sense would go underground longer than he need? When they have their land, they can plant their potatoes in the spring, and lift them in the summer, and eat them through the year, and the last of the year please themselves about when they work in the mines. For there is each of them a free Irish gentleman in his own mind, paying his rent and living of his own. So if they have no potatoes, they cannot eat, and if they cannot eat they cannot work in the mines, or anywhere else, and if they do not work in the mines they cannot pay their rent and they will be turned out. And that is how it goes.'

And that is a clear enough explanation for anybody, thought Father McGuire, *and we will drive in peace the rest of the way.* But in a little while, the stranger said, 'I have never seen country like this.'

It gave the priest a little satisfaction. It was a barren, incredible country. The soil was thin, an inch or two over the barren rock, no more. Everywhere the great stones thrust up, the bones of the land, grey as the priest's face, and as haggard and as tight drawn. It was a weary land. There was no room here, surely, to plant potatoes, not single roots, let alone whole patches. Nobody could live here. Yet people did live here. There were the occasional cabins of rough stone, dry-walled, always long side on to the road. There were the hosts of children, more like scarecrows — anyone could see that it was broomsticks that masqueraded as arms and legs. And if there were children, there must be parents.

'What do these live on?' Talleyman asked.

'They do not live. They starve.'

'Everywhere like this?'

'Everywhere in the Island.'

'I thought it was only at the coast, around Eyories, and such places.'

'Ah, 'tis very bad there. But it is worse inland.'

'But what do they all live on? In normal times?'

'There are no normal times in Ireland. We have lived on the edge of famine for years, and every ten or twelve years it comes. This time we have had it two years running. Last summer it was very bad, worse than it had ever been, till the harvest. There was a good harvest last year for those who had land and seed to plant, but the people were so poor there were very few of them could do more than rent the land and leave it to lie fallow. And who, anyway, had the heart to plant? So we are all still hungry.'

'You yourself?'

'I live with my parish. I hunger with my parish.'

'But your parish is not here?'

'I was born down there, in Castletown. I came back to see to my father's farm, for he died in the winter and so did my mother and two of my brothers. So 'tis my sister-in-law has the place now, and I have been able to get her enough seed potatoes to plant for herself.'

Talleyman was silent, he did not ask how the priest's family had died. The priest marked this down for politeness. The car stopped outside a stone house, in better than usual repair; it looked as if someone had started to demolish it and then stopped, rather than if it had fallen down of its own accord. There was a sign outside, once painted, now worn to a monochrome. With difficulty it could be read, showing that this was at once a shop, a corn dealer's, a livery stable and an inn. The horses were to be changed. Talleyman got down stiffly. He went into the little room, rapped on the counter with a sovereign, 'Have you any hot punch? For myself. And for the reverend gentleman here.'

The man did not realize, thought McGuire, *that I would have been served first, anyway, and perhaps he would never have been taken notice of at all unless I had been with him. But the man has manners, I will say that for him. Such courtesy deserves a compromise between truth and tact.* He pointed out of the door to a hovel opposite.

'Would you like to see inside that house?'

'I have seen too many. My stomach will not stand more.'

'Still, do you be looking carefully. That is a man of substance in this country. He has a field there, you see — perhaps half an acre, perhaps less. He has a dozen rows of potatoes, and a patch of turnips, which shows he is a man of educated tastes. And the rest of it is down in grass, and he will be having stooks of hay off it by the end of the year. You see, the hay will feed a cow, and pay the rent.'

'I have heard that said of pigs.'

'The cow will give milk, and there is no problem about paying the rent, because it can graze on the townland, and he can sell the butter — there's shiploads of it go out every tide to England. Sure, if only the people could eat the butter and live rent free for a year or two, we would have no famine. And the corn, too, there's a hundred tons of it going out of the country every week, while the government steamers are going out and in to bring the yellow maize.'

'Why do they not eat the corn?'

'Wheat is not for eating. Potatoes are what they eat, and nothing else. And if they did eat it, they would lose their land, and land is for potatoes. If they lose their land, these people have nothing.'

Talleyman considered, as they left Adrigole behind them and sat, blue with cold, on the rocking car. Then he asked, 'What will cure it?'

The priest considered. There was a need for courtesy. This was an Englishman, it was plain now, and there was no knowing what influence he might not have among the Constabulary or the landlords. But he had been well-mannered, and generous with the toddy. And Father McGuire had never really thought about this question.

'What indeed?' he answered, because this answer at least was safe. 'What but the intercession of the blessed saints and the will of God?'

'But would you want independence? Would that not help? The Young Irelanders are wanting it. There'd be an Irish Parliament again, like there used to be. A separate state from England. Would you not want that?'

'Look now, when there was an Irish Parliament it was a Protestant Parliament, and it was the Westminster Parliament that gave us emancipation. Now that Protestantism is off our backs, and the true faith has its independence, sure is not that all the independence that anyone could want?'

'But political independence?' Talleyman pressed. The priest looked hard at him. There was no knowing, no knowing at all.

'I'll have no talk of politics in my parish. We did have some of it, and who was the leader but the Protestant Vicar's own son, and it wasn't long before his own father tossed him out of doors, and there was an end of it. If I found any more Young Irelanders that I knew of, why, I'd denounce them all by name from the altar steps. And then there'd be cause enough for them to emigrate, because nobody in this place would be wanting anything to do with them at all.'

'But imagine that Ireland controlled her own affairs.' Talleyman pressed his neighbour, relentlessly: humorlessly, brutally, Father McGuire thought, not showing any perception of the reality of the situation. Here was an idiot savant, a man intent on information and nothing else, not able to reason or extrapolate. 'If an independent Irish government controlled the flow of corn and butter — then would you suffer from famine?'

There must be no more of this. Father McGuire replied, 'The famine is the will of God.'

3

'The famine is the will of God,' boomed Canon Delauny all down the length of the dinner table in Ballyfine House. For all this was the private dining room of the Baron, a mere cubbyhole a long way from the great Hall that had seated ninety guests and a servant to stand behind every chair, yet it seemed echoing and empty here with only seven of them, and Michael Flannery and the two girls to serve them. They all listened to the canon, the three servants who were not in theory able to understand the talk of their betters, Talleyman and Mr Roding, Foster the Yeomanry captain, Jane Roding and Harriet Delauny. Mrs Roding watched, and did not listen. She watched the soundless movements of the parson's lips behind his high white stock and wondered. Michael Flannery had heard it all before and too often. It was not his place to take notice of what the Protestant parson said, and he would make sure that the two maids forgot all about it.

Mrs Roding wished only that the evening was over, and she could go to bed, could return to the fine world of dreams, in which alone she heard great music and fair speech and the subtlety of actors' declamations, and the crying of her babies, three soon dead and this one now grown into a great girl, who frightened her sometimes. Her husband and the Ulster captain wished only that the vicar would cut himself short and let them get on with the meal and settle down to the serious business of drinking their way through Lord Denain's cellar. And the two girls sat quiet and still, wishing that the old man would stop and let them hear something from the visitor, this Englishman come out of the great and shining world of the other island, where there was talk and dancing and pleasure, where men could walk unmolested and women not worry whether their husbands or fathers might never come home at all: and where, most of all, there were people, hosts of people, new, new people.

'It is the will of God, and the greatest blessing the country ever had,' the vicar of Ballyfine went on. He addressed himself directly to Talleyman, sitting opposite him. He ignored the rest of the dinner party. He was used to sermonizing, and it reassured him of his own importance in the eyes of God. The others had all heard this before, in every sermon and every speech of their lives, they lived with it: but it might well be necessary to impart the facts of life to a foreigner. It would teach him reality.

'The inhabitants, of the poorer sort, are all Romanists, as you must know, Mr Talleyman, and their ears are fast closed to the message of the Gospel. I have laboured in this county for the better part of thirty years trying to turn the people to a true love of the God whose blood was shed for their sins, and to a real respect for the Queen's Majesty. But I have not until now been able to make the slightest headway against their Papist superstition and their priests. They pray here to graven images, you know,' and he leaned confidentially across the table, 'but at last, the Irish are beginning to turn from the heathen ways.'

'You mean they have seen the hand of the Lord in the famine? Have they come to you to teach them?'

'Of course, they have not gone so far as to do that, for their priests do not let them. But the failure of the potato has given us an advantage over the peasants which we did not have before. I have been receiving consignments of cornmeal, privately, from a charitable trust in certain parishes at home — especially from Fen Dilney which is a small town on the edge of the Fens, where Lord Denain has an estate, and I suppose some influence.'

'The present Lord Denain has never been near the estate.'

'How do you know that?'

'My father rents that estate. From Lord Denain.'

'Rents it? The whole of that estate?' Surely this could not be true, legend made that estate cover half a county.

'Not the whole of it. Lord Denain retains the Dower House. And its garden: about five acres. But the other six hundred acres we rent. My father wishes to buy the Estate. He lives in the Manor house. He has improved it. But Lord Denain is unwilling to sell.'

Roding, sitting between then, looked from Delauny to Talleyman. Had the youngster the slightest idea of the effect his words had? Even the parson was looking slightly surprised. If his father really did rent that estate, if he really could offer to buy it — sure, this was someone to know, to cultivate. But the vicar was droning on, 'That town has been very good to us. And I have spent a great deal of my own money.'

'Far too much from your stipend,' Roding put in. He had a duty to his own daughter, and there could be no letting Talleyman think that the vicar had money of his own. And somehow he must make the point later that he had land himself. 'You will ruin yourself out of kindness.'

Amen to that, thought Harriet Delauny, sitting next to Mr Roding, and smiling sweetly across at Jane, who was between Talleyman and Foster. She was in her three-year-old best gown, and if it had fitted her at fifteen, it was now hardly suitable for mixed company, since the dip of her bodice now pointed too clearly to the … the … portions of her anatomy it was not proper for gentlemen to have their attention called to. It made her blush to think of it.

'I own,' the canon agreed, 'that perhaps I have been over-generous, especially since the Parish is not well endowed, but depends almost entirely on the tithes for the stipend of the incumbent.'

Michael Flannery had cleared the first remove of salmon and turbot and leek soup. He began to bring on the second remove of mutton cutlets, and roast beef, and a couple of boiled chickens.

'The tithes,' asked Talleyman, ignoring the disturbance, 'are paid by…?' He let his voice trail off.

'The farmers,' explained Foster, kindly. It might be different in England.

'Who are, by religion…?'

'Mostly Catholics,' the canon confirmed. 'But Lord Denain is the lay Rector, and therefore Mr Roding collects the tithes for me along with the rents.'

'Do have some potatoes, Mr Talleyman,' Jane Roding interrupted. She saw the look of surprise in his eyes, remembered what Philip Suttle had written, 'an innocent, and needs to have simple things explained to him.' 'Oh, but we have plenty; it's only the improvident poor who didn't plant enough last year who are short now.'

But the canon went roaring on, like the sea, 'It is the wisdom of our settlement here in Ireland that the people, wherever they live shall find a minister settled in every parish, as indeed is the case in England. If they do not come to him for spiritual sustenance, then it shows that they are wilfully sinful. There is no need for the poor to seek the comfort of these Maynooth priests, who strip them of every penny they have—'

'And they cannot have much after paying their rent and the tithes.' The vicar was not quite sure what Talleyman's contribution meant, and decided to ignore it.

'As I was saying, I have been able to administer a little relief of my own, and for the last two years I have kept a school in my church. Every child who comes, providing he behaves himself and stays the whole time and is respectful and repeats his lessons and if he brings his own container, can carry away a whole pound of cornmeal.'

'That is most conscientious of you. A true father in God, teaching his own people their first lessons, every day.'

Yes, thought Jane, *this is an innocent, to say things like this. The vicar is giving him a strange look.*

'No… I am prevented by my duties about the parish, and the burdens of scholarship, Mr Talleyman. I am writing a refutation of Mr Newman, which will put an end to his pretensions for ever. If this work is to be thorough, it must be sound on the Fathers, on Chrysostom, Tertullian, and especially Origen.'

'Oh, a discussion of Chrysostom is most necessary,' Talleyman agreed.

The canon was about to expand, caught the look in Talleyman's eye, and instead, 'I take the Services on the Sabbath, but my daughter and Miss Roding are unceasing in their attendance, everyday.'

'Do you teach reading and writing, Miss Delauny?'

Harriet was confused at being addressed directly. Jane had expected that, watched with malice.

'Oh, no, nothing like that.' She was nervous. Whatever she said her father would complain of later; if she spoke too little or too softly, she would be called childish, yet if she spoke out at length, she would be a brazen strumpet. She was used to being told that she was a disgrace to her family, to her poor dead mother and the three little ones who all lay in that churchyard way up in Kerry. And she had often enough had her brother flung in her face, but at least he had escaped, to Trinity College and beyond. Yet Talleyman's voice sounded kind, coaxing: it was a voice the three cadets had heard, sometimes in the engine room as they tried to puzzle out the laws of the expansion of gases.

'What do you teach them, Miss Delauny?'

'We teach them to say the catechism, and the Twenty-third Psalm, and the Athanasian Creed—'

'That is the true foundation of doctrine,' the canon still boomed.

But Talleyman was still asking Harriet, 'By heart?'

'Oh, yes by heart.'

'But how do the peasants learn to read?'

'They do not,' the canon spoke flatly. 'There are no schools for them, they would not know how to take advantage of education.'

'I have been into many cabins. The people were very poor. Yet many could read. I would say about one grown man in three. They ask if I have newspapers. They want to read news of politics. Of the arrest of Mr O'Brien.'

Roding felt that he was being left out of the conversation. If there were money like that around, then there was no point in letting the Delauny's make all the running. Besides, he had never heard of Chrysostom, since he was at best an inattentive listener at the Parish Church, being more inclined to be a Presbyterian himself. So seeing a topic on which he could contribute, he explained, 'They used to have what they called hedge schools. Some old man who could read and write would come round, on tramp really, and stay in a cabin through the winter. Everyone would bring in some potatoes to feed him, and he would teach children to read, and in the spring he'd go back on tramp again.'

'Not only reading, and writing as well,' put in Foster, seeing a gap and wishing to help his fellow Ulsterman, 'but some of them knew Latin and taught a bit of that. How do you think all these Maynooth priests got their start?'

'How else, that illiterate crew,' boomed the canon, 'than by being taught by beggars. But we give them the true learning that leads to salvation, and bring them to a real knowledge of the one faith and the love of God.'

'So all the people of the townland come?' Talleyman was boring into the canon again, making him squirm. He felt he ought to counter-attack.

'At first they were very awkward and stubborn, but of late more and more children have been coming to us. And a child cannot eat a whole pound of meal a day so that if a man has eight children as many of them have, he may live tolerably well and have most of his family saved, even if he does not want to see his own soul safe into eternity.'

Mrs Roding at last managed to catch her husband's eye. She slid in her question, 'Shall we go to the drawing room?' Her voice, lacking the comparison of sound, produced now merely by force of habit and training, was beginning to collapse. 'I am sure you would all be glad of a dish of tea.'

The company rose, still talking. Harriet was sorry she had eaten so much. It had been the third remove of a turkey and two hares that had done the damage, irresistible, before the trifle and the jelly. She wondered how they would fare later in the week, because it was essential that her father now invite Mr Talleyman back. It was a pity that she would then be obliged to have her dear friend Jane in the house at the same time. But if the Rodings could borrow Mary Flannery to cook for the evening, then surely she could borrow her father to wait on table. There must be ways of arranging matters to her own advantage. But her stomach was straining against her stays, and it was one of her headache days. Why did women have headaches? It was not fair. At least eating was some consolation.

The canon moved in front of his daughter to give his arm to Mrs Roding. This allowed enough confusion for Harriet to move in front of Jane, so that Talleyman had no choice but to offer her his arm. Harriet knew very little about Talleyman. Perhaps he had money — she had gathered that from the talk at dinner — but obviously he had no land; he was merely renting it, or at least his father was, like any peasant. And he was only a navy officer, and therefore far below even Captain Foster socially, for he at least was a captain in the Yeomanry. But Foster was married, and there was no hope of escape that way: and Talleyman came from England, where anything might be possible. So she left Foster to Jane, who liked him no better than she did.

'You know England well, Miss Delauny?'

'Indeed, and I have never been there, Mr Talleyman.' She was only too conscious of it, and that her voice was Irish. She could tell that she spoke with a very different accent from Talleyman, and surely from any young ladies he might be knowing across the water, so she was hoping that her voice would be sounding strange and attractive to him, as it was the gossip it would. But she was afraid that she would only sound ignorant and savage.

'But your father spoke of England as home,' Talleyman reminded her.

'You're the only one here, Mr Talleyman,' put in Roding from behind them, 'that wasn't born and bred in this Island.'

'But … home? England?'

'What else would you be calling England?' asked the canon over his shoulder, putting down all other conversation. Harriet was used to that: she could not understand that other people might sometimes find it irritating. 'Can you name any part of our civilization here in Ireland, any part of our literature, of our music, of our religion that did not come from England? And was it not our ancestors that brought them? Why, the first Delaunys came over in Strongbow's time.'

And the first Suttles, thought Roding, *were just that, stemming from a sutler who went to the Flemish wars with Marlborough and cheated this estate out of the debts of a Dutch general that came here with William, God bless the King's memory.* The little procession down the vast corridor had reached the drawing room, the whole length of the west wing distant from the dining room. The corridor was icy chill, their breath hung in the light of the candles, but the room they entered was warm with the peat that had smouldered all day in the grate. The canon, with the air of someone perfectly at home in another man's house, threw unbidden a log on the fire.

Harriet leaned her weight on the arm under hers, manoeuvred Talleyman to a sofa. She felt her father's eyes on her as she sat. She remembered the long lines of young men she had been set out to meet at hunt balls and routs over the last year, all across two counties, all good Protestants and with each forty or fifty acres clear, and all the advice her father had been giving her on how to behave and to make herself agreeable. *None of them*, she thought fiercely, *not some pale curate with a fine relation who promises him a living in the bogs, or a dull and drunken squire even if he has a hundred acres. I will not stay here all my life, I know that. I will have... I know I shall have...* She asked Talleyman, abruptly, 'Do you know Philip Suttle very well?'

'I suppose I do. We were midshipmen together. We were in a gunroom for nearly three years. It was mostly on the West Coast of Africa. You cannot know what a gunroom is like. Smaller than this. All crowded together. No privacy. No room for privacy. Towards the end of the commission, it got better.'

'How did it get better?'

'Blackwater fever. So many died. Worse the second time.'

Harriet looked sideways at him. A man out of the great world she had promised herself. But was it then a world like Ireland, where people died in such great numbers that all one remarked on was that it made more room? Or was he talking for effect? She decided that he was merely doing that, and ignored it. She went on as if there had been no excursion into Africa. 'I knew Philip well once. You know, before he succeeded — before his father succeeded—' she was getting flustered, made an effort to talk coherently. 'The present Lord Denain was vicar here. When he succeeded he gave up the living, though there was no need to, you know, he could have put a curate in and kept the stipend, but he gave the living to my father because he was patron now as well as incumbent, and so we put a curate in the living my father has in Kerry and came to live here because it is more … well more central and more convenient for towns. But when I was a child, we often stayed in the Vicarage here for the company.'

'Where were you before?'

She caught the tone in his voice. He was making conversation; she really wanted to know: that was the difference.

'Oh we were twenty miles across the Long Bay, up in Kerry, and very far from company. But it was knowing Philip very well that I grew up, and even when he went to sea, it was often he was coming back till his father — for of course that was in the old Lord Denain's days before anyone ever thought that Philip's father would ever be Lord Denain himself — well, when his father came into the title he took it into his head to go and live in England and he hasn't been back here since. But Philip used to tell us such tales of the sea nobody could believe them, they were quite impossible.'

But that was all talk. What she wanted to ask was, didn't you know him very well then, or surely you would have heard of me? Didn't he *ever* speak of me, didn't he tell you about the elm trees behind the Vicarage with our names in the bark, didn't he tell you of all he promised, didn't he, didn't he? She wanted to ask all that, but how could she, sitting here with all these people listening, watching, even Jane there opposite with Foster and her narrow cat's eyes on every move, her ears almost twitching to catch the sound, snatching at what was being said...

Harriet did all she could, asked, 'Have you seen him lately? How is he?'

'I saw him about four months ago. Near to Christmas. He was remarkably well. It was in London.'

'What was he doing in London?'

'He was spending his patrimony. As far as I could tell. At any rate he took me out to dinner. I was glad of it. It was a very fine dinner. I wish I could have done it more justice. I had been working. I was very tired that night.'

Harriet almost asked what they had eaten, but restrained herself. If she pressed further it would look suspicious. Instead she asked, 'What were you doing in London? Were you working at the Admiralty?'

'I had lodgings in Clapham. The food was not very good. I was working at Napier's yard. In Lambeth. I was setting up engines. They paid me three pounds a week.'

Harriet was taken aback. In her world, no young men of consequence worked *for* anyone else. Even a peasant farmed for himself, and if he did work on his landlord's farm it was to pay the rent, not for money. The better sort might have professions or be in the army, even the embodied Yeomanry. Even being a land agent like Mr Roding came more under the heading of obliging a friend. The fiction was that Mr Roding's attention to Lord Denain's rents and to the vicar's tithes were a favour which sadly interfered with his administration of his own little demesne in Armagh. It was, of course, only a minor compensation that while he did it he had a whole wing of Ballyfine House to live in, and firing free and candles and the shooting and the run of the cellar because one gentleman could not refuse another the occasional bottle of wine, and all the dairy stuff and the vegetables from the gardens and the peaches from the hot house and keep for his horses. And if there was any money involved, a flat fee or a commission on the rents collected, then that was a private matter between his lordship and his friend. Meanwhile, Harriet sat in these splendid apartments, splendid at least by candlelight, and asked hopefully, 'You were studying these engines? For the Admiralty?'

'I suppose you could call it that. I was very glad of what they paid me. A mate's pay is only half a crown a day, you know. And half pay is — less.'

Harriet's experience did not include young men who talked of such trivial sums as these. They might discuss their gambling debts, indeed, or the cost of clothes or horses or even of land, but they did not mention incomes, not in such tiny sums. She moved back to safer topics. 'But he was well?'

'Who? Oh, Suttle? Never saw him better in my life. Fat as butter.'

'Did he talk about coming to Ireland?'

'Oh, no, shouldn't think he'd do that. Might get shot at, you know.'

At that moment, Captain Foster loomed over them. 'Miss Harriet, I must take my leave for a moment. Must go on my rounds, you know, and arrange an escort for you. I will return when it is ready.'

'An escort?' Talleyman queried.

'I was shot at myself a hundred yards from where we are sitting a month ago,' Mr Roding said across the room.

'That's why we have the Yeomanry quartered here.'

'You find it convenient?' Talleyman asked Foster.

The temporary soldier found it difficult to express himself. This idiot sailor clearly had not the slightest idea of the state of the country he was splashing around. Convenient, indeed, to be embodied and brought all the way down here from Ulster? On the other hand, though, to be living here at the government's expense and not at your own, and have free stabling for your horses and all the time in the world for hunting and a house like this to live in — he could only try to answer diplomatically, 'Yes it is quiet convenient. My men are under canvas in the wood — quite impossible in winter, but now the spring is well on they are very comfortable. We have a cookhouse in the stables and we keep our powder in the wine cellar.'

'Powder?' Talleyman sat up, almost making Harriet spill her tea. 'In this cellar? You find it convenient? Is it safe? I have been through *Excellent*.'

What that meant, Foster could not imagine. Probably some naval term of commendation. He answered, 'Oh, quite safe. It is locked up. I sleep in the house, and there is no danger of the Molly Maguires getting at me.'

Talleyman said softly, as if musing, 'I met a Father McGuire on the way. Any relation? Were you really shot at, Mr Roding? What did the police do?'

'Oh, the Constabulary are all of one piece with the Irish, and for all the great Superintendent Trant could do that is supposed to know every move the traitors make, when he came here after I was near killed, there was a devil a man to be caught.'

'And the remedy? More soldiers?'

'Oh, 'tis agreeing I am with the canon, that the Famine is the best thing that ever happened to Ireland.'

'You would like to see more people die of starvation?'

That, thought Roding, *is a sight too direct, but the whole thing here is too far gone to be hiding anything.*

'If there were fewer of the murderous dogs in the Island, the rest of us could lead a decent life.'

'I thought the same of slavers. In Africa.'

There was a short silence. Roding was trying to work out what that comment meant. The vicar was asleep. Mrs Roding sat immobile, trying to follow the drift of feelings by the expressions on the faces. The content of the discussion was beyond her comprehension for ever. Jane Roding rose and crossed the room. Talleyman stood, let the two girls rearrange themselves on the sofa, then sat again between them. Harriet seized on the moment. She asked, 'Will you not tell us something about Africa, Mr Talleyman?'

'Oh yes. Good shooting there.'

Roding pricked up his ears again. The canon was awake.

'What did you shoot?'

'Goldbeaters, mostly.'

'Goldbeaters?'

'They form a principal part of the exported wealth. You have heard of Goldbeaters' skin?'

Roding nodded wisely. The canon made an effort to regain control of the talk.

'Why are they called Goldbeaters?'

'They have a peculiar habit. They search the sands of the mangrove swamps for nuggets of gold. They clutch the nuggets to their breasts. They ascend into the branches. They beat on the branches with the nuggets. This disturbs the slag weevils which live in the bark. They come out. The Goldbeater eats them.'

'The Goldbeater is a bird?' asked Jane, suddenly.

Talleyman looked shrewdly at her.

'Oh, no. It is a mollusc. The shells are much prized as a garment. That is why the skin is so delicate.'

'How wonderful and inscrutable are the ways of the Lord,' said the vicar. 'I have read of this in Herodotus.'

'There is a longer treatment in Pliny,' Talleyman assured him.

'I will use this as an illustration in my book against Mr Newman, to show how from among the lowliest forms of life some good may come.'

Foster returned. Soon Harriet stood in the corridor, wrapped in her mantle, embracing Jane, dear Jane, who was going to have Talleyman to herself for so much of the time, who would be able to ask for news of Philip whenever she liked. But because the horses were waiting — oh those damned horses, she could blaspheme in her mind at least, always so important, more valuable than any people, never to be overworked, kept out in the cold or wet — because of the horses she had to be bundled out into the dark wind and leave Jane with this prize. Good luck to any steam engine that would do away with horses. She wondered what a steam engine was really like. She had never seen one, only pictures in the *Illustrated*. And there had been a few glimpses of steamers passing close to shore in the Long Bay. At least, if the thing had a fire in it, it would be warmer than a carriage.

In the carriage, she pretended to be sleepy, so excusing herself from conversation with her father. Talleyman, she thought, could be of use. Trade he might be, and not very important trade, if he had to work while he was on half-pay. She was sure that army officers never went on half-pay unless they wanted to, and then it was to return to their estates. Of course, Philip would never have gone into the navy if there had been the slightest thought, when he was only thirteen, that he might come into a peerage. Nevertheless... Talleyman might be more important than he seemed. She began to see Philip's scheme. She was to be polite to him, and there would follow the invitation to Fen Dilney, where she could regain her Philip at last. That must be the scheme. He need not tell her, he could depend on her to understand the way he thought. But to be sure — she must get Talleyman out of Jane's way.

4

Talleyman climbed the hillside close behind Jane. Her feet clung securely to the slippery path. They stopped near the edge of a wood and looked down at the great house. The drive went from the door and out, almost straight, half a mile across the park to the lodge gates. Beyond this gate, across the road, in its own twelve acres, stood the vicarage, fine in its red brick and its pillared porch. And further on from the main road was the church, ill-repaired, tottering.

That morning Talleyman had sat at Matins, in Lord Denain's pew, making a third of his representatives with Mr Roding and Jane. In the opposite front pew, across the aisle, Harriet had been sitting. At the back of the church eleven thin ragged children crouched uneasily, tried to make the appropriate noises at the responses, after the blessing seized their pounds of meal from the vicar himself, and ran. Between the children and the gentry sat Captain Foster and his thirty Yeomanry, splendid in their warm blue Hussar uniforms. And no one else.

Talleyman had already been for a walk that morning, before breakfast. He had found the Catholic chapel. It was simple, a mere barn, but in good repair. He had never seen a service anywhere so well attended that half the congregation stayed outside, on the steps or kneeling in the mud.

He asked Flannery about it, catching the butler in his pantry polishing the silver after the midday dinner.

'Oh, yes, indeed your honour, there is no question there that you saw the same children twice this morning, although I would not be having you tell the canon about it, for it would be breaking his heart, and there's Father McGuire wouldn't be wanting to hear about it either. Sure, there's many a family that choose one child out of the house to risk damnation for them, and send it to the Church School every day for the meal.'

Flannery waited a moment, expecting a comment. It was a little time coming. He was ready for the visitor to say something, like 'a pound of meal is worth a catechism, eh?' and give him a nudge or a wink. But Talleyman stood for a long time, looking at him minutely, and then, suddenly, 'You're the bo'sun, then, Flannery.'

Flannery looked at Talleyman, did not answer.

'I never knew a ship that the bo'sun didn't run, Flannery, whatever the captain and the commission officers thought about it. It's only you who matters here.'

'I beg your honour's pardon?'

'You run the house, don't you? You run the estate. Don't you? You can tell the people how much they can pay; how little they can risk. You tell them when they must pay. If they have to. That's right, isn't it, Flannery? And it's you who gives the warnings. That's right, isn't it, Flannery?'

The butler stuttered.

'You can't hide it, man. It's clear for anybody who looks. This is your country. The gentry — they don't control it. You do. And up at the vicarage. The housekeeper. She's called Flannery too. Your cousin? Your sister? Your daughter?'

'My eldest daughter, sir. She had three years in a convent up at Tralee, through the kindness of my brother that is priest of a parish near Sligo, but she had a long training here as well with my wife and Mrs Roding. So that although she is still young, we thought she would be as well for that post as any other, and not as oppressive for Miss Delauny as an older person might be—'

'We thought? Who thought?'

'Well, your honour, it was Mrs Roding and I and we thought—'

'A Catholic housekeeper for a Protestant vicar. A strange country.'

Flannery had no comment. And how else would you have arranged things? But what Talleyman turned to next was worse.

'Mr Delauny. Young Mr Delauny. The engineer. He is often at home?'

'Oh, no, your honour, he never comes home, not now.'

'That is a pity. I have met him. Several times. He is working hard. Out there in the West. He needs a rest.'

'Indeed, and so they do say your honour, and 'tis terrible times they are having out there at Eyories, as you have seen for yourself, and it's not even Mr Roding will dare go out there any more, that was afraid of nothing till the boyos had a shot at him in the dark and missed him by the width of a cow.'

'There's a lot of shots fired, Flannery, and not many hits. 'Tis frightening, if nothing else. Why does Mr Delauny not come home now?'

Flannery had heard the tone of that last question, coming hard on the flippant comment. It was a tone he had not heard for a very long time, not since the old Lord Denain had been in Ballyfine, not the one that had been vicar, but the real old devil. But he recognized it, the unthinking voice of authority, assuming that it had a right to know, seeing no reason why it should not be answered, and answered with truth. But to Flannery, there were half a hundred reasons why it should not be answered, and as many ways of evading authority, born of five hundred years of practice. Whether there were more reasons to parry questions about young Delauny, or about the likelihood of being shot himself the first time he put his head outside the lodge gates was hard to tell. Perhaps half truths…

'There was trouble about a woman. Someone he wanted to get married to, and the vicar would not have it. So they are not married, but the lad dare not come back here.'

'I see.' And the pressure, unbelievably, was off. Of a sudden, Talleyman was walking away, and Flannery saw that at the foot of the stairs Jane was waiting for him, in her walking clothes, her stout boots. The pressure was off, but for how long? For this was a navy man, out of a Queen's ship, and when would he be returning to ask more of his straight questions that went so near the truth? What would he ask next? Or not ask? What did he mean by saying so straight that he had seen Delauny in the West, that it was time he came away? Flannery watched Talleyman go. *Sure, this was a hard one, and saw too clear. Bo'sun, then did he call me? Control it all, then, do I? Saints help us, but I'll show him he's right but he'll never know a thing of it.*

Talleyman kept up with Jane on the steep hill path. But he was panting.

'You move fast. Over such rough ground.'

'Oh, it's all a matter of being used to the country. When I first came here, for my father to be agent to the Old Baron, we were all children together and we used to run about as barefoot as the children out of the cabins, Harriet and Philip and Lawrence and me. We learnt the tricks of the bogs and the turns of the path. I'll wager, Mr Talleyman, that I could go from here to the Long Bay and back faster than you could in a Bianconi or with a troop of Yeomanry, and you'd never see me once on the road. And I'd be slow compared to many of the men who live around here. Now, look around you? Can you see the cabins? And the smoke of the peat fires?'

'I can see more cabins than fires.'

'When I was a child, I used to come up here and count the fires, and never get the count the same twice running, but I know there were over a hundred. Now, can you see even twenty fires? And there's cabins that have no fires because there's nobody alive in them, and others because there's nobody in the house with strength to go out the cut the turf. For turf cutting is not hard to do, if you've learnt the knack of it, but still it takes strength, and it's strength they lack. They won't have strength till the potato harvest's in, when July comes. Then they'll be lighting their fires again, and it'll all be like the old days when I was a child. Oh, but it's a dreadful time it has been, indeed.'

'Why did you all stay here? Why did you not find somewhere else to go?'

'My father cannot go because he has the rents to collect for Lord Denain, and the demesne farm to work. And he has his own rents and lands in Armagh. And my mother would not go and leave him here, and I could not leave my mother, because I hear for her. So we stay.'

She did not tell him about the letters from Philip Suttle that had asked the same question. And they had told her more. She knew this man, from the letters. Limited, they had said, able to tackle any problem provided a few hard strokes with a hammer would solve it. He was only one of the many Philip had described over the years, Fat Jack Pither, poor Partridge, Pentstemon — she wished that he had sent Pentstemon, he seemed more interesting in spite of his age. So many names that were never people till this one. Now she had seen Talleyman, he was turning into someone in his own right, and she found that disturbing. Nothing had prepared her for a man whose father could bargain with Lord Denain, and in this townland where the Baron was next to God in power, that was something to marvel at. Only a manufacturing somebody, but nevertheless, somebody. Not a man of imagination, Philip told her, not subtle, with no insight ... she could handle him. Only the Goldbeaters lurked in her mind.

He was still arguing with her, 'It would be advisable to go. If the harvest is better if there is less strife — or more strife — perhaps then you could leave your father here. You and your mother could find a welcome at Fen Dilney. My mother — my sister Arabella—'

'It may be possible, Mr Talleyman, thank you very much. Now, perhaps since my mother looks to us to join her for a dish of tea, we ought to be going back down the hill.'

He stretched out his hand to help her down the path, the bare earth was slippery under her feet. He held on to her fingers, and she sensed that there was enough excuse in the ground to make it reasonable, or at least to make any objection unreasonable. After a few yards, the path was easier, and she was able to take her hand from his, but still felt that she must take his arm. They came further down, where the woods hid them from the house, from everything. She kept talking brightly, so as not to think of anything else, to stop him thinking or make him reply in his odd short sentences. *And of course*, she thought suddenly, looking back to the tales she had read, *it's the speech of a man used to saving his breath, used to shouting over the noise and clatter of workshops and engines and the creak of masts and ropes.*

'Yes, here is where we always used to look for the first primroses when we were children, and I am sure that if the ground were dry enough for us to venture from the path we would find some but alas the ground is quite impracticable and I don't think we can risk our shoes in the wood and if we did we would be so late and my mother would be waiting for us, and worrying, she does worry so, you know, and it is very hard to console her when she can't hear anything we say and always thinks we are keeping bad news from her. And Flannery would be so disapproving, they say that even old Lord Denain, not Philip's father, the great Baron, was afraid of Flannery, and no wonder. His father was out in the 'Ninety-Eight, and he has the most awful tales of people being shot to death or piked or cut to pieces with scythes or hanged off bridges to drown if they didn't strangle. But that was all in the past, and in the east, around Waterford and Dublin, and not here, although now — ah!'

She had slipped. It was a genuine fall, and she was sure it had nothing of coquetry, whatever Talleyman might think. Her heel went from under her, and the other knee bent and she almost sat down on the path as if it were a chair. But her left arm was on his right, and as her grip tightened, automatically, and she squealed, his left arm curled around her, supported her, held her, lifted her against the fall and pressed her hard against the front of his coat. She felt the harsh rubbery front of his mackintosh, and smelt it, all mixed with the smell of cigar smoke and a faint background of harsh soap and salt and the sea. It was a smell of man, and yet a different smell from the one she was used to at balls and suppers when the farmers' sons would try to get her into a corner, dark and warm and snug. This wasn't a snug corner, and the smell was different, but the result was the same. She was pulled to him, and was furious to find herself for an instant, mechanically, against any conscious will, turning her face up to be kissed. His face pressed against hers, his lips were on hers. She pushed back at him, kept her body unyielding, her lips tight pressed, her eyes wide open to stare into his — she had noticed before how brown they were but not how soft, like a spaniel's. She pushed him away as soon as she felt his grip slacken.

'Mr Talleyman! How dare you!'

For a split second she considered smacking his face. But the moment passed, and she excused herself after all that there had been provocation, and perhaps all the innocent talk about going into the wood for primroses had not been the wisest topic. She had given him the opportunity. And besides, to slap him would turn this all into an open quarrel, one not to be supported, not to be carried on for another week while they lived under the same roof. And if it were carried that far, making it up would be as passionate as the quarrel, and where would they be then? And under Harriet's scornful questioning eyes, too, it would be too much. Besides, she had not really felt offended to the smacking point, or she would not have hesitated.

'Miss Roding! Jane!'

'Mr Talleyman. That was not polite.'

'Miss Roding! Please! I have known you—'

'For at most three days. Do you act so, Mr Talleyman, to every young lady on three days' acquaintance?'

He looked so abashed she almost laughed. This *was* a spaniel; if only his ears were longer — the thought made her want to laugh even more. But Talleyman would not be put off, returned to the charge, 'For three whole days, Miss Roding, from the time I saw you first, on Friday evening. Miss Delauny … she monopolized me…'

'She was very polite to you, sir.' She was doing her best, and much good it did her. If she were to hear about this she'd turn green.

'I am not concerned with Miss Delauny. Miss Roding! Will you … will you … may I speak to your father?'

'No, sir, you may certainly not speak to my father. At such short notice! It is unthinkable.' *The old devil, he'd pack me off with you as soon as he could find a car, he'd have old Delauny reading the service at eleven o'clock at night, and drink for a week in relief at getting me off his hands. I swear he'd marry me off to Bronterre O'Brien himself if he had a chance.* 'You must keep your feelings to yourself. If he thought that you had taken advantage of this visit to try to sweep me off my feet, there would be trouble indeed. Men still fight duels in Ireland, you know. Perhaps after a few months, when you have been without my company for a while you may consider whether your feelings remain the same, and then perhaps you may wish to ask my father whether you may visit us again.'

'But Miss Roding … may I hope…?'

'I cannot stop you hoping.'

'May I write to you?'

'No! You may not write to me.' That would make life unbearable, with the letters that came now from England, always addressed to Mary Flannery in a dozen different hands, but always the secret mark on the corner that told her who it was. More letters that could not be hidden — yes, her father would soon be trying to be rid of her.

'But at least tell me. Is there another? Is it Mr Delauny?'

And that was the end of it, because at the very thought of it Jane collapsed in laughter, hooting uncontrollably, Talleyman thought, like any cadet in the cockpit. After that, there could be no serious discussion. Only hopes for some other time, alone.

5

Jane knocked at Talleyman's door, scarcely a knock, more like a scratching on the wood, soft, small in the huge night, the long dark corridor. There was silence. She wondered if perhaps he were downstairs already. She knocked again, a little louder than before. She heard the squeak of the bed, another long silence, and then the door was opened a crack. Talleyman was holding a candle. The delay, she realized, had allowed him to light it, and pull on a dressing-gown. She turned the slide on her dark lantern, and he in reply hid his candle behind the door. She had had to take the risk, and knew it was a risk when he stammered, 'Miss Roding — Jane—'

She cut him short, whispering, 'There is someone in the house.'

He came awake, properly, at once. He looked over her wool day dress, down to her shoes, said, 'Go back to your room.'

He shut his door on her. She returned to her own room, fifty paces away and across the corridor, and went again to the window, looking down into the courtyard. She had barely glanced out when he was tapping softly at her door. She let him in, turning him away, in her embarrassment, from the rumpled, still warm bed.

'We learn to dress quickly at sea,' he told her. She took in the pea jacket, the trousers over his nightshirt, and heavy boots, too. 'What is happening?'

'I can hear noises down there in the courtyard, at the back of the house. I thought I could see someone moving in the court. It is very dark, but I think they have a window open. And the noises might have been a handcart.'

'I see. Why did you not call your father? Or the gallant Captain?'

'You saw how much they had to drink tonight. And I could never make my mother hear.'

'I thought that Lord Denain had shut up all that part of the house. Surely there is nothing there to steal?'

'There is a door to the wine cellar there, under the main staircase, handy to the dining room, and this window opens close to it.'

'You think they are after the liquor?'

'I think somebody is after the powder.'

He was silent a moment. Then he asked, 'No sentries at all?'

'You remember that is why Captain Foster sleeps in the house — all he does is sleep.' She could not help saying that even if it sounded a little catty... 'He has the key — no, one of the keys. My father has another one, and Flannery has a third, or neither of the others would be so sound asleep now. But I think that Foster believes that there is so much powder that nobody could move it without making enough noise to wake the county. Besides, if they did steal it, the theft would be known at once and the Yeomanry would scour all the country round till they found it.'

'Why should anyone steal all that powder?'

'I told you — there are men here who were out in 'Ninety-Eight, and that was a civil war and most horrible. Don't you understand — we hourly expect it here again.'

She was proud of that play on words, it showed that she was still cool-headed. Philip would have been proud of her. It was good to see Talleyman's eyes narrow. She hit at him again: 'The army knows that even if the navy doesn't.'

'The army is asleep. We keep our watch.' He slid the pistol out of the inner pocket of his jacket. It was a huge thing, eighteen inches long.

'What on earth—'

'One of Collier's revolving flintlocks. I wanted to buy a Deane and Adams, but it was too expensive. So I altered this. Look, the new hammer comes down here, and I have drilled out each cylinder to take a percussion cap. I did the drawings at *Excellent*, and the machining at Mr Napier's yard.' He was like a small boy with a toy, his whole manner of speech had changed.

It seemed a pity to spoil his fun, but, 'I have this,' and she reached under her pillow for the squat Belgian pepperpot. He looked at it curiously.

'Double action? No, you can see … can you fire it? Have you fired it?'

'I can hit a running rabbit — if it comes close enough. I fire all the chambers once a week, and I reload them — it keeps the damp out. I change the percussion caps every two or three nights.'

'Why?'

'I told you. A powder keg.' She could match his speech.

'Your father let you have this?'

'No. Philip Suttle. He said, one success, and the police and Yeomanry will just run away. The rebels will have all their arms for the picking up. Then the looting will start, and we must look after ourselves. But they have to start somewhere.'

'That's logic. How much powder?'

'I heard Captain Foster talking about a five hundredweight cask, and cartridge cases to be filled. And there was shot as well.'

'Maybe two tons of lead. Enough for a small battle. They'll need several men. And ropes — unless they repack it into small bags first. Now … look, someone is moving. See, by the pilaster. In the shadow.'

'Will you shoot at them from here?'

'I know my own marksmanship. And at night. Perhaps in the day, at three feet… I will go to the cellar. Stay here.'

'I am coming with you.'

'You will do no such thing.'

'Indeed, and I will. I will hold the light for you. And more, Lieutenant, you would not leave me here unarmed. With me, you have an extra pistol, to surprise them. Six more shots.' When he hesitated, she added, 'If you were not here, I would have to go down alone.'

For a moment she was still afraid he would refuse her, but he only said, 'Stay ten feet behind me. Pray do not shoot me. Not if you can help it. Or if you think it necessary.'

They went along the narrow passage to the steep service stairs that led to one end of the great front gallery. They peered out from the small door hidden in the bookshelves. The grand staircase, leading up to the closed bedrooms of the first floor, and the great state rooms, was about halfway along it. About, not exactly. The French architect had designed the house to the nearest half-centimetre: the Irish masons had worked to the nearest whole brick. There were no right angles in Ballyfine House.

The back of the house had been in shadow, but the moon shone in here through the tall south-facing windows, showing that the Hall was empty except for the humps of the sheeted chairs. Jane stood a moment to count them, satisfied herself that there were no extra shadows, nothing there she did not know. She could feel a draught of air, though none of the front windows was open. The intruders were working through the small window in the alcove behind the grand staircase, that led into the back court.

The hall was empty, but there were noises coming from behind the grand staircase. Jane tugged at Talleyman's sleeve, and pulled him with her along the gallery, and into a space between two cupboards. She strained to keep her booted feet from grating on the oak floors: she had taken the hint from Talleyman, and was not going to have her feet trodden on. She had played hide and seek here often enough in the old days, with Philip and Lawrence and Harriet, in real dread of being caught by that horrid figure, the old Lord Denain. She felt that nobody would have dared to steal powder from *him*. So she knew every hiding place here, every inch of dead ground. From here, you could see the window into the courtyard, and the little door that led behind the grand staircase and down into the cellar, and never be seen yourself.

A man came out of the cellar. He was carrying a knapsack, full and very heavy by the way he leaned over with it. He turned his head to call back, not loud but still not trying to whisper, to the man behind him, 'Will that be all, then, Patrick?'

'Indeed, it will, or there'll be not enough left to hide what's gone or finish the job. But we haven't roused the man yet. We'll never have him at this rate.'

'Michael's gone to throw a stone at his window. That will bring him.'

Jane tried to understand what he meant. Talleyman, she guessed, would never have caught a word of the thick South Cork accent. But she felt him take the dark lantern from her, and he walked softly, even on the bare boards, after the man with the bag into the open window to the courtyard where another man waited. He reached the wall three paces after them, as they began to push their handbarrow away. He put the lantern on the sill against one side of the window. He pressed himself against the other, and leaned forward to open the dark slide. The yellow light flooded the courtyard. It picked out the men, their handcart with its wheels padded with rags. Talleyman shouted loud, in a voice enough, she thought, to wake her mother.

'Stop there! Stop! Or I fire!'

Between her and the light thrown back by the lantern he was silhouetted. But there was more light on his back. She remembered why she was there, and looked at the cellar door, from which a softer light came. And then there was a man silhouetted in his turn against it, setting down his own lantern on the stairs. He had something in his hand, maybe a pistol, maybe a club, she did not wait to see which. It was something she could not afford to see used, and that was enough for her.

She pulled back the hammer with the thumb and finger of her left hand. She could hear Philip's voice in her ear as she swung the revolver up: *don't think about aiming, just point — you never miss anything when you point your finger.* And then she heard him again: *get close and be certain.* So she took three long steps forward.

Jane pointed her hand at the man in the cellar door and pulled the trigger. She coughed in the smoke. She was almost deafened, she had never fired the thing indoors before. But she remembered to turn the cylinder, cock the weapon again. The two men outside, not leaving their handcart, broke into a clumsy run, as Talleyman turned to Jane with a face of anger, perceptibly caught himself, turned again to the window and fired somewhere into the blackness where the men had been.

He faced Jane again, his face now blank of anger. *This*, she thought, *is how he controls himself, and controls men by restraining himself. What would he be like if he did let himself go? Wolf? Or vulture?*

'Why did you fire? You frightened them off. I could have held them.'

'Look there!'

She was unable to say more, pointed to the cellar door. Talleyman brought the lantern over. The man was lying on his face across the door sill, his feet on the cellar stairs, his lantern by his ankles. And there was a pistol by him. It had been necessary, then. Philip had used to say, if you must kill, then a man will lie as dead as a rabbit. Talleyman turned him over. He did not groan, just flopped vaguely limp where he was let lie. The sailor looked up at her.

'He is dead. Thank you. He would have had me. Do you know him?'

She forced herself to look at the body, at the thin face with the three days' growth of beard, the lips drawn back over the teeth. It looked like the woodcuts she had seen in the chapbooks and cheap tracts warning against the dangers of another 'Ninety-Eight — or looking forward to them. This was how the men looked, their faces strained and wild, alive but no less frightening than this dead man. A flood of pictures swept through her mind, she heard the screams of the mob, felt nails at her face, hands at her breasts, she floated as it were above herself, felt her legs spread apart — and she blushed to feel a glow of half-pleasure, half-pain, a physical shudder. She announced, 'No, I don't know him.'

'Not even the clothes?'

'They all dress alike, this frock coat. He is no one from around here.'

'Then how did he know?'

'That there was powder here? Sure, and where else would the Yeomanry keep it? Or how to get to the cellar? There's half the county knew, all the families that built the house, that have served in it — that paid for it.'

'Did you see the men who went through the window?'

'Not to know them again. And I did not know the voices either, but they were … well, they did not come from this end of the county, but still they were Cork men, West Cork. Not Kerry men, for instance. I'll swear to that.'

'Well, let's be rid of him. No point in an inquest.'

Talleyman picked up the dead man and threw him bodily down the stairs. Jane heard the soggy bump, and tried not to be sick.

Talleyman waited a moment, then, 'I'm going down. Wait for me.'

He looked around a moment, and then tore down a curtain from the window behind them.

Jane warned him, 'But there may be more down there.'

'If there were, they'd be up already. Especially now he's gone down again.'

He picked up the intruder's lantern, and with that in one hand, the pistol in the other, the curtain wrapped curiously around his chest, went into the doorway. Jane retreated to her first hiding place, closed the slide on the lantern, and waited, shivering, with her finger still on the trigger.

There was no sound of a voice from below, or of a shot. Instead, they were the noises of things being moved, of heavy weights disturbed, rolled across a stone floor. There was a gurgling sound. Then the tread of feet on the stairs, intentionally heavy, and Talleyman's voice, 'Miss Roding! Do not shoot me. Please.'

He was with her, again. The bulge of the pistol showed in his pocket, but the lantern and the curtain were gone. There was a glow from the cellar stairs. The lantern? No, it was too red for the lantern, and it was flickering, growing.

'What…?'

'There will be no inquest. Not on a shot man. Perhaps on a burnt one, if they find enough. We both fired through the window. He died in the cellar, on his own powder mine.'

'What's that?'

She was as jumpy as a frightened hare, and she knew it and could not control it. This was hammering on the door behind them, into the agent's wing.

Talleyman told her, 'I bolted that door behind me. I did not want to be taken in the rear.'

The clear half of her mind seemed to answer: *but you were so taken*, but she remembered the way the man had fallen, the horrible choking noise, the look on his face. She tried not to retch and leant against the wall. Talleyman had her by the arm, was hurrying her along the gallery away from the fire, away from her own part of the house. She looked through the window, saw the movements outside.

'No, no,' she shouted. 'Look, the mob's there, they'll kill us.'

She reached for her revolver. She could not find it, and that seemed to her a dreadful thing, till she saw it in Talleyman's hand. At the far end of the Hall there was a French window in place of a sash, but it was locked as well as bolted.

'Out here,' Talleyman muttered in her ear. He picked up a chair. With one, two, three short strokes he beat out the glass and then the frame itself. The smoke was all about them now. They could look back and see flames coming up between the treads of the great staircase. But still she pulled back, couldn't make herself leave, till Talleyman, seizing her roughly by the upper arms, bundled her out in front of him.

'The powder — any minute now!'

Jane still screamed, 'They're after us — look, the pikes!'

Then she realized that the fire was glinting on the muskets and fixed bayonets of the Yeomanry, rushing around like frightened sheep. Talleyman caught at a figure.

'Sergeant Bothwell! Stand fast there! Get your men into order. No man to go into the house. It will go up directly. Get your men into order there!'

Bothwell seemed overcome by Talleyman's appearance. He asked no questions, seemed only too glad to have someone give him orders. He bellowed at his men, 'Stand still, all of you. Markers on parade! Now, get fell in, will ye, get into line. Stand still...! Let's have you numbering off then, so we can see who's not here.'

Talleyman ran further along the terrace to the front windows of the agent's wing. There were windows alight here. He shouted up, 'Mr Roding! Captain Foster! Come out by the side door. Don't go into the main house. There is a fire in the cellar.'

Somebody shouted back, but who Jane could not make out. She felt that she could not move. Talleyman turned again to the sergeant, fussing over his roll call, 'Do you know for any buckets?'

'A few, sir, in the stable.'

'Then send men for some. Get a bucket chain ready, down to the lake.'

Jane pulled at his sleeve.

'Can you put it out? Can you make it safe?'

'We cannot go in before the powder goes up. We can put the fire out after that.' Then, with a sudden desperation in his voice, 'Why doesn't it go up? Why doesn't it go?'

Now the control has gone, she thought, as he broke from her and ran back to the house. He was halfway back to the shattered French window when the powder did go up. There was a heavy ccffffrrrrrrrumping noise, a roar rather than a bang, a crushing feeling at the pit of her stomach. She had expected to see the whole front of the house fall outwards, or the sky filled with the bursting roof and tables and chairs and books and beds and plates and carpets all sailing upwards like the pictures in the chapbooks. But there was only a flaring out of the cellar gratings and the shattering of the windows in the long Hall.

The Yeomanry yelled at the explosion, and to a man ran the hundred yards to the other side of the ornamental lake, where they stood stock-still looking at the red glow in all the windows of the hall. Jane felt that she could not move now, could not run out of the smoke that billowed all over her. And then Talleyman came back to her, and even in the flickering light she could see that his face and clothes were smoke-blackened and torn, but that he was smiling in a satisfied way. He told her confidentially, as imparting a trade secret, 'Velvet doesn't burn quickly.'

'You mean…?'

'They left about thirty pounds of powder. I put the man against the four casks of brandy, and heaped the powder over him. But loose. Blasting is a skilled trade. Unless you lay it properly, powder just burns. The peasants can't know how to do this. I laid a fuse with the curtain. Then I set light to the stairs. This was not an explosion, only a rush of flame. If we act at once — water and wet sacks.'

He turned away from her and she could hear him bellowing orders at the sergeant, haranguing the troops across the lake. After a while she sensed men going by her, with buckets. Talleyman came back to her, Mrs Roding on his arm.

'Look after your mother. Perhaps she can see what happened.'

Jane found herself sobbing, clinging not to her mother but to him, pressing her face against the rough wool of the pea jacket, rubbing the tears from her cheeks.

'That man — in the cellar. I killed him, I killed him, God forgive me, but I killed him. What shall I do, I killed him!'

She did not think about what she was saying, only thought aloud to him. He said softly into her ear, close so that she could feel his warm breath, 'You did your duty. Do it again. We saw no man in the cellar.'

He went a little way into the darkness, but she could still see him, a black shape against the redness of the house. Her mother clung to her. The lawn was crowded with people now, peasants from the cabins nearby, and others not known, from far off. They looked at her insolently, and she felt terrified, wondering if they knew, if anyone had recognized her there in the hall. There was a trooper standing near her, his carbine on the cock. Talleyman's doing, she realized, for Foster's only thought was to get his baggage out of the house.

Was this sailor, she wondered, as unsubtle as Philip had said, when his first thought had been to make sure that there was no inquest, that she would not be labelled as the Ascendancy girl who had killed a starving peasant, and that he should not be known as the man who had come to Ireland to bring food and brought death instead. Were there not people who would be very well suited by a story like that? And at whose windows were they going to throw a stone? Oh, this was politics again, it was all politics in Ireland, and she wished that she could be out of this wild land and anywhere, anywhere else that was safe and quiet.

Now it was Canon Delauny touching her on the arm.

'You must both come to the vicarage.'

'Thank you, sir, but I think we will be quite happy here. See, the fire is almost out, and it was not in our wing. We can go indoors again quite soon.'

'Oh, no, my child, can't you see? There is not a pane of glass left, not even in your wing.'

She pulled herself together, told herself to be sensible, even if it meant being grateful to Harriet.

'Thank you, sir, we will be very pleased to come with you. But have you seen my father?'

'He is up at the house with Captain Roding, trying to see if any of the pictures can be saved. But poor Michael Flannery — have you not heard? He was struck down tonight, on the road, when he was going to see the Papist priest. I suppose someone had a grudge against him for serving Lord Denain. They took all he had, and left him lying in the ditch. Luckily, his hurts are not serious.'

'All he had on him? They took his keys, I suppose?'

'Oh, yes, all that. One of the Brogan brothers found him and brought him to the vicarage. His daughter is looking after him. For once it is a good thing to be in a vicarage with twelve bedrooms.'

The canon laughed. Jane shivered. Flannery, hardly hurt then, but his keys gone from him in an honourable way. There was nobody to be trusted. It was not his window, then, they would have thrown a stone at. The lines were drawing firm.

6

'It has been done several times, but we were not sure,' Superintendent Trant, dapper and gleaming from his well-polished boots to his sharp trimmed moustache, looked warily at Talleyman in the vicarage drawing room. 'They would steal most of the powder, and blow up the rest to make us think it was all destroyed by the Yeomanry's carelessness.'

'I thought as much,' Talleyman agreed. 'I note from the *Illustrated* that there has been one great house blown up almost every month all through this winter. It seemed too inefficient to be true, even for Irish Yeomanry.'

'And yet you saw nothing?' *There's not much in this one*, Trant thought, *how should I expect him to understand what's really going on*. 'Nothing at all?'

'I saw nobody I could put a name to. No one I would recognize again.'

Trant would have snorted if he had thought it polite. There were enough complications in his life without stray sailors wandering about the country and shooting into the air. Revolt and sedition and thefts of powder and political assassination were his private province, and he had come hotfoot from Dublin to look into the affair. He knew what he was doing, and there was no room in his tidy scheme of things for unplanned eruptions from the sea. He merely wanted to know whether Talleyman's presence had been in any way essential to the unpleasantness, whether he had been the spark to fire the powder or whether his presence had been entirely incidental. It seemed like the latter.

'Nothing recognizable?'

'Only shapes. There was nothing to see. Only fire and darkness.'

'And the one masked the other,' put in Jane. She felt desperately that she must fog the questions somehow, distort the answers, confuse this policeman, however great his reputation.

'Yet you fired at the shadows?'

'They were noisy shadows,' Talleyman was defending them.

'But you fired twice? Captain Foster is adamant that there were two shots, the one that woke him and the one after it.'

'I fired. Then Miss Roding fired. She was excited.'

'You are lucky to be alive, Mr Talleyman, begging Miss Roding's pardon, there have been more men killed by their friends behind them than ever by their enemies in front.'

'So I am told — daily. My Captain discourses on it. He has a great distrust of firearms of all sizes. He holds that they ought not to be allowed in a ship of war.'

Trant deftly avoided this proffered change of subject, and offered a new one of his own.

'Have you seen anyone strange around these parts lately? Anyone wandering? Pedlars? Punch and Judy men? A man in a white coat?'

'No, nobody like that,' Talleyman sounded positive. *Ah, well,* thought Trant, *there's no harm in laying a false trail for the benefit of the right people. Try the other tack,* 'Or the man in the cellar?'

'Was there a man in the cellar?' Talleyman looked as calm as ever. *Oh, a hard one, this,* thought Trant, *there'll be no shaking him ever, but that Miss Roding, she looks fit to die at that.* Talleyman was saying, and sure it sounded natural enough, 'If I'd thought there was a man in the cellar, I would not have turned my back on the door. How do you know there was a man there? Have you caught him?'

'Oh, in a way you may be saying that we have caught him. We found him an hour ago, in the cellar still, for still's the word for him.'

'Did he die in the fire?' Jane felt sick, this was where it would all come out and she and Talleyman would be caught, for murder and arson, each the other's accomplice and each guilty of the other's crime. But she must keep herself calm, let nothing slip.

'It's not a very pleasant thing to talk about, Miss Roding.'

'Life in a famine is not very pleasant, Superintendent.' She felt pleased that she was able to keep up a rational conversation, return logical answers as if she were discussing the weather or the latest fashions. Trant could see her pride, and guessed the effort it cost her. *She's on edge*, he thought, *and no wonder, for it was only the night before last and the memories are now coming back that were too close, yesterday, to hurt. But they cannot add anything, they are memories only of feelings, of terror and pain. If this solid young man, with never an ounce of imagination in him, could not tell what he saw, what could she say of any use?*

'If I may say so, when a man has been near to a barrel of gunpowder and half a dozen of spirits when they take fire, there's no further asking how he died, not who he is either for there's nothing but a few bones and buttons. But you didn't see him, that's obvious.'

The door opened. Harriet entered, doing her best to act the lady of the house, to control at least the hospitality if not the course of the action. Trant eyed her. *This one is making a brave show at being a woman*, he thought, *but it's a child she'll always be. But sitting here is a full woman, that'll not break, and another of the same kind bringing in the tea tray. Aye, and this one is more of a woman yet than either of the two fine Ascendancy girls, and better looking too with her red hair and blue eyes.* He had already got all he wanted out of Mary Flannery, and that book was still open against another time. She had reeled off to him, very convincingly, the tale of how her father had been found all bruised and muddy, and that well before the fire started, and even the canon would vouch for that. And there had been no reason to send any word up to the big house at all, because sure wasn't there another set of keys in Mr Roding's study so that if he needed another bottle he had only to go for it. But while the others were in the room, Trant felt he could not push further.

'It seems there is nothing more you can do for me, nor I for you. It seems that there is very little point either in arranging an inquest on what we found, for there is no proving that they are not a relic of 'Ninety-Eight, or even of Cromwell's time out of the floor of the house that was here before this one. I thank you, Miss Delauny, but I cannot stay for tea. I must be off to my work, for there is a constable who thinks he has found where those rascals took the handcart. We will soon hunt them down.'

'Is there need for that?' Talleyman asked very quietly.

Trant looked at him, said nothing.

The sailor went on, 'They do no real harm. They blunder about in the dark. They shoot at men at ten feet and miss. They burn down houses where no one lives. They steal powder and never seem to shoot it off. I do not think they have the wit to store it. They are harmless.'

'What would you do, then?' Trant asked direct.

'Remove the provocation. Take away the Yeomanry and send them back to their farms. Concentrate the regular troops where it is clear that they are here to keep out invasion, not to hold down the country. Let the Constabulary put up their guns. Make government, law enforcement, something the people do for themselves through the police, not something that is done to them. Bring in food. Let the people have security for their land. Let men get benefit from their work. Let them live like ... free men.'

The three women were all looking at Talleyman as if they could not believe what they had heard. Trant was shaken too, but then he thought, *sure, 'tis an innocent we have here, not knowing the country at all, or how we live. And if there's many navy officers think that way, then the sooner they're all back to Plymouth the better.*

He retorted, smoothly, 'And was it peace and contentment and paying of the rent that followed at Eyories from giving them meal, Mr Talleyman?'

'That proves my point, Superintendent. They would not take it from *us*. When we let young Mr Delauny have the meal to issue through his clerk, then they came for it, and they worked on their jetty also. They would not take it from us — we were outsiders. They see Mr Delauny as one of themselves. They will take it through him. They will save themselves alone: so they tell me.'

There was nothing more to be said. Mary Flannery slipped from the room in front of the Superintendent, to show him out to where James O'Shaughnessy held the horse for him, and a good reliable man he was, married to Mary's cousin.

Over the teacups, the two girls avoided the awkward subject Talleyman had flaunted before them. Harriet felt that any mention of her brother was in bad taste, where her father might overhear. But the situation was too good not to exploit. For the first time Harriet had the house full of guests: her guests, of course. In face of all these people even Mary Flannery had been obliged to pay her employer's daughter a little deference.

Talleyman had certainly treated Harriet like the mistress of the house. He had behaved better than she had expected.

There was the way he had come in, the morning after the fire, eager for breakfast but first insisting on washing off the filth of powder and soot. And then, hardly had he sat down, but he had leapt up again and was out in the yard in an instant, with his big pistol in his hand, taking the caps off the chambers. What Irish gentleman would have had such respect for his hostess? It showed what mixing with a Lord did for you.

Of course, Philip, being a Lord or as good as one, would have behaved even better. He would have gone after the thieves and brought the handcart back, powder and all, and the rabble with it in chains. They would have been afraid of him, she knew, and he would have been afraid of nothing. And a good shot like Philip would not have let them get away in the first place.

When she married Philip, Harriet thought, she might let him go back into the navy for a while. The uniform was so becoming. And not as a midshipman, the way she had last seen him, or as a lieutenant: the Admiralty would hardly let a Lord go to sea except as captain of his own ship. But that was all yet to come. Surely Philip would have to come home now to inspect the damage, and take her away.

And, then, Jane could have Talleyman. She would do very nicely for him, before she got too old for anyone. Neither she nor Talleyman, of course, was really first rate, noticeably dashing. They would be welcome at Denain Hall in Wiltshire, wherever that was but surely close to London and the centre of fashion and balls and levees, and they could make part of the background to the brilliant life Harriet would lead with Philip. One of my husband's officers, you know... but not for the greatest occasions. After all, it was only trade money, from boilermaking. Respectable, perhaps, but Harriet was not going to be just respectable: she intended to be the brilliant wife of a brilliant peer.

Yet, there was stiffness between Jane and Talleyman. They sat opposite each other across the fireplace, sipped their strong tea, ate their soda bread: there was nobody in Ireland made soda bread like Mary Flannery, it was a pity that she would not be wanting to live in Wiltshire, but perhaps, again, it would not be fair to her to take her to such a fine busy place. But these silent two … there must be some way of getting them together. So she asked, 'Must you be going back to your ship on Friday, Mr Talleyman? You are perfectly welcome to stay longer.'

'I am expected, Miss Roding. I must go.'

'Will you be hiring a horse?'

'I will join the Bianconi for Castletown.'

Harriet allowed herself a mental sniff. Philip would never have demeaned himself to travel by a public car, or without a servant. That would do very well for Jane, who was only, when all was said and done, a farmer's daughter, but the canon was a professional gentleman, and his daughter would expect better than this. So Jane need not be overawed. There would be another chance.

'In the summer, my father goes to Cashel for his turn as canon in residence. Oh, there is nothing in the world so gay as Cashel in the summer, Mr Talleyman, and you must come and visit us there. All the fashionable world comes from as far as Waterford and Cork, and there are balls and routs and concerts and conversationées and nothing but gaiety from morn to night. And perhaps you would like to come to us, too, Jane dear?'

'The vicar has already asked my mother and myself.' Jane knew her voice was edgy, harsh, a fine cutting mood. The impudence of this chit. A month in Cashel may be better than nothing, but not much better, and if Talleyman were there, then much, much worse. Perhaps Mary Flannery had a letter. She would see, but in any case she would write herself, now, to him, and ask: please, please, take me out of this dreadful place, take me soon or lose me for ever. Yet she dared not write: or lose me to a hard and clever man, who will spare no one to get what he wants.

She rose. 'I have a headache. I will go to my room. I must ask you to excuse me.'

Talleyman rose as she went out. He told Harriet, apologetically, as if defending someone who had already, strangely, adopted his own staccato speech.

'I think she is not well. She was brave during the fire. Bravery is a great strain. And is not Ireland a great strain? To live here?'

'How can it be a strain to live in Ireland, Mr Talleyman,' and if weaker souls break, why, she who would reign in Denain Hall and entertain the great must be of sterner stuff, 'when we have comfort and firing and soda bread for our tea?'

7

'It's you must ask him to come again,' Harriet told Jane. 'It was to you he came the first time, it would only be decent.'

'We did not ask him,' Jane objected, 'not that time. He wrote us and asked, on Lord Denain's recommendation. It was Lord Denain he was visiting, in fact. It's not our place to ask him to the estate. There is no need to see him back at all.'

'Have you no gratitude?' Harriet asked. Sure, and wasn't it gratitude the girl ought to be having to anyone who would point her surely to the only way she'd ever get a husband. 'If only for waking you before the house blew up, you owe him for that.'

'I owe him nothing,' Jane insisted. 'When the house blew up, my mother was in bed in our wing still and never noticed it, nor got hurt at all.'

And there was no point in it at all, she thought. *The man is barely out of the place, the noise of the Bianconi's wheels hardly died away, and here this stupid thing is wanting to write after him like any housemaid. What degree of delicacy or tact is there in that? If she wants him, let her do her own pleading. My letter writing is better directed elsewhere.*

'If he did come, it would at least break the monotony again,' Harriet was still pressing. 'The summer goes so heavily. Life goes so slowly itself.' *And in the end*, she thought, *it is not at all boring it will be, when Philip comes back for me.* Jane took her up.

'And was it not two days ago that you were telling Mr Talleyman how bright and exciting it was in Cashel in the summer? You won't be bored there, I'll be bound. Why do you not write to him and ask him, firmly, to come to Cashel in the summer? That will be more exciting.'

'I have invited him in person. There is no use my writing as well, but if you should ask him…'

In the end, they both wrote, but neither told the other. There was no answer till the end of June, when each received an identical note, regretting that Mr Talleyman had been sick, which had prevented both his answering their kind invitations earlier, and his acceptance of any further invitations for the summer. Neither girl told the other of the reply, but each, later in July just before they went to Cashel, wrote regretting Mr Talleyman's inability to give any promise, and assuring him that he would be welcome.

Yes, if he comes, Jane thought, *then there is an end of everything. Once I see him, once I hear him talk, then it will all be over. Now I understand what it means, that love and fear are close allied.*

8

The landlord of Clancy's Hotel, that is to say Clancy himself, watched Talleyman get off the Bianconi in the square at Castletown. The car was going on to Allihies, where the last copper mines were, in case there was anyone there wanting to get back, as there often was. But the only passenger arriving was this one, who was getting down opposite where the houses looked across the water at the island. Ships sometimes still came into Castletown, to load copper, or sometimes to water after loading cargoes at Allihies. There was a jetty at Allihies, and some reason for it, not like the crazy thing they were building at Eyories, where there was nothing at all to take out and even less to bring in. Occasionally warships lay for weeks at a time anchored between the island and the port, but not often in peace time, if you could call this peace with the French out again. There was no ship of any kind in sight from the Quay now: *yet*, thought Clancy, *this is a sailor. I'll lay any money on it, a sailor for sure, I've seen that look before.*

He watched the tall sailor standing in the road, looking round him, a little unsteady on his feet, bewildered. He had a bag with him, a leather one with handles and a brass lock, heavy from the way the guard of the car handled it putting it on the ground at his feet. The sailor stood looking down at it in a puzzled way, as if he had never seen it before and yet knew whose it was. He suddenly bent to pick it up. The movement nearly overbalanced him. He swayed upright, and looked at the bag as if asking why it was dodging away from him in this mischievous way. Then he bent his knees with exaggerated care, and this time got the bag handles firmly into his hands.

Finally he straightened up laboriously and stood there, holding the bag and swaying backwards and forwards on the balls of his feet as if the bag were trying to overbalance him. He gazed around him the while as if he were looking for something but could not see well enough to find it.

'Drunk, and what else d'ye expect,' grumbled Clancy aloud in the empty square, because, he would argue, if a man had not even himself to talk to then he was in a bad way for friends. 'A sailor, and how long he's been sitting on that thing with one ear in the wind and nothing at all to do there's no knowing. And he's bound to be having a bottle with him, and it's finished the lot he has already because there's no sign of it in his hand. Oh, I'll not be having him in my house, to come rioting and breaking everything about us and shouting for women and with old Molly Flanagan dead and rest her soul there'll be no one to find them for him, and drinking all the good porter and whisky too and hard it is to find any to make the bare drop to bribe the excise man with let alone any to sell to any stranger that comes along the road. I've had enough of sailors in the best times, and a misery it is when the ships are in and the money is not worth the trouble it is it isn't. Or it wasn't then in the well times, and now with my wife dead and the potman, and old Molly Flanagan that used to pay me for the use of the room there's nobody in the whole town to help, or to hinder either come to that.'

But Talleyman was leaning on the bar, and asking, 'Can you let me have, if you please—'

The publican noted with the eye of experience the slurred speech and the mouth filled with saliva, the tongue too big for its seat and the flushed face. *Oh, this one is full of the hard stuff all right, and there is no telling what he will do and nothing sensible that was for sure. Better cut him short.*

'No! I've no drink to sell ye, no drink whatever now, and it's going away to annoy some other hotel you ought to be. Not so far along the road, and a mile or a bit more up the hill and it's called Malone's and that's not a far step for a man like you with plenty of flesh on your bones.'

'No. I don't want a drink. Not that kind of drink. Something hot. Have you any coffee?'

'And who would be making coffee for you when you are in the state you are and disturbing people who only want to be left alone for the rest of the time that the Holy God will give them and sure that's not long here with the typhus and the relapsing fever and all the other dreadful things that's around and me alone here in the hotel and all to do myself and no wife nor anybody left to do a hand's turn, and it's coffee you're asking me to make for you now and sure it'll be a seven-course dinner you'll be wanting next. Och away with you and find your ship and be out of here and let us all alone.'

Talleyman looked at him as if he could not understand that he was being refused. Then he lumbered past Clancy, almost brushing the landlord out of the way with the big bag swinging in his left hand, and sat down on the only chair in the bar. He took a handkerchief from his pocket and buried his face in it. His long body shook and he made retching sounds.

Clancy told him sharply, 'Now, it's not being sick you're going to be here, is it, and nobody but me to clean it up and it's in the street you ought to be doing that. Out with ye, now, it's a respectable house this is and I won't have any of this nonsense about the place when 'tis all clean and tidy.'

Talleyman took no notice. He seemed not to hear what was being said. He stopped coughing, and said, very low but most clearly, in a tired voice, 'I have a headache. A headache. Have you any coffee? Or tea. Please? Only hot. Hot.'

'And 'tis no wonder that 'tis a headache you're having, and all the drink taken that there's been. And serve you right and better it would have been if you'd stayed in Cork and listened to Father Matthew and didn't come out here and show your drunkenness in front of us decent people.'

Talleyman was silent for a while, as he leant his head on his arm, and his arm on the bar counter. Then he asked, 'If you have nothing for me to drink, then—'

'No nothing at all. I've told ye a hundred times, the best thing for you is to get away and leave us alone and the further the better.'

'I want to go. I want to reach Eyories. The ship will be there. I must reach Eyories. The ship.'

'Then go there, indeed, because there's nobody wants you to stay here, or stopping you walking away to a hundred ships.'

'I must go. I... I can't walk. Not to Eyories. Have you a horse? Or a car? To hire me? Is there a car here? I can hire one. Or a horse.'

He kept his free hand over his eyes, not looking at the light at all. *The drink takes every one of them a different way*, thought Clancy, *and there's some as won't dare the light when there's a glass or two in them.*

'I've got no horse to hire you, and that's the truth, for who would be wanting to hire horses around here when there's respectable farmers that haven't the price of a meal between now and midsummer, and even if I had one I wouldn't hire one to ye, not the way ye are now, and not responsible, as I could swear to any magistrate if there was any trouble you were causing. There's better men than you are to walk the whole way night and day to get a bit of bread at the end of it, aye and died of hunger too and never got there at all and there's no more you can do than that, and no less I'd be having you doing.'

'I shall sit here. I will stay here. I can't walk. I can pay.'

Talleyman bowed his head on his chest. In a moment he was shaken by a bout of coughing worse than before. He almost fell from the chair which rocked back on two legs under him: but he recovered himself with what Clancy knew to be the luck of a drunken man. He seemed unable to speak more. But he had said enough.

Clancy suddenly had a vision of this big drunken man sitting there in the bar all the night and frightening away any real customers that might turn up, although there had been none since that Swedish ship came in and watered and stayed not more than the six hours between the two points of the tide, for it was thinking it was Milford Haven they were in, and didn't Joseph Aherne's boy young Francis go off in her and him pleading to the Captain and crying to take him to America or Sweden or Africa or anywhere only away from here where he had buried his father and mother and all the other Ahernes, and those Swedes didn't spend much either. And in the morning he'll wake up in a fury and a head on him like a volcano the size of a mountain, and there's nothing he'll remember but that I refused him the drink and even a horse to get away from here for all that I told him to go, and whatever he says now he's got wrong to his head it'll be worse in the morning, and it's steadier on his feet and with his fist he'll be in the morning. So Clancy told the sailor, 'Will you be waiting here, then, for a while, and it's a bit of patience you ought to be having and perhaps there's something I can find for you, if I have a little time to go and look. And be easy now, there's a good man, and don't do no more damage and just you be sitting quiet till I come back. But where to look or to start to look I don't know at all because there's not a hundred people left in this town that used to be so lively, and happy we all were till that steamer came up the water between us and the Island and 'twas the black smoke of her that brought the black blight over the potatoes and it'll never leave us till the steamers are entirely put down. And with all the houses empty who on earth would be having horses to hire ye, or a car for that matter. There's nothing left in the whole place at all, and nothing for you, I can be telling you that for a start since it's nothing but bad luck the steamers have brought us since you first came.'

Clancy was suddenly aware of how shrill his voice was and how tired and frightened he had become, and he almost wept where he stood. He cut himself short in alarm, and went out into the street. If there was any luck he could be having at all, and the Saints knew that he needed some at last and for that matter didn't the whole of Ireland need a bit of good fortune for a change, perhaps when he came back the drunken sailor might be asleep and there would be a chance of tumbling him off somewhere in a ditch and he would never remember where it was he was turned out of. But along the street and up the hill were the Hurleys, and perhaps there was something there because they still had a piece left from the time when they had been people of substance, and kept a livery stable if you could call three horses spare on the holding a stable, but at any rate they were used to hiring the beasts out if they still had any beasts, but likely now they had nothing, nothing at all like the rest of this fated town, and so they'd soon be dead and there'd be nothing left in the end but a hummock or two by the strand where the houses had been like where the cabins had been that were pulled down over the peasants' heads. Yet as Clancy went out into the street, there was James O'Shaughnessy that came out of a doorway, and had watched all and was now come,

God preserve us, to ask Clancy all about, and wasn't it one of the Brotherhood he was?

So it was half an hour before Clancy came back, and the eldest Hurley boy with him, Mr Hurley himself being indisposed to come and intelligibly so since he had not a coat to his back and his breeches in holes they were. The boy had brought with him the main capital possession of the Hurley family, being a donkey and cart, the animal in better condition than the vehicle. They found Talleyman still sitting in the bar parlour.

'Here is young Michael Hurley, and himself the only support of all his family and a good honest boy he is, and has brought his beast and the car for you to get a bite for his fatherless and motherless brothers and sisters and no other way for them to live.'

'My da says it's a guinea to Eyories, take it or leave it, and ye can pay me before ye leave,' put in the lad. Clancy gave him a foul look, for that was no way to make a living, contradicting your own friends when they tried to help you a little on the way. Talleyman did not answer but leaned forward in his chair and went into another coughing fit. The lad pulled at his sleeve.

'A guinea, a guinea it is, and no less. Me and the car. And the beast. A guinea, your honour, only a guinea, and we can go now.'

He saw that his loud voice had penetrated the Englishman's stupidity. Talleyman was fumbling to bring out a purse, catching it on the edge of his pocket. He fidgeted to open it. His hand was shaking, and he was unable to grasp a coin between his fingers. Suddenly he jerked forwards impatiently, and spilled the contents of the purse on to the bar counter. Five or six sovereigns were scattered on the dark wood, catching the light from the door as they rolled, and catching Clancy's eye as well. Three of the coins rolled off the edge of the bar on to the floor, among the dirt and the scanty straw. Clancy and the boy went down on their knees and scratched for the money like hens in the yard, trying to outsnatch each other and spitting like cats in their greed. But the boy got none. Clancy stood up and thumped money bravely on the counter.

'There, your honour, all safe and sound and not a penny of it missing.' And he slid the two sovereigns along the counter among the others. If it came to the worst he could kneel on the floor again, and find the other sovereign as easily as he had just slipped it into his waistcoat pocket, if it didn't slip out again of its own accord. He did not think it would come to an argument, but if it did, this man was a good head taller than he was and drunk enough not to care about being hurt and anything might happen, and no counting on Michael Hurley to be any help. Clancy did not like fighting, not in his own front parlour where it was apt to damage things he would prefer not to have damaged, like himself.

But Talleyman did not argue. Either, Clancy thought, he had not the wit to count or the strength to bargain. He peered at the coins on the counter as if he could not remember where he was or what they had to do with him. He blinked, and after several stabs with a forefinger, pushed one of the sovereigns to the lad, who grabbed it and shouted, 'A guinea, I said it was a guinea, your honour, a whole guinea. My da said to have a guinea and not to come home without it or he'd have my hide.' Then, to push home his point, 'A whole guinea, or my da won't let me go.'

'My eyes, it's my eyes,' Talleyman mumbled. 'The light. Hurts my eyes. The light does.'

He scrabbled in the pockets of his paletot, but found nothing. He clumsily opened the buttons of the garment, and fished aimlessly in the recesses of his frock coat. When he found some change, he looked at it in some surprise as if he had not known it was there. After examining the coins closely, holding them near to his eyes, he held out half a crown to the boy, saying, ''S all right. All right. Take it. 'S all right.'

Young Hurley looked at the money, and then shouted in Talleyman's ear, 'I'll take it to my da, first.'

He dodged from Clancy's hand and out of the hotel, his bare feet slapping on the pavement and up the street. Clancy turned back to Talleyman, explaining in a placatory tone, 'Sure, why, 'tis all right your honour, all right after all and he'll be back directly and take you wherever it is you'll be wanting to go, and sure isn't it a fair price to have the lad and the car all to yourself for the whole day, but his father is a real terror and there's not a man in town but does go in fear of him, and no wonder the boy's in a hurry for his da will have the hide off his back and the donkey's as well if he's not paid directly, but he'll be back never fear.'

He saw that his malignings of old Hurley who was a meek man and as arrant a coward as ever faced a loaded bottle of porter at close range were not needed, that they weren't at all. Talleyman had slumped forward again, his head on his arms on the counter. He might have been asleep, but it wasn't certain, so it was best for an honest man to remain content with what providence had put in his way. Therefore Clancy merely watched him till, after about twenty minutes, Michael Hurley returned. Together, somehow, they urged Talleyman out into the light rain. They coaxed him on to the cart, sitting in it with his back to the donkey, and his bag beside him. And so Clancy saw him off.

'Drunk, and well rid of him we are,' he told Michael, 'and 'tis to Eyories, as you know, you have to take him, and it's up to you to make the best of it for what you've got for it.'

'It's a long way I have to go,' Michael objected, 'and me with not a bite inside me as yet today and perhaps nothing when I come home again to supper.'

'Then thank Mary and Joseph that you ate yesterday, and I saw it, and if your father doesn't drink it all tomorrow then I may have something for ye on the slate. And 'tis cheap enough for getting him out of the town, and leaving us all in peace, and there's a fine public-spirited lad you are then, now isn't it so?'

'It was a sovereign he gave me, you'll tell my da that, Mr Clancy, and no more, a sovereign and nothing else.'

'You're a good boy, Michael, and I'll tell him that if only you'll get this one out of the town and a fair piece on his way.'

And indeed to God wasn't it a great thing to have them now out of a town that was as empty as sin and nothing to keep the hotel going and not even the Punch and Judy man to come and drink a quiet dram here and sure why was it ever he came when there was not a penny anyone could give him no matter how Mr Punch crowed, but 'twas useful he was to show how it was even a Mr Punch could beat the Constabulary whenever he wanted.

9

So it was a fair way then they were on the journey and the lad with half a crown and nothing else to keep him warm under his sodden rags against the spring rain and the beating wind that drove it horizontal into them. Talleyman had undone his paletot in the hotel, and had not buttoned it up again. He lay almost flat on his back with the rain soaking into his frock and velvet waistcoat. His hat rolled on the boards of the cart. Sometimes he opened his eyes, but mostly, the boy noticed, he kept them screwed up shut. Now and then he had his dreadful fits of coughing, from deep down in his chest.

There was nothing for Michael Hurley to do to keep the donkey on the road, for wasn't it the only road there was and didn't the beast know it as well as anyone? So he could spend some time on listening to what Talleyman said as he lay there. Some of it was unintelligible. There were strange names like Pentstemon and Napier, and nonsense words like Owerri, and he seemed very concerned about a partridge, and where was it now. It must be the drink that was talking, he was rambling in the drink, and not in the fever, for Mr Clancy had said it was the drink and didn't Mr Clancy sell the stuff? And it was only the Irish got the fever and never the English with their fine clothes and their strange food and their money. Oh, it would be a fine thing to have money, to have sovereigns in your pocket to throw carelessly on the bar counter.

Yet it never occurred to the boy, any more than it had occurred to Clancy, that this petty filching of a coin here and there, and the hard brainwork that went into making a stray pound, were hardly worth the labour when he could easily roll this sailor over and take the purse and everything that was in it, and nobody to stop him or take any notice at all. That would have been wicked: but neither Clancy nor the boy thought in terms of real evil. What worried the boy was how to get this vast piece of silver, half a crown, changed into sixty halfpence, that could be hidden here and there and explained away after. He was already finding out that the planning and execution of a swindle was far easier than the problem of fencing the swag.

But there were other things that Talleyman said, and the lad could follow and knew now what this was all about. There was talk of this O'Connor, now, and how he was going to bring out all the people against the English and burn London with a charter, whatever that might be, although sure wasn't a charter something like part of a ship? And it was all going to happen on the tenth of April, and wasn't it April by now, though which day of April Michael couldn't think. Yet if that were the day, then sure it was easy to understand what he had been told to do, and it was still a good piece to the place.

And still some way short, the boy became aware that Talleyman was nearer to control of himself. He was sitting nearer to upright in the cart, and talking more coherently. And suddenly he was talking to Michael Hurley, directly, and saying, 'Now, lad, and what does it mean to you if Ireland is independent? It won't give you any more to eat. So who's going to get anything out of it?'

He seemed to be waiting for an answer, but Michael couldn't think of anything to say except 'gee-up' to the donkey. But his passenger seemed to be hearing answers where none were spoken.

'That's right. But not only the French. Who'll have the power then? Not the Englishry, that's the whole point of it. But somebody will have power.'

It disturbed Michael. There was nothing to comfort him but the dusk and the knowledge that they were almost at the place arranged. They were pulling up the slope, towards the two rocks. There was a good excuse. Michael had been shouting his encouragement to the donkey for some time, and as usual the animal paid no notice, knowing better than the lad what it was about. But now Michael pulled the beast to a stop, and ran around behind to put a stone under the wheel. Then he caught at Talleyman's arm, and urged him, 'You'll have to walk here, your honour, the poor animal can't manage it, we'll have to be walking up to the top of the hill, and it's all downhill after that. And the bag, your honour, that great big bag, he can't manage that either.'

Coaxing, pulling, he manoeuvred Talleyman out of the cart, got him to stand on the roadside. He pulled the bag across the floor of the cart and broke its fall to the ground. Then, moving as fast as he could manage in the cold, Michael Hurley leapt on to the cart, hauled the donkey's head round, and whipped the animal into a trot, downhill towards Castletown. For now he had done what James O'Shaughnessy had told him to do, and no less, and there was seven pounds of taties he was promised for that, a reward beyond any money for unbuyable they were.

Behind the two great rocks, James O'Shaughnessy saw Talleyman on the road. A big man, as he knew, but swaying on his feet. It ought to be easy enough. He moved forward, and the others came behind him, all good boys they were, ready to do anything for Ireland, Noonan and Brennan and John Doyle, Malachi's son. It was a pity that they hadn't been able to get a pistol, but never mind, they would give him a hiding he wouldn't forget as long as he lived before they killed him.

But it wasn't as simple as that, not at all. The bloody man, drunk or whatever he was, could still stand up, could still move. There were four of them to come at him from all sides, and he said nothing, didn't challenge them, but at once began to try to open the big bag. And there was word from Flannery already that he had packed that big pistol in it, and there'd be no getting it out in a hurry, even if it were loaded. They could be on him before that, and sure the pistol itself would be useful in the good times to come. Still, there was no point in risking it, and it was Noonan who threw the big stone at him, and hit him in the ribs. It made Talleyman stagger, almost drop the bag. There was no time left to open it.

Yet as the four Irishmen came at him, Talleyman straightened up and swung the bag in a circle round him, from one side to another, so that there was no way to take him. *Ah, but 'tis like a wolfs his eyes are, that fierce and evil*, thought O'Shaughnessy, and there's nothing to do but to wear him down, because he can't lift that bag for long. And true it was that as they danced in on him, and dodged the swinging weight, they saw the movements grow slower, the arms begin to droop. And then it was easy, after all, to be clever. They knew the trick, not to wave a good stick about and beat him over the head but to stab in with it, into the body. So first Talleyman dropped the bag, and then he was bowed over double, clutching at his stomach and ribs. And then, sure that was the time to go for the head and the back of the neck, till he was rolling on the ground, and now to put the boot in. And they heard the cart wheels and the man shouting.

Lawrence Delauny had heard of it all from Malachi, who was proud that his son should strike a real blow for Ireland. And pleased indeed he was to see Mr Delauny, who was too fine a gentleman to do anything more than planning and designing, go off for once to get the real dirt on his hands. So O'Shaughnessy was taken aback to see Delauny come over the hill and bear down on them with a face of mortal anger on him. For Lawrence Delauny was shouting 'Stop! Stop!' at the top of his voice. He jumped from his trap and ran to the struggling group, pushing between Talleyman and his attackers. Talleyman was rolling on the ground, his hands over his face.

But when the hail of blows ceased, he looked up at Delauny, and said, 'Oh, my good friend. You've saved me.'

Then his eyes shut, and there was no denying that he was out as a dead moon.

Delauny spoke harshly, 'What d'ye think ye're about? Did you want to kill him?'

'Aye.' It was O'Shaughnessy, hard, uncompromising. 'Was it not himself killed Foley, there in the cellar? For it's shot he must have been, and he never came out alive. So here's a life forfeit, and by God, we'll take it.'

'And what'll be the end of that, I ask you?'

'Justice.'

'That's as may be. But I'll tell you what the end is sure to be. Here's a sailor killed, an officer, off a man-o'-war. There'll be all hell let loose to find the man who did it, and it won't be the Constabulary who go through the townland, although it's all good lads they are, nor the Ulster Yeomanry either that we can lead a dance where we like. It'll be the Marines first, that'll burn every house between here and Cork, and the regular soldiers after, pure English, and no more mercy in them than in a tiger.'

'Sure, and won't they be too busy? There'll be enough for them to worry about in their own country, O'Connor will see to that.'

'You haven't heard? It's been over four days now.'

'Heard what? It's not all of us, Mr Delauny, that are so well paid out of the relief that we can afford newspapers.'

'It's over. All over. There was twenty thousand police on the streets in London. O'Connor, the lot of them, were afraid to march, or start anything. They took the petition to Parliament in a cab. There was no Chartist revolution. The English soldiers have nothing to care about. They'll stay here.'

'So it's on our own we are, then?'

'No. It's just a bit delayed we are. But what of it? Did the food come in? Has the American ship been?'

'That was yesterday. And food was all it brought.'

'So that's it, then. We'll be having the jetty finished first. And let me tell you this, James O'Shaughnessy, it's better off we are without O'Connor and his mad ideas of doing everything by argument. Perhaps it'll work over there in England, but even there not likely. Wait, there's the word, wait and be sure. There's Himself that's back from France, and waiting for his trial, and indeed that's a better time for it all. So wait, till we have what we need.'

'And until then,' said O'Shaughnessy, 'we'll just kill *him*.'

'Ye'll do no such thing.'

Delauny was standing astride Talleyman's body. He spoke calmly, quietly, but wondering if he could hold these men back, how far he could go and keep some measure of control, or faith in the future.

'*Ye*'ll not kill him. Put your hand close to him. Feel the heat come off him. It's the fever he's got, and only half chances that he'll live anyway. But let me have him, and live or die I'll get the value out of him. What d'ye think they'll do to someone who finds an officer left for dead on the road and brings him in? Let him live or die, so he does it in their hands, and it's twisting the English around my little finger I'll be. Now, before he comes to again and sees you — go!'

I've held it, Delauny thought, *I've kept them with me*. The four men had melted silently into the rocks at the roadside, into the pools of twilight blackness. Delauny bent himself to pull Talleyman to his feet, lever him somehow over the back board of the cart. Then, another struggle to get the long legs folded in. Last, the big brown bag went into the trap beside its owner. It was at this moment, as Delauny pulled himself up to his seat, that Talleyman opened his eyes again, and asked, very clearly, before he relapsed into his sweating sleep, 'Why? Why? All I did was bring them food.'

Lawrence Delauny cracked his whip, urged the pony on over the crest and down the long hill into Eyories. Before he reached his own cottage, he turned aside, and followed the sunken track to the Tower. He had been heard before he came in sight. Although it was nearly dark, there was a marine outside the gate, bayonet fixed. He came forward, and shouted, as if afraid that Delauny might not understand.

'Halt! Who goes there?'

'Come and help me,' Delauny shouted back, as loudly. 'Get your officer! Help me with this!'

Sergeant Bunton emerged from the gate shadows.

'Now, now, Mr Delauny, sir, there's no need to be shouting. The officer will be out to see you directly, as soon as he's finished his wine, so please to wait quietly.'

'Then it's a life will be on his conscience and on yours, Sergeant, and it's looking in here you'd better be.'

Twenty yards was the nearest he could get the trap to the steps. The sergeant came, slowly: he wanted to show that if he came at all to a civilian's summons, it was out of pure politeness to a man who was equally polite in addressing him by his proper title. There was no necessity to come, any more than there was a necessity for him to take any notice when the surveyor said, 'And you'd better bring half a dozen of your men, too.'

Bunton came slowly to the trap, and looked in. He started back.

'Is it a dead man you're bringing us, Mr Delauny?'

'Dead he is not, but he soon will be unless you get him into the warm.'

'I'll get the officer.' The sergeant bumbled off. *Obviously*, thought Delauny, *nothing in the drill book covers this*. But almost immediately, Lidderdale came out, running, in his short mess-jacket. He leant into the trap, reaching over to cradle Talleyman's head against his chest. He cried, 'Tal, my good fellow, Tal, what is it, my dear friend!'

The sergeant was behind him, with five marines carrying blankets and a hammock. In a dozen skilled economical movements they had Talleyman cocooned against the night air, and carried between them into the gate. The sergeant picked up the bag.

Lidderdale turned to Delauny, 'Thank you for bringing him in. Thank you for your trouble.'

The sergeant touched his hat politely to Delauny — on no account could he be accused of saluting a civilian — and followed his officer inside.

The surveyor was put firmly in his place. And that place was outside the Tower. Talleyman was back in his own world. And Delauny had been told, clearly, without anyone bothering to waste breath on saying it in words, that this was none of his business.

It was when he was unhitching the pony from the trap that he saw the sketchpad lying on the floor of the carriage where it had fallen from Talleyman's inside pocket. Inside his cabin, in the light of the turf fire, he looked through it. The faces stared up at him, from the page: his father, Harriet, Roding, Trant, a face he did not know that must be Foster. And at last, on a separate sheet that he could tear out and set aside in his book of tables in his surveying library, the face he was looking for.

10

But when Delauny went the next morning to return the sketchbook, there was a different welcome. He had been in two minds about going at all, but then it came to him that Talleyman's habit of sketching was so well known that someone would come to look for it. And the soldiers were better off inside the Tower than roaming outside, looking into things.

'The officer would like to see you,' Sergeant Bunton told him, and brought him into the Tower, where the lower floor was turned into a wardroom. There was some kind of fabric on the stone floor, Delauny noticed, glass put into the embrasures, curtains hung over them, furniture, beds. Talleyman was lying in one of the beds.

Lidderdale was leaning over him, stood to say, 'He seems very bad. Is it the concussion from the beating? It was very good of you to save him.'

Delauny looked down at the lieutenant. He answered curtly, 'Don't be more stupid than you can help. That beating was nothing. He's got the relapsing fever. I've seen it often enough.'

He was disappointed when the Marine did not argue, merely asked, 'If you have seen it, then you must know what to do. There are no doctors in this half of the county, I know that.'

'When does your ship get back?'

'I expected her today, but now I know she is delayed. Three days, at least.'

'Look, he's soaking, he's sweating himself to nothing. Has he had anything to drink?'

'No. I tried to give him some coffee, but he won't take it. What else?'

'Have you lime juice? Of course you have. It's sharp, it'll make him open his mouth.' Delauny looked across the officer to Sergeant Bunton in the doorway, said savagely, 'Look to it, sergeant.'

Bunton also knew the voice of authority. He moved, fast.

'Now, let's get him out of this shirt. Has he another nightshirt in his bag? Is it aired? Get him into the bed, keep him warm. And more coal in that brazier. Keep the room warm.'

'He's too hot already,' objected Lidderdale.

'That's the body's way of fighting the fever. If we keep him hot, we help him. The sweat doesn't matter except it makes him catch cold.'

'It may be something he caught on the Coast,' Lidderdale suggested. 'I've not been out, thank God, but the men who come back are not the same.'

'No, this is common around here.'

'I've got him in bed,' Bunton reported. 'But I can't keep his hands off his eyes.'

'It's the light. They can't stand the light. Can we cover these windows with something denser?'

'Sailcloth do, sir?'

'Cover them with your own trousers if you like,' Delauny was curt, 'but cover them. And rig a curtain over the door.'

'He's talking,' said Lidderdale. 'He says his head aches.'

'So it will. If he's livelier, and we can get his head up, we can try the lime juice. Now, lad, try a drop of that, will you, then …

that didn't go far, did it? We'd better have a big jug of it here, well diluted.'

'How long?' Lidderdale asked.

'Till he's better, of course, or till the ship comes. And till the doctor comes.'

'Not much a doctor can do,' Lidderdale was cynical. 'Only say, put the patient to bed, keep his strength up, keep him warm, give him plenty to drink.'

'Then we'll do that.'

Bunton spoke, 'We got cabbage and oatmeal and a bit of dried beef all fried up for dinner, sir, not to be too greasy to turn him like.'

'A good thick soup is more like it. Can you do that?'

Two sailors were now covering the windows. When the room was in twilight, Talleyman moved his hands from his eyes, and seemed a little easier, not turning so much or trying to bury his face in the pillows. Bunton brought the soup, and they tried, the three of them, to spoon it down Talleyman's throat, but he refused it. He did take more lime juice. Bunton suggested putting a little rum in it, to 'make him sleep'.

'I'm not sure we want that,' Delauny told him. It was true, he just did not know. Talleyman was breathing heavily, in a kind of light doze, sweating heavily. He was not delirious. Occasionally he spoke, quite rationally, but only to make the same complaint of a headache.

'He's still as hot,' said Lidderdale, 'but dry.'

'Now we have to cool him. Find a sponge.' Delauny wondered where he was getting this voice of command from, what was making these soldiers obey him. Was it merely that they were trained to obey any firm order? They got Talleyman's nightshirt off, and lifted him to sit up. Delauny began to sponge Talleyman's back. Suddenly he felt his hand caught and held, tight. He did not withdraw it. It seemed to be a comfort to Talleyman. Lidderdale kept on with the sponging. The hand-holding seemed to be a comfort to Talleyman, but Delauny found it a comfort too. As long as Talleyman had strength to hold like this, he would live.

He drank, eagerly, a great deal more lime juice. He did not sweat. Delauny wondered where the liquid was going. In the afternoon, they tried some more soup: Bunton had mixed in some curry powder, 'to give it more taste for him,' he explained later. Talleyman swallowed several spoonfuls, and then began to retch. Bunton snatched a bucket, and Lidderdale held the patient while he vomited into it. Delauny could only lend one hand, the other was still held fiercely. After that, Talleyman lay exhausted, very still, but still clutching.

Why am I here, thought Delauny. *Now they know what the trouble is, these men can do it as well as I. I ought to be out there, I ought to be measuring the stone in the quarry, seeing how I can make up for the lost days in the rain. I have a million things to do, and here am I nursing an Englishman.*

He drank some soup himself, and regretted the curry powder. Finally, he had gently to disengage his hand, and go outside to a lavatory. Almost immediately, Lidderdale was after him.

'You'd better come back. We can't do a thing with him.'

Talleyman was sitting up in bed, held back by Bunton and another Marine. For the first time he was rambling, but coherently, intermittently.

'Partridge,' he was saying. 'Like Partridge. Partridge was taking too long to die.' And later, 'They're coming, they're coming, I'll have to do it. It's Partridge.'

'There, there,' Delauny told him. 'We won't let you go. Lie back, we've got you safe.'

The slats of daylight that came in round the sailcloth curtains faded. A slight glow came around the screen from the coal brazier. Delauny dozed, trying to stay awake, but always pulled into an uncomfortable crouch by the gripping hand. Gradually in the small hours he came quite awake. Something was different. Talleyman's hand, still holding tight, was not dry but clammy again. Delauny whispered into the dark, 'Bunton!'

'No, Marney, sir,' said a strange voice. 'The Captain and Sergeant Bunton are sleeping. It's my watch.' This, Delauny could just see, was a sailor, not a Marine.

'He's sweating again. I know what's coming. Get a bucket.'

'A bucket? Aye, aye sir.'

'An empty one. And another full of water, if you can. And any waste rags. Call the Captain.'

Talleyman was tossing now, and groaning. He was running with sweat. Suddenly there was a great spasm of movement.

'Christ!' called Delauny. 'The bucket!'

There were four of them and they got the blankets off Talleyman and held him over the bucket till the diarrhoea had passed. Delauny took the clean rags and warm water and washed him down, tenderly. The spasms continued for about an hour, and then stopped.

'Clean nightshirt,' Delauny ordered. The stench in the room was unspeakable. 'Get him into the other bunk. Now he's warm. Open those windows, get some air.'

'But the light?' Lidderdale objected.

'That was the end. He'll be all right now, at least till he relapses, if he does.'

'Is it infectious?' asked the marine officer.

'A bit late to ask. It may be, but it seems to be carried in the dirty cabins. If it is, then all your men will have it soon.'

'That doesn't matter. Only I don't want it into the ship. If it is infectious, we stay till we all have it.'

There was a low sound from the bed, almost a panting. Delauny went over. Talleyman was awake, making no effort to sit up, not struggling. The big brown eyes were open, focusing well. He spoke quietly, composed, calm.

'Oh, it's you. I thought it was... I thought there was a woman here. It must be the eyes. I thought there was a woman here.'

He turned over on to his side, facing the window, and went off into a peaceful sleep.

PART III: SUMMER

1

'I thought it more suitable,' said Lord Denain, 'to tell you of my decision in person, rather than leave it to the lawyers.'

'Most considerate of your lordship.' *He is going to say no again*, thought Josiah Talleyman. Not much of a club, not much of a lunch. The old man really was a miser, then. It might have worked to bring say a quarter of the price and roll it in front of him in gold, real sovereigns, thousands of them, to be counted and piled in stacks, fifty by fifty. But even a quarter of the Fen Dilney Estate would have been too great a weight to carry, turned into gold coins, to hold in the hands, even in the mind. It was a figure that could only exist on paper. A pity. This was the first land he had rented as land, not as a place to build a factory or to run a railway over, but as land to own, to ride over, to work.

'I have been much vexed over it,' Denain went on. 'I have talked it over with many advisers — lawyers, agents, my neighbours, other friends...' He made a wide gesture which seemed to imply that the whole of the House of Lords had been called in to help in the discussions. 'Even with my son.'

'I informed my sons. I do not discuss things with them. But you have, then, come to a conclusion?'

'The discussions with my son were on the terms you last offered.'

'Were those terms a stumbling block?'

'Half in cash, and half in what I suppose we must call a speculative venture.'

'A shipbuilding yard today can hardly be called a speculative venture.'

'All steam engines are speculative ventures, Mr Talleyman. I tell you I cannot express the relief I felt when I got down alive at Paddington. If God had meant us to travel by steam, Mr Talleyman — but that is another matter. I had misgivings about the terms, although my son had none.'

So that's who's been forcing them up, thought Josiah Talleyman. *But that's the end.*

'That is as far as I can go, my Lord. As it is, I would be diverting to the purchase moneys which I can more profitably invest in that very shipyard, and gain a greater return.'

'Then why spend it in this way, Mr Talleyman?'

'It is land, my Lord. Be honest — is a man anything unless he owns land?' *There was no point in concealing it now*, thought Josiah Talleyman, *the decision was made. So I cannot have these fields I have worked on for five years. But if the old fool really has friends and influence, then he may know others who may be willing to sell me something as attractive — but not for this price. The chance is gone.* 'When I own land, I will feel that I am … someone.'

'Are you not someone already? You are as well known as, let us say, Mr Hudson.'

'But I am nobody till I own land, a substantial piece of land, and own it, so that I can leave it to my son after me.'

'You are well enough known for me to be certain that the little estate you are trying to buy from me is as a drop in the ocean of your industrial properties.'

'Industrial properties do not give me the one thing I need, the thing that will make me somebody. And land gives it.'

'And the one thing is…?'

'Independence. For me and for my heirs.'

'But with wealth you have independence, surely?'

'My wealth is dependent on my customers, Lord Denain, on their wish to buy my goods and their readiness to pay for what they receive. But if they change their wishes, if the fashion alters, if their bankers fail them, if their governments — for I must admit that many of my customers are, regrettably, foreigners — then I have nothing. The only thing that gives independence is land, and that I mean to have.'

'And now you have it.'

'I beg your pardon?'

'My solicitors have written to yours this morning, accepting your last offer.'

'But, my Lord, you have refused steadily for the last two years to consider the sale of the estate. Why have you changed your mind now?'

'I need the money. Before, I only desired it. Now I need it.'

'For building? I knew that the house your uncle started to build was conceived on a vast scale, but—'

'No. It is not for the building. Somehow I will complete that, with God's help, but the money is not for building.'

'Then, for what? Forgive me, my Lord, but you arouse my curiosity.'

'I have seen the pictures your son drew, of the Irish on my lands.'

'The ones printed in the *Illustrated*?'

'No, not only those. He sent my son a whole portfolio of them. It was ... it was ... if you do not know the country, if you do not know how the people struggle to live even in the good times, or how they scrape for nourishment when there is no famine, you cannot understand how I feel. I am an absentee landlord now, Mr Talleyman, and they threaten to shoot me if I cease to be an absentee, but I have been a country parson there. I cannot be absent and do nothing. Half the price, then, is to be in your shares. That is Philip's advice, and they can be his after I am gone, if they are worth anything. Do not misunderstand me, Mr Talleyman. I am sure that they are of value now, and I will keep this conversation secret, but you have not now encouraged me to think of them as being, let us say, as safe as houses.

'But I will have the other half in real money, and I will spend it as I want. Ireland is finished, Mr Talleyman. There will be no rents from it for another twenty years. Do you know how much I got this last year from the whole of the Denain estates in that island, after all my outgoings, and the agent's fees? Thirty-one pounds and ten shillings. The people are ruined, and more will die this year. There is only one thing to do to help them, and that is to make them leave the country. I intend — I will say it this afternoon in the House, I will make a speech and say it — I intend to pay for taking a thousand families from Ireland to America. From my estate, as far as possible, but I will help others, rather than see them starve. That will account for most of my share of the sale money.'

'And your son is in agreement with this?'

'He is in agreement. He must be.' *Oh, this is a good 'un after all,* thought old Talleyman. 'I had hopes that he might have joined us today, but he has gone, he told me, to visit friends in Wales.'

'He now has my permission,' said old Talleyman — he felt in the mood to be generous, and this was a father who wouldn't stand any argument, he'd tell the minx when he got home that they had better draft out the banns 'to call upon my daughter'.

'That would be very appropriate,' Denain agreed. *Now, when it comes to the marriage settlement, we will see which way that land goes. There can be a peerage in that family, and Fen Dilney can go with the title, after all. And as for the sons…*

'I've made Tom into a gentleman,' said old Talleyman. 'He's an officer now, and can go to the levees, which is the first in the family. Now he can leave the sea, and come back to live

177

like a squire, like your son does. I've kept him out of the works, and he'll stay out. The works is good enough for my other boy, Richard, but Tom'll stay on our lands. Now I can have him back from the sea, and the next thing is to get *him* married. There's not much two old codgers like us can do, so we'll have to think deep on it.'

'Will you try to have him back now? If he stayed in the ship when he had the relapsing fever, will he be content to come home before the commission is over? There may still be war with the French.'

'There's always like to be war with the French,' said old Talleyman, 'like there's always trouble with the Irish. And always trouble with them in London too. We had that first affair in April, when they had the troops lining the streets for the Charter, and what a fraud that was — they say half the signatures were forgeries. And then last Whit Monday, riots in Croydon and that M'Douall with thousands of them in Bishop Bonner's fields all shouting "On to Whitehall!" It's all an Irish plot, my Lord, it's all an Irish plot, and the French to take advantage of it all the time.'

2

That same day, near the end of July, *Santorin* was in the Long Bay again. The weather was good, Pentstemon felt it was even fine enough to talk to officers in the open air, on his side of the quarterdeck. He called Talleyman, and said, 'It's you for the dreaded Tower, young Tal.'

'Oh, I don't think so, sir.'

'You've not been there yet. You missed two turns when you were too sick to go.'

'I might relapse, sir.'

'That,' said Only in a tone of resignation, 'is too much to hope for.'

'But the engines—'

'You had a week's leave and four weeks' sick and incapable, and the engines worked well enough.'

'But not perfectly, sir, not like they are now.'

'Young Tal,' Pentstemon told him firmly, 'there is the Tower and Mr Mallow there eating his heart out for the refreshing taste of hard tack and duff. Are you going to deny him that pleasure?'

'One of the mates could go, sir. I feel I might relapse at any moment.'

'Then you may take Mr Cricklade with you. He will run your errands and pretend that he has heard, vaguely, somewhere, of the duties of an officer. You may have Sergeant Bunton as well, and a few marines as well as the seamen. And do not worry. We will go down as far as Cork for the mails, and be back in three days with whatever soft whisperings on paper may have come for you.'

'I am sure, sir, I would be more use in Cork. We have to look for iron. We have to repair Number Three boiler.'

'Pellick can do all that, and he can post any letters which are burning your pockets into holes. Though I suppose that you can find a post office here, or in Castletown, to take letters to Cashel.'

'It is not fair, sir. Do not laugh at me.'

'You're our only bachelor in the wardroom,' Only pointed out, 'and we are all in a hurry to have the wedding over before we leave Ireland.'

'There is no question of a wedding. Not yet.'

'We could send a landing party, if it would help.' Pentstemon laughed within himself, it would settle the lad for life if they could get him settled with some colleen. And not a bad catch himself, either. Young Tal was keen enough, they had all seen the portrait he had drawn of this Miss Roding. If there were doubt, it seemed to be on her side. The woman must be mad, or perhaps she was simply a very good fisherwoman. 'But while you're ashore, stay at Eyories. No pounding off inland, no matter what opportunity offers.'

'There's no justice,' Talleyman grumbled. 'You'll sight the French. Their fighting's over in Paris. They'll want to come at us, to keep the mob quiet.'

'If we meet them at sea, we'll ask them to wait till we come for you. After we've warned Admiral Napier, in Cork.'

'Thank you very much … sir.' Talleyman gave Only a baleful look, and went to get his gear together. Mr Senescall began to muster the seamen for the Tower.

'Harrison, Yeoman of Signals. You'll be the petty officer. Then Norris, Eaton, Harding, Braybrook, Adams — that's all the matelots. Now be respectful to Sergeant Bunton and let his Jollies have a bit o' peace.'

'What officer's going?' Harrison asked.

'Mr Talleyman.'

'Oh, no. Oh, I'm not going with 'im. 'E's bloody mad, 'e is.'

'He's all right.' Senescall felt it necessary somehow to support the officer, however he himself thought about it.

'At sea, 'e's all right,' said Harrison. 'But I was in the *Argyle*, in Africa, and I knows this, once 'e gets ashore, the land goes to 'is 'ead, like, and there's no 'olding 'im. Look last time, wasn't it in all the papers, no sooner do 'e get away from the ship but 'e burns a mansion down?'

'No arguing, lad, you're going,' said Senescall. 'True, rather you than me.'

3

'And did you relapse?' It was still in the Tower, but the late July sun was bright through the embrasure. 'Did you not have a relapse?'

'Only the one, and that was slight. Doctor Hampson said it was due to good nursing that it was no worse.'

'But they were very cruel to keep you in the ship. Why did they not send you ashore to get well?'

'They threatened to do that, but I was very determined. I would rather stay with people I knew. More sherry?' Talleyman crossed the carpeted Tower room to the sideboard. 'Besides, I did practically no work for weeks. I just sat on the quarterdeck and sketched, or read novels. I never read a novel in my life before, and Only has two hundred. He's had a misspent life, if you ask me.'

'Your brother officers seemed very grateful,' Delauny admitted. 'They presented me with a very handsome piece of silver almost as soon as they had you aboard. I wonder where they got it at such short notice.'

'They stole it.'

'They what?'

'It was almost as bad. It was Captain Pentstemon's sugar bowl. They bullied him into giving it, to be paid for out of Mess Funds. He gave in against his better judgement. He will not let us forget it. Pellick engraved it.'

'I will treasure it always.'

Rowe cleared away the soup plates, served curry and a mound of rice. Cricklade waited patiently, feeling that he could have eaten the three portions himself. After Talleyman's illness,

Pentstemon had ruled that there ought always to be what he called two officer-like creatures in the Tower at once, in case of sickness. Collins had guffawed at that, said loudly, 'Blast these boys, they split up the back.'

Cricklade had not understood that. He was glad he was ashore with Talleyman again and not with Collins. His elders were talking, and he was supposed to listen, and learn.

'I see your jetty is nearly finished.'

'It will soon be ready, as far as it goes.'

'If your work here is at an end... I do not quite know how to say this. My father has friends who build railways. Mr Hudson, for instance. Or docks. If you should wish to work as an engineer in England, there would be no difficulty.'

'My work is not finished. Work in Ireland is never finished. And how could I leave. The blight is back again this year.'

'Merciful Christ!' Cricklade knew that this was not blasphemy, but a prayer. To himself he said *Amen*.

Delauny went on, 'I may have to leave myself in the next few days. Because of the blight, my trustees are holding a meeting, but the place and day are not yet certain. You see, if it's money for this townland I'm wanting, for example to build a road to this jetty from Castletown, then I must be there to argue for it. They may want me to work elsewhere. You don't know about things like this. You're a warm man, aren't you, Talleyman?'

'Am I? My father, certainly, has money.'

'Then what are you doing at sea? What are you in the navy for?'

'It's better than the Hundred and Tenth of Foot.'

'What do you mean?'

'My father is not a gentleman. He knows it. He wants me to be a gentleman. So he always said he would not have me meddling in the firm. I must not be a boilermaker. He would make me a gentleman the easiest way, by turning me into an officer. When I was young, all I knew was that army officers didn't do anything and did it with horses. Naval officers went to sea. In the family I grew up in, going to sea meant steamers. We made boilers for steamers. So when I was a brat I yelled I wanted to be a sailor. When I was twelve I was sent off to learn to be a sailor. This is the first steamer I've been in. I think the term is irony.'

'You enjoy the steamer?'

'Why do you think I have been able to find excuses all this time to stay in the ship and avoid the Tower? The Captain's mad, doesn't believe in steam. They're all mad. If we fight, they'll put the boilers out, and try to manoeuvre under steam. The Captain likes the paddle boxes — says they'll make good boarding platforms. He still wants to fight Navarino. They all do. Have some duff. It's Rowe's masterpiece.'

'But you don't have to go to sea? Or come to Ireland?'

'No, I suppose not. Do you have to work *here*?'

'Well, 'tis something I am doing for Ireland. I have had offers from America, but they are not desperate. I don't know the people there like I know these. But we can't go on here unless we get more money. Have you thought of drawing any more pictures for the *Illustrated*?'

'You saw them? They only printed a few. The others were too bad to print, and I had some too bad to send. I went into many cabins near Ballyfine House. I was flea-bitten in them as any peasant.'

'Is that how you caught the fever?'

'I don't think so. I've been flea-bitten and lousy before — can't help it in a ship. But will nothing else help?'

'Only one thing will help this country. Independence. If we have the land, then we will be able to help ourselves, ourselves alone.'

'That's what my father wants, land. He thinks if he owns land, then I will be a gentleman. It's too late for him.'

'If we hold the country, then we can do something with it. We can build railway lines and make the country one. We have the coal at Killenaule, and sure there must be iron somewhere in the country. Then we can keep our own corn in the land and break this dependence on the potato. The men will work in our own factories, and 'tis then, you English look out.'

'This cheese is English, I'm afraid. But with it—'

'Now, don't go wasting your fine brandy on me, for it's wasted it'll be on a palate like mine. I took the precaution of bringing a little something, and I can assure you that it's at least a fortnight old, and I am positive on that point for was it not a great friend dear to my heart that made it?' He placed a stone jar on the table. 'Ah, it's a good thing that 'tis hardly coastguards you are and not the Excise at all because there'd be none of it you'd be getting it then.'

Cricklade noted that as the evening went on and the bottles emptied, Delauny's voice changed subtly. At first, he had spoken in the quiet precise accents of an educated man, the trained engineer. Now he was exaggerating his Irishness, in phraseology, as well as accent. Later in the evening, he was to speak a smoother English again, the relics of a vicarage upbringing.

'No, 'tis never a penny of duty that this will pay, I'll swear that, and the old man up in Kerry that makes it, 'tis in mortal fear he lives of the Peelers that would break up his pipes and pour the good liquor into the heather and not much good that does to the pasture itself, and put him into the jail they would too if they could catch him. Now, how d'ye like it?'

'Why, I like it middling well. It's … a change from cognac. Is this what they call poteen?'

'Arra, indeed, 'tis the holy fluid itself, and there's no being a true Irishman till you've drunk your own volume of it, as I have many a time. The wine of the country it is, and, faith, there's the boyos up in the hills that make sure that I'll never be going short of it.'

'So you have good friends up in the hills, then? Come, Mr Cricklade, you are not drinking. And our guest has been so good as to bring it for us.'

'No, sir, I couldn't, it's spirits, sir … my parents … I promised…'

'Why, and isn't it wine you've been drinking all the evening?' Delauny laughed at him.

'Only a sip, sir.'

'But isn't that the pass sold altogether? You can't be almost an abstainer, my boyo, for 'tis like being almost a virgin, and you couldn't face Father Matthew like that.'

'You drink your rum, don't you?' Talleyman asked, more kindly.

'Oh, no, sir, I give it to the gunner, sir.'

'You must *drink* it, Mr Cricklade. It is not given you for pleasure but to make your water safe to drink. You must *learn* to drink it, or the men will laugh at you.'

'Yes, sir. I … oh, no, I can't, sir, please…'

'We'll make a punch of it for you. Rowe! Hot water and lemon and sugar and nutmeg!'

Cricklade sipped miserably at his punch. It was not as bad as the raw spirit, in fact it was quite pleasant.

'That's better. You must learn to entertain your guests gracefully.' In the lieutenant's eyes, Cricklade read the clear message, *finish that glass if it kills you*. He prepared to die, decided that death might not after all be too dreadful, and finished it. Then he laid his head on the table and let the waves of talk wash over him.

'And were there no famines when Ireland had her own Parliament?'

'But it's not only a Parliament I'm talking of, and I'm thinking of what some might want that's been too long in America...'

'... a pawn and a knight, and I'll still beat ye.'

'No. Here is five shillings on it. With that we must start even.'

'Then you have white...'

'... and the railways not come any further than Thurles, and no telegraph either, and what state is that for a country to be in...'

'... A Parliament is not really for debating. It provides men who can be ministers. Take decisions. Run departments. Manage your railways.'

'There is no need to have these heads appointed from Parliament, out of all those debaters. The Americans do not do it that way, their President appoints all the servants of the state, and their Congress has nothing to do but argue. Now, Mr Talleyman, from what you have seen in Ireland, can you think of a better way of managing a country like this, where there is not a man but born with a silver tongue in his mouth and no more sense of time than a tree trunk?'

'I see your point. I do not know if I can accept it, not after the poteen. Shall I take white again? This match to settle all...'

'... mate. So it's a sovereign I've taken off you now, and t'would be conscience-stricken I'd be about it if I weren't thinking of all those wonderful boilers making the money for you and wondering how long before we make our own boilers in Ireland, although it's enough steam we all blow enough as it is. But if I'm to be arranging things in the morning in case I have to go off to my Committee, then I'd better be going. Your youngster doesn't stand up well to drink, does he?'

'He'll do. I have to get him fit to pass for midshipman by the autumn. Half the day, this is a schoolroom.'

Never a word about the girls, Delauny thought, *not all the night, and I saw two letters lying there as plain as brass one each from Jane and from Harriet by the writing on the envelopes and there's a deep one he is at that. There's a thing to show you can never trust an Englishman yet, or understand the English mind. And yet, there is something about him ... true, if he insists that I saved his life, then even if I did there is still something I am owing* him — *affection, acceptance of a kind, what we went through in this room when he neared death and held my hand for courage. It is something that lies between us, and I can never forget it.*

He looked round for his coat, but Talleyman was saying, 'I have here some property of yours.'

'And what's that?'

'Only some handkerchiefs your sister lent me, with your initials sewn into them. After the fire. They've been well washed — any complaints to Rowe. And your coat.'

'Oh, and that is very kind of you. You can see me in the dark in this and know me a mile away in the moonlight.'

Talleyman laughed. The two men tripped and stumbled their way across the cobbled courtyard. Out of the shadow, a marine sentry came to attention, opened the gate.

The sailor said, looming a head over Delauny, clasping his hand firmly in two huge palms, 'Goodbye, my dear Lawrence.

Take care of yourself on the road to Dublin. Do not let the Moonlighters get you before you reach your committee.'

'Oh, 'tis only about as far as Kilkenny I've got to go. And that's a thing they never do, kill Delauny on the way to the Committee, oh, no, the Moonlighters would never do that, nor the Mollies neither. But don't you catch your feet wet and another fever with it yourself, for I may not be back then for a while to look after you.'

They stood on the threshold, and then the sentry watched them embrace, briefly. Well, and he'd never have thought that of Mr Talleyman. The lieutenant stood back. He watched Delauny get into his trap, and then wavered his own way to the Tower room. Rowe thought his officer looked slumped, as if a spring had broken.

He heard the order, 'Let's have some black coffee, Rowe. Some black … black … tee-hee … black coffee. And strong.'

'Yes sir. I've had it on the go all the evening. I thought it might be wanted, sir.'

'Good man. Have you got the child to bed?'

'Yes sir. He needed it.'

'Tha's right. I've not got relapsising fever, Rowe. I'm drunk, Rowe. Drunk in the line of duty.'

'Very well, sir.'

Talleyman sat down very heavily, his hands on the table, his head on his hands. When his coffee came, he blew on it, noisily.

'That was a gambit, Rowe.'

'A gambit. Yes sir.'

'You don't play chess, do you?'

'No, sir.' *What chance to do that, or anything, on the Marines' mess-deck.*

'A gambit, Rowe, is an 'schange of a material loss for a material, no that'sh wrong, a pos'shnal 'vantage. Got it right. Very tiring, Rowe, very tiring, playing chess b'low standard. Very tiring, loshing to a man who plash chessh like a cattle drover. Indeed, Rowe. Know what my material loss is, Rowe?'

'No, sir.'

'I'm not feeling very well now, Rowe. That's a material loss. And I'll have a head in the morning.'

'Yes, sir.' *Thanks for the warning, I'll steer clear of you.*

'Know what my pos'shonal 'dvantage is, Rowe?'

'No, sir.'

'Hoped you would. You've been here all evening. What were you doing, not lishtenin? Blowed if I know where it is, either. Musht ha' dropped it somewhere. But it's not here, Rowe, it'sh shomewhere out on the road to Kilkenny.'

4

Sergeant Bunton went below, as he called it, which meant up the stone steps to the lower floor of the Tower, to warn Talleyman. The lieutenant was eating a hearty breakfast, as if it was running over the bogs he had been the last two days and nights, not sitting up and talking and drinking. It was eight o'clock, officers' breakfast time. The sergeant and his six marines and the six sailors had had their breakfast at the proper time, ship time, half past six, and Talleyman had been there to watch them.

Since then Talleyman had done his rounds. He had satisfied himself that all was secure, that there had been no attempt on the meal store by night, that the chickens had been fed, that none of the seamen had too obviously had women between their blankets overnight, that the Marines were sober. He had gone round with Sergeant Bunton at his elbow, and he had seen those things he was expected to see, according to the rules of the game. The sergeant was pleased with a lieutenant who knew the rules, and that was more than he could say for some. It was a very good day indeed, with the white clouds covering half the sky, streaming in from the sea but very high so that with luck any rain would go over their heads and fall in the hills. It had been worth the risk of turning all the bedding out to air on the grass, even if it did mean keeping a permanent sentry over it.

Talleyman had worked his way through four eggs and half a pound of bacon. Now he was well into the ship's biscuits and marmalade. *Got to keep his strength up*, thought Rowe, *and it's a pleasure to have an officer who will take advantage of the chance. That's a lot of weight he's lost since he had the beating, but he's putting it back again, all right.*

Now Talleyman was reading a four-day-old newspaper that had come in the day before with the weekly postman from Castletown. *It's a pity*, thought Bunton, *to disturb a gentleman's peace and before he's reached the first cigar of the day, but it's got to be done.* He knocked on the open plank door, and entered, saluting.

'Begging your pardon, sir...'

'Oh, come in, sergeant. Have a cup of coffee.'

The coffee was always offered, always refused. Such were the rules of the game.

'No, thank you sir. There's a sail in sight.'

'A sail? That's early. *Santorin* is not due till tonight at the earliest, or perhaps tomorrow morning.'

And that, thought Rowe, *is not what he told the surveyor last night. I remember he said she wouldn't be in till the end of next week.*

'It's not *Santorin*, sir. It's a schooner, the yeoman tells me, and it's just come round the land from the way of Allihies.'

Bunton affected not to see Talleyman wince. When he had first taken the Queen's shilling twenty years before he had been under both the influence of alcohol and the impression that he was enlisting in the Fourth Dragoon Guards. He still persisted in the belief that a ship was an inanimate thing without gender. But not without personality: they were all misbegotten and evil-intentioned. Talleyman stood up.

'I had better come and see. Rowe, try and wake Mr Cricklade if you can. He didn't want any breakfast.'

He picked his telescope from the rack, and put on his hat so that he could respond to salutes. The Tower roof, reached by an outside staircase, was domed slightly so that rainwater could run into the guttering. It was surrounded by a six-foot parapet, pierced by arched embrasures, so that sailors could think themselves on the upper deck of a ship, looking through ports. Talleyman steadied his telescope against the side of an embrasure and looked west.

'You are right. A schooner. A big one. Two hundred tons about. Wouldn't you say so? Wind's on her quarter. I can't make out her colours. Where would you say she was built, sergeant?'

The sergeant knew the rules. This talk was a way of passing the time. There were few other ways of making the day go tolerably in the Tower, other than by irrelevant conversation, since there was a shortage of things to be cleaned. He screwed up his mind for a polite response: he reasoned that if his lieutenant was puzzled about where this thing came from, there was one safe reply, 'Not in these parts, I shouldn't say, sir.'

'No, I'd agree with that. A New Englander, perhaps. See how the bows fine away there. Nothing to go on, of course. But I think I've seen the type before. No knowing who owns her now. Wish I did.'

'You may well be right, sir.'

Sergeant Bunton was a soldier by trade. The fact that he had spent a great deal of his life inside warships, often being by years the most experienced seagoing man aboard, was incidental to his way of life. His lack of curiosity about any ship, even the one he happened to be in at the moment, was total and absolute. To relieve his boredom he looked idly around him for fluff on scarlet coats or dust on boots, while Talleyman carried on with his examination.

'I don't suppose she'll bother us, sergeant.'

Bunton's gaze, travelling round the roof, was suddenly fixed. He felt disturbed. He worked his conscience hard, sought for precedents. There were none. He was forced in the end, at the cost of intense personal anguish, to call an officer's attention to a phenomenon not connected with the sea.

He suggested, 'If you was to look at the shore, sir…'

Talleyman swung round. Then he crossed the roof to look through another embrasure. The sergeant looked over his shoulder. Four roads converged on the head of Delauny's new jetty. Two came from east and west, unmade tracks but fit for carts. The others, metalled once, perhaps in Oliver's time, came from inland, one over the hills from Castletown, and the other from Kilmackowen.

'There's movement on the roads,' said Talleyman.

'Yes, sir.' *What the hell does he think I meant, then, bloody volcanoes?*

'Donkey carts. Donkey carts coming from everywhere. On all the roads. Must be … a hundred of them. And more coming. What are they doing?'

'Going to meet the ship, sir?'

'Can't be. There's no knowing she's going to call here. If she does, what use to them? They've nothing to sell here, and no money to buy with. Those carts are all empty — see them bump. Unless they're selling their donkeys and carts.'

Talleyman was scanning the roads, counting under his breath, his lips moving. The Yeoman of Signals was standing near, trying to catch Bunton's eye. Bunton saw him, and gained fresh courage.

'I begs your pardon, sir, but I thinks that Harrison knows something.'

'He looks fit to bust. What is it, Harrison?'

'I know that ship, sir. She's been here before.'

'Has she, now? I'm not surprised to hear it. See how close she's coming along the shore there. We can see the rocks, in this light, but he can't. But he knows they're there. Or he's got a mackerel for a pilot. What do you know?'

'She did come in when I was here before with Captain Lidderdale. She did lie out there and unload a lot of corn sacks and got it ashore in her own boats. Took them a lot of trouble, it did. We thought it was a relief ship out of America. Mr Delauny the engineer did come down and have breakfast with Captain Lidderdale that morning. And the Irish came down with their donkeys, like this, but not so many, to take the meal away.'

'Oh, so this is Mr Delauny's relief ship. Anything in the log about it?'

While Harrison flipped through the log, Cricklade came up very dishevelled and sleepy, and still clutching a mug of black coffee. He blinked at Talleyman, and then blinked more through his telescope. Since it was the same model as Talleyman's, it was a couple of sizes too large for him to handle. It did not help that he could only just get his face over the level of the embrasure, and that he could not manage to hold the telescope still. He could do that better from the chains in *Santorin*. He was too proud to ask for a box to stand on, although there were several lying around. He did not realize that Harrison kept them handy for that purpose, but was afraid of hurting Cricklade's feelings by offering openly.

'Look, sir, when you was sick at sea.'

'Now, hear who she is,' and Talleyman read from the log. It was all there in Lidderdale's fine firm hand. 'Inspected Schooner *Cayuga* of Gloucester in Maine, out of Boston with a cargo of corn paid for by the Boston Relief Fund for distribution among the poor of the region. Distribution effected under the supervision of Mr Delauny.' He looked at Harrison. 'Did Captain Lidderdale go into her?'

'Oh, no, sir, he just looked at her through the glass from here, and walked on the shore when the boats grounded, with Mr Delauny. He said if it were famine time, nothing weren't going to be very regular. And he hadn't seen any Customs officers very eager to come on board her, and it weren't no problem of ourn.'

'I think we'll give them a little more attention. I'll go into her if she anchors. Or if she moors at the jetty.'

Talleyman drank coffee, till it was clear that the schooner was indeed going to moor.

He said to Cricklade, 'I can't help if you've been up all night. First lieutenant said I was to have a restful time. Didn't say anything about you resting.' Then, to the group around him, 'The sergeant's in charge. Mr Cricklade, you'll come with me, and Harrison too. Best suits. This is a formal visit. Not a formality.'

5

Captain Langer was intent on mooring the schooner. The supercargo stood by him, as he had all the way up the Long Bay, murmuring hints, directions, warnings. Working carefully, they could bring her near enough to the jetty for the men there to catch a thrown rope, and then another, and at last to work her alongside, at the far end where the water was deeper. The Mate drew Langer's attention to the officers coming.

Langer was used to being bothered by men in British uniforms. In fact, he was getting rather bored by it, repeating the same story again and again. The officer here the last time had wandered down and watched the unloading from the shore. That had been a redcoat, and come down all unbuttoned, his soft hat on the back of his head, smoking a cigar. But this one, Langer had him in the glass. A long beanpole of a man, wearing his blue frock coat all buttoned up, and his cocked hat on, and a sword on his belt. And there was a youngster trailing behind him, and a sailor.

Langer called to the supercargo, 'Get down into the cabin, James Brennan. Have all the papers out in order, and a bottle of rye. I think this one will want to see something. We'll have it all easy and quiet, d'ye hear that, and not a word out of you that you can avoid.'

The gangplank had hardly touched the jetty before Talleyman was up it in long strides. Cricklade and Harrison stayed at the foot.

'Good morning, Captain.'

'Good morning, Lieutenant.' Langer thought that it was worthwhile seizing on this nominal disparity in rank. 'And to what do I owe this pleasure?'

'I am glad you find it pleasant. I am head of the Coastguard in this area. You have no objection to my inspecting your ship? After all, you are now within the Queen's dominions.'

Langer could think of half a dozen replies to that, and thought it politic not to use them.

It was better to offer, 'Would you not be the better for a dram?'

'So you speak the language. That is a very Christian suggestion.'

'This way then, Lieutenant. I think you will find everything in order.'

Talleyman took the log and the untidy bundle of other documents from Brennan, hardly looking at him. He sat down at the cabin table, and stretched out his legs. He almost filled the saloon. *Acting big*, thought Langer, *showing that he has no care for anybody. He'll laugh the other side of his face some day.*

'Chartered, I see, by the Boston Irish Relief Association. But your own property, Captain Langer?'

'Altogether my own all clear, and never had another owner. I saw her built in Marblehead—'

'Where?'

'In Marblehead, Lieutenant, near Salem.' *And if you listened properly, instead of keeping half an eye on the papers and half an ear on me, you'd do the whole job.* 'I know her like I known my own body, better, perhaps, because I've seen all over her inside, and between the skin and the ribs.' Langer waited for the laugh. It did not come. He went on, trying to be distracting, 'There's an art in building, you know, when you can please yourself what is made. It's a temptation to try for speed, the most you can get on the length, but if you go too fine there's no room to carry anything. Speed is only worth having for perishables, or for seasonal markets like tea, or passengers…'

'Cornmeal is not a perishable.'

'I take what charters I can get. And I have … connections with several Irish gentlemen in Boston. They need a ship that can get into these small harbours, and they cannot fill a big ship quickly.'

'But you should have cleared customs.'

'There is a note in the log. We spoke to a Customs cutter off the Fastnet. Since we were bound here, they did not ask us to clear in Cork. They had met us before.'

'You have been here before?'

This questioning, thought Langer, *is closer than I like, and this time of all times. Where's that bloody man Delauny that was supposed to arrange things? I've not had such attention for years, not since the old days, that was a risky run. But the navy style is what I always remember, and I've got through it before, on the Coast. I'll weather it again, talk my way out of it, beat him down with detail.*

'I have been here twice before, but this is the first time we have lain at the jetty. The first time was in the autumn, when the work was hardly started, and the next time not so long ago … see here in the log … then we could lie behind the jetty in smooth water, even if we could not tie up. But I believe now we can lie here at least for eight hours between tides, and that'll be time for us to unload. Before we could only bring small bags, because we had to tranship into small boats, like they do at Kumasi, but this time we have the big sacks, a hundred pounds at a time, and save a great deal of trouble unloading. D'you see, last year, there was only enough money collected for the one cargo, but here we are with the second for this year, and more to come. You'll soon be used to seeing me around, Lieutenant. Why, look who's come aboard. D'you know Mr Delauny, Lieutenant?' *And he's been long enough coming, and no thanks to him we haven't had damage done.*

'Good morning, Mr Delauny. I hope you had a peaceful night. What we left of it. I will be with you in a moment.'

Talleyman returned to the log, while the other three watched him. He worked steadily through the log, sidetracking expertly to the letters and charters, rearranging the bundle. His lips moved in calculation.

He spoke aloud, 'Yes, with those winds … we met them also … three weeks to get here, five weeks back, three weeks eastabout again … that will be about right.'

But it is right, Langer told himself. *He won't find a thing wrong with those charters and log entries, they're all genuine. Even the Society is genuine, as far as anything can be genuine in Boston. And there's real grain in the bags, all of them, if he wants to feel, and a few of the top ones fit for him to open. If Delauny hadn't come, I'd have tried showing him the colour of a roll of bank notes, but now we'll let the surveyor do the talking. It's for his benefit, more than mine.*

Talleyman turned to Delauny, 'Pray, what are all these men doing here? And their carts?'

'Why, Talleyman, they have come to collect their grain.'

'They come so pat when they are called?'

'You only saw the ship when she moored: she would have been sighted from the mountaintops last night, off Allihies.'

'On the open ocean. But … do you mean to issue the grain directly to them? And indiscriminately? Or to the most needy? If anyone knows the deserving cases, you do.'

'It's not as simple as that, Talleyman, and yet simpler still, one might say. Now this is a charity with which my Trustees are intimately connected, and yet it is not indiscriminate. The cargo has been paid for by individual Irishmen in Boston, and sent to their families. I have the list here. Look, Thomas, this is not charity. These men are not beggars. It is their own sons and cousins who are sending them back food from America to tide them over the bad years, so that they will not lose their land here. You understand, do you not, that it is a matter of being Irish. The people stick together, and look after each other. We live for ourselves alone, we are helped by ourselves alone.'

'For yourselves alone. That is why the people here refuse the food the navy brings them. Each sack Captain Langer brings has a man's name on?'

'Not literally, but that is the principle. See here, Thomas, we need not be a burden on your state, we have food for ourselves that the Irish have bought, and worked for, in America, for their own. Being Irish, my friend, is more than living in Ireland, more than being subject to the Queen. It spreads all across the world; we will look after ourselves alone.'

'Then will you superintend the distribution?'

'Myself? I'm afraid not. I told you, I have to go to the meeting of my Trustees, and I am already late.'

'In that case…' Talleyman looked around the cabin, from eye to eye. 'There may be disorder. I will send down a few marines. They will keep order while you, Captain, make the distribution.'

'Now, Tom, do you think that these people will make a disorder when they have their own food in their midst?'

'Why, *Mister* Delauny, do you forget what state the country is in? Captain Langer, have you heard the news? Martial law has been proclaimed in this Island. I can show you *The Times*, if you wish. General Hardinge is in command, at Kilkenny. Habeas Corpus is suspended. The whole land is a powder keg. I cannot risk a spark. Not here, where I am in command.'

So that's it, thought Langer, *being on his own has gone to his head. Next he'll be telling us he's king of Ireland.*

'Now, Lieutenant, it would be better to have the Constabulary here, because at least they're Irish.'

'There are no Constabulary. I would prefer it, I know redcoats are disturbing. But we must have order. I will make a small show of force.'

'I will protest about this, Lieutenant, to our Consul at Cork, and—'

'Protest if you wish. This is for your own protection. These men are not responsible. Last week at Dingle I was in a ship. It had been loaded with corn to take away. It had been robbed. The people of the town stole all the corn. The Captain was killed defending it. I must see you safer here. Your Consul would protest enough if I let you be killed.'

Talleyman stood up. Langer noticed that he had left most of the whisky in his glass, indeed if he had touched it at all. Delauny went in front of them up the companion, on to the deck. The American sailors had the hatch covers off, and looked to the supercargo for the word to start unloading. The tackle was rigged to the mainsail gaff.

Talleyman spoke, 'Mr Delauny, perhaps then you would be off to your meeting. Mr Brennan, you may unload some of your sacks on to the jetty if you wish.' *Oh, he got the name from the papers*, thought Langer. *I mustn't let Delauny say any more, he's done his job, and I can handle it now.*

'Perhaps, Lieutenant, Larry here can go and explain to the people of the place what you are doing? I don't want the sight of the redcoats to frighten them all off.'

'Yes. Go and talk to your ... compatriots, Mr Delauny. Now, Captain, I will go back to the Tower for a few men. Not many.' They were on the quay now. 'I will leave this officer here for your protection.' Cricklade suppressed a startled squeak. 'I will also leave this seaman in case he is needed to run errands.'

Talleyman caught Harrison's eye over Cricklade's head. Cricklade caught the glance and felt better. Then Talleyman reached down and tapped the pistol thrust into the cadet's waistband.

'Careful with that or we'll see the end of the House of Cricklade.'

Langer and Brennan laughed, the American seamen joined in, and all the Irish at the head of the jetty saw them all laughing together. Even Delauny, climbing into his trap, felt the tension slacken. Well, that was all he could do. Could anyone do better? It would all come ashore now, and be shared out, and the redcoats to help in it. Well, and was not this a trick to boast about from Cork to Derry? He whipped up the pony and went off on the Kenmare road.

Harrison watched Talleyman walk away alone. He did not himself feel very easy in his mind, either, left to look after this cadet, with nothing but his cutlass and a couple of pistols. Talleyman's manner had spoiled the seaman's stomach for standing on the quay. He watched with envy for the officer's sheer nerve as Talleyman came to the head of the jetty and walked straight past the line of donkey carts without appearing to notice them. The peasants noticed him, though — silently.

Harrison turned his head back, and fixed on the American sailors unloading the sacks from the hold. They were handling that corn like gold, he thought, lowering each sack gingerly on to the jetty, never letting one fall. Heavy sacks? That size ought to be a hundredweight, but the way these men were working … *well, we always thought that the Americans weren't much cop, and if they can't lift these sacks, it's true.*

Cricklade also watched the men working on the tackle. He found it more comfortable than watching the crowd of peasants at the head of the quay, a ragged army, all dressed alike in the eternal tailcoats and billycock hats, a generation out of fashion. There were a great number of them now. He had tried counting heads, but when he had reached two hundred he had lost count, and there were many more after that. He wondered what he should do if they all came marching along the quay. Come to that, he realized disturbingly, he had no idea what he was supposed to be doing here at all. Was he looking after Harrison, or the other way about? Or had they been left because Talleyman thought it safer for one man to go back than three? One thing he had already learnt from the rules of the game. The seamen would see him through. He stood still and trusted Harrison.

6

Sergeant Bunton watched Talleyman come back. He had the corporal and the ten privates of Marines drilling outside the gate of the Tower. They had brought in the bedding. Eleven was an awkward number to form square, but that was the only evolution in the drill book they had not worked over already that morning. The squad came to attention as Talleyman came past them. The officer returned the salute, and then beckoned Bunton to follow him to the roof of the Tower.

Bunton stood there and watched Talleyman as he paced to and fro. This was a familiar sight to him. He saw it more often on quarterdecks, and at a higher rank level, and he seldom knew the result. But this continual striding, this snapping of fingers, this sudden stopping to stare into the sky or out to sea, he had seen it with a dozen different captains. They seemed more puzzled when they were dealing with matters on shore. *They ought to have a Marine officer here all the time*, thought Bunton.

But here, plainly, was an officer in a quandary. Talleyman was weighing something up. He was wondering, obviously, whether he could do something questionable, whether he could risk a court martial, or ridicule, or Pentstemon's displeasure, balancing one thing against another, gains against losses. But what things? It wasn't a sergeant's job to think, but Bunton couldn't help wondering, worrying. There were tales he had heard about what had happened in 'Ninety-eight, and he didn't like them. They were as bad as anything he had heard in Africa. But come to that, he had heard tales in Africa about Talleyman: a nasty man to cross was the word on the lower deck. The man who'd broken his nose for him — oh, that was a horrible tale. Anything might happen, any old Coaster would tell you, with Talleyman loose in Ireland. Whatever it was, Bunton wished the lunatic would make up his mind and get on with it. Bunton only wanted to be told what to do.

Talleyman suddenly snapped open his telescope. He handed it to the sergeant, and indicated the growing pile of sacks on the jetty. Bunton looked at them obediently, then handed the telescope back to the lieutenant.

'How do those sacks look? To you?'

'Look, sir?' Bunton pondered. How the hell ought they to look? He chose a word at random. 'Heavy, sir.'

'I think so, too.'

And what's so odd about that, Bunton wondered. There was another silence, then sharply,

'Sergeant!'

'Sir!' This was a different tone, thank god, this was orders at last.

'Fall in your Marines with their muskets. Serve out … oh, twenty rounds a man. Full water bottles. No knapsacks. Ready to march in … three minutes.'

'Sir!'

Bunton ran down the steps from the Tower roof. He barked his orders to the corporal, ran back into the lower room of the Tower. He rolled back the canvas that did for a carpet, unlocked the grating in the floor, dropped into the magazine below. *Twenty rounds*, he thought, as he handed the packets of cartridges up to Rowe. *That was a lot, it showed Talleyman expected more than a squabble. Water bottles — that meant a long day. No knapsacks, that meant they wouldn't be going far. No living off the country here in Ireland, no sleeping out either in the rain: but we'd better have a couple of biscuits each in our pouches.*

Bunton had his men in two lines when Talleyman came out through the gate. There were two sailors behind him, with cutlasses and pistols through their belts. That left only three matlows in the fort, Bunton realized: he hoped they'd have the sense to keep the door closed. Talleyman was wearing his pea jacket again, and his soft hat pushed to the back of his head. Instead of looking jaunty, it merely gave him a desperate air. *Is he afraid of spoiling his best things?* thought Bunton. *No sword, either. But this is more like it, when an officer dresses as if he expects trouble, instead of coming on it by surprise. And there will be trouble?* Bunton hesitated. Then, for the first time in his life, justifying himself that there was no Royal Marine officer present, Bunton gave an independent order.

He shouted, 'Detachment! Fix … bayonets. Slope arms! Right turn! Following the officer… Quick march.'

The little force marched after Talleyman down the sunken road. Seeing the crowd in front, filling the way from hedge to hedge with donkey cart, Bunton moved them into single file. He double-spaced them, to make their passing take longer and make the force look bigger. The corporal marched behind Talleyman. Bunton brought up the rear, and the hairs on his neck bristled with fear.

There was silence as they went by. Other days when the Marines had been marched around to tire them out, and soak up time, there had been at best a little badinage, at worst, curses as the redcoats went by. But now nobody said anything, the men just watched. And all men, Bunton noticed with little joy. No women, no children at all, when in Ireland you could hardly put a foot to the ground without stepping on two babies. And not many boys, and those there were youths really, never a one as young as Cricklade.

And this silence, Bunton thought, *was it the bayonets that did it? But Talleyman had not countermanded the order.* Now that they came to the head of the jetty, Talleyman jerked his hand to the sergeant, pointed at the ground. Here there was room to move. Bunton could halt his section, and give them something to do, check their dressing till they rattled, put them through a spot of foot-and-arms drill, anything to steady them — Christ, he could do with some steadying himself. It was the hush that was so bad. It was men, all silent, that meant trouble: it always had, in Africa.

Cricklade, at any rate, was glad to see the gleam of the bayonets above the heads of the crowd. He had been standing too long there on the jetty, looking at a thickening crowd of Irishmen, all in their tattered frieze coats, who just looked back at him, at him and at the sacks that were hoisted out of the ship, one by one, so carefully. He felt ashamed of his good clothes, of his thick cloth jacket, his stout shoes, of the money that had been paid to the outfitter in one lump which could keep a man going here in rent for a lifetime. He wondered if it were right that he should even be here, well fed, in the face of these … these scarecrows. Yet no scarecrow would ever have such a desperate face as the mildest man he could see now: turnips were too fat to carve like this.

Langer counted the Marines and swore under his breath. This time it was Brennan's turn to comfort him.

'There's no need for you to worry, Delauny's done the work, didn't he tell us so? We've got protection, and it's the man's life that's paying for it. And what have you to lose, anyway?'

'What? I've got my ship to lose, that's what.'

'Why, and that's but a trifle, and already paid for. If they catch me, then I'll be hanged, and am I caring about that?

Watch you, now, it's helping us to get it ashore the soldiers will be in a moment.'

'I'd feel a sight safer if that Delauny were still here.'

'I've heard things from Malachi Doyle. Larry's never a care in the world but how to keep himself on the Committee, for there's some of the others that are dead set against him. So he'll get there with the news that it's all safe ashore, and he'll be safe himself till the great day comes. And the Queen will give this officer a medal for helping the starving Irish, and if she doesn't the Irish nation will when we're free whether he wants it or not.'

But Langer was not much cheered. He watched the Marines draw their line across the head of the jetty. Talleyman and the two sailors passed through the line, pausing only for the officer to say to Malachi Doyle, in a voice of menace, 'You — out!'

Langer came forward to meet Talleyman. He was not comforted to hear the order, 'Sergeant, have your men load. Do it so that the people can see it.'

Bunton called his orders loud whispering to his men that they were to count to six, not three, between movements, to make it more impressive.

Langer protested, 'Lieutenant, there's no need for that.'

'I must make a show of force. It will save trouble. Not now, but later. Sergeant! Bring your men to the Order. Then send the corporal and two men with me. I need sentries at the gangplanks. You stay here with the rest.'

'Sir!'

The ramrods slid back, clacked into their clips. The musket butts grounded on the cobbles with a single crash. The Marines were stood at attention in a single line facing the patient peasants and their patient donkeys. Talleyman walked back to the gangplank with Langer, the two matelots following.

Behind, Bunton and the corporal made as much fuss of detaching two men from the line as if they had been trooping the colour, going through a litany of coming to attention, and standing at ease, of numbering off and falling out, of stepping back two paces and closing up, of stretching out the line again and recovering dressing. *It made as much noise as if a whole army had been there*, thought Bunton, *but the army could never have done it in the style that comes as second nature to Marines*. Bunton took his place at the right of the line, but facing along it so that he could divide his attention between his men and his officer.

The corporal and his two Marines thumped down the jetty and slammed to attention in front of Talleyman.

'Sir!'

'Sentry go in front of the gangplank, Corporal Clapp. No one to go in or out of the ship without my permission.'

'*Sir!*'

'I think that you may continue unloading, Mr Langer.' Cricklade felt Talleyman's hand on his shoulder a moment. The cadet stiffened. He had become a little easier in his mind when he saw redcoats around him, but now he realized that though Talleyman's voice was steady, his hand was shaking. 'So Mr Delauny helped you the last time?'

'Oh, yes, he has been of the greatest help to us. He has given the relief association so much information and practical help, and has been the leading spirit…'

'I am not surprised to hear it. I know his family. I have relied very much on his judgement. You would do well to follow him. The people trust him. If he were still here I would not feel so uneasy.'

For a last wild moment, Langer still felt hope. *If this Englishman did know Delauny as well as that, knew his family … had it all been arranged even better than he had been told? There were many like this Englishman who felt for Ireland, who had been persuaded, or loved, into sympathy, who would do what they could, with the advantage that since they were not Irish they could be discarded in the end. And after all, what was Delauny but a converted Englishman? What had Brennan said, that there was a limit to how far the people* would *trust him, being a Protestant. Yet somehow he had fixed this Englishman, brought him over, worked from that lucky accident of stopping the boyos, and see how it paid off. He had settled him, bribed him perhaps, because there was money for sure poured into this Young Ireland, and hopes of a tenfold return.*

Well, perhaps Brennan was right. Play our cards properly, and we can make the British navy itself a laughing-stock. They would have these Marines pile their arms yet and help with the sacks. Langer shouted to his men to carry on with the unloading.

'One moment,' said Talleyman. He walked away from the gangplank towards the main hatch. Langer had heard no word spoken, but he saw that it was Harrison alone who followed the lieutenant, the other two bluejackets still standing with Cricklade. This then was a service where men knew each other, acted on the inflection of a voice, the twitching of an eyebrow. He stood and watched, rigid. In that moment he knew that it was over, and there was nothing he could do, with one of the seamen, unobtrusively, holding a pistol on him. Above, on the deck, Brennan held to the mizzen shrouds and watched in silence. Talleyman stood under the sack of meal hanging from the tackle above his head, his hand tucked into the breast of his pea jacket. He spoke out of the corner of his mouth, 'Cut it open!'

Harrison drew his cutlass and slashed up, carving down the side of the sack in a ragged line of frayed jute. The tautness of the fabric stretched out by the weight of the meal helped him, pressing against the edge of the steel. The meal poured out with a rush, blowing in the wind, covering Harrison and all around with white, blowing in the wind, spilling to float on the water on the far side of the jetty. Only meal, for a moment, and Langer prayed that it was one of the right sacks, but then he stopped praying and cursed God in his heart. Out of the gutted sack, with a clatter and a ring of iron, fell two heavy objects, long and narrow, wrapped in oilskin, and six smaller packages. They lay on the cobbles.

There was absolute silence. The men at the tackle stood and watched. Langer was like the statue of a dead king. Only Talleyman moved, motioning with his little finger. Harrison sheathed his cutlass. He bent and with his clasp knife cut the yarn around one of the long parcels. He unwrapped it, turning it over and over on the jetty. The muskets fell out, one by one, three of them. With dreadful care Harrison set them in a pyramid, interlocking the piling swivels as if he were bivouacking, fixing the sheathed bayonets. He opened one of the smaller packets. Two boxes of fifty cartridges each, and a packet of percussion caps. He held them up for Talleyman to see.

Talleyman turned in the silence to Langer. Talleyman's hand was out of his breast now, it hung slack at his side holding his frighteningly large pistol, his finger not on the trigger but lying along the barrel. Bunton saw it, far off, and called his men to attention, and then to the high port as being more frightening. He waited for a movement in the crowd, saw none, mistrusted the quiet and called his men to the Aim. Talleyman spoke.

'I did not see these on your bill of lading, Captain.'

Langer could not answer. But the spell was broken. Brennan broke from the group on the deck. There was no way out for him along the jetty. He took five paces across the deck, to the opposite shrouds. He pulled himself up on to the gunwale. He hung for a moment before he would jump into the water.

Talleyman shot him. Without challenge, without a word or flicker of his face, bringing up his pistol hand in a smooth swing. The sailors saw Brennan fall all slack into the water, sink, reappear again a moment, his face loose and vacant, his eyes open, a sliver of blood about his lips. Then his boots filled and he went down.

The pistol smoke curled into the air in a white smudge, was carried inland by the wind, the wind that carried the echo among the hills as a signal, that brought the first sight now of *Santorin*'s black smoke coming up the bay. The run was over. The work was in vain.

There was a shouting and a squabbling noise from the land, a shrieking and a wailing, a rumbling of a hundred little carts, the clattering of small hooves, as the donkey carts were turned, pulled round, the asses whipped into a gallop. Many of the men nearest the jetty valued speed more than property, and left their carts to run up the road and off it, over the hillsides, into the bog and rocky moorland, dodging behind solitary trees or the hedgebanks, shielding their faces as if they were afraid of being recognized. Everywhere they went, anywhere, only to get away from these redcoats, from these terrible men who killed without speaking, as coldly and dispassionately and fairly as they gave away meal. It was over, then, the jetty was wasted, the ship taken. All the muskets they had been promised, for which they had come from furthest Clare and Kerry, all gone, lost, in the hands of the Marines. The redcoats had beaten them.

At the jetty head, Bunton grunted. He was sweating. He could do, he reflected, with his rum ration. He brought his men back to the high port, and then to the At Ease. But the corporal and his two remained at the ready, and the matlows drew their cutlasses. Now, if there were danger if would be in

213

the ship. But there was no more danger, it had passed. Langer had sat down on the jetty with his head in his hands and was vomiting on the cobbles.

Only Talleyman seemed unconcerned, blowing down the barrel of his pistol. As he reloaded the chamber, Cricklade asked him, 'Why, sir, why? How did you know? And why did you shoot that man, without challenging?'

'It was the shape of the ship. And the smell.'

7

'It was the shape of the ship,' Talleyman repeated. 'And the smell.' They were in Pentstemon's day cabin.

'You must not be so cryptic, young Tal. Remember, you will have to explain all this at some time or other to higher authority, although what higher authority can be conceived of than your captain I find it hard to say, but we cannot depend on our enlightened and popular administration to understand the workings of rational minds.'

'Will we need to explain even to them? We are under martial law.'

'So I believe, but we have only *The Times* for our authority. I have had no official instructions for some days, for weeks even. On this service I feel abandoned as the country does. There is certainly no communication with Dublin from here. The report may well have been true when it was written, but for all I know it may have since been contradicted. What do you mean, the shape of the ship?'

'Look at her!' *Santorin* lay about a quarter of a mile offshore. There was a pile of torn sacks on the jetty, a great heap of flour blowing into the air, covering the moored schooner, the salt water. 'A clipper. Built narrow and sharp at the bottom, a fine sweep to the counter, and no room for a big cargo. Not for any ordinary cargo. A special cargo. She was built on purpose for it. A perishable cargo. And then there was the smell.'

'A smell?' asked Only from the basket chair. 'A smell of the cargo?'

'You have never been on the Coast. That American has owned her since she was built. He was proud of that. But he could never clean out that smell.'

'But what smell?' Only insisted.

'A smell we all know from the Coast. The smell of men. The smell of slaves.'

There was a silence. Only had heard Talleyman talk in laughter, in disappointment, in the momentary fear that comes to all men at sea, in the anger of a good officer at work badly done. But this was a note that Only had not heard before, a note of anger and hate intermingled.

'I told you I had seen worse than here. I had my mid times on the Coast. It was men like Langer that made the Coast worse than here.'

'The man says,' murmured Pentstemon, from the scuttle, 'that he did it all for the sake of liberty in Ireland.'

'And no liberty in Africa?' Talleyman leaned across the table facing Only. 'I knew that smell. Of slaves. They can never clean it out. Then I knew it was wrong. No man who has been in that trade can ever do right after, for it corrupts into the soul. I can smell a slaver a mile off, and when I smelt him, I knew there was something wrong. *I knew.*'

'And if you had been wrong?'

'I am an accountable person.'

'But *I* am the responsible person,' said Pentstemon from the scuttle. He still did not turn towards them. 'I am Captain of this ship. If there is an enquiry, then I must answer for everything you do, right or wrong, with my approval or without it. But let me tell you this,' and he turned towards them now, 'if you had been wrong, Tom, even if you had been wrong, then you did the right thing. And you were not wrong.

Ah, come in, Mr Collins. Have you finished? How many muskets?'

'We counted eight hundred sacks with six stand of arms in each, so that makes four thousand eight hundred muskets and bayonets, and a hundred rounds apiece. And in some casks of butter in the captain's pantry we found a hundred pistols. The muskets are US Army pattern of 1841, Captain Lidderdale says—'

'And who are we to contradict him?'

'Anyway, they're better than ours. And the pistols are made in Hartford by a Mr Colt. Revolvers, very good-looking.'

'With all that, it's a wonder she stayed afloat. Thank you, steward, put the coffee down for us. I regret, gentlemen, that I will have to pass around the sugar in a jam jar — sometimes I have a distinct feeling that life is getting out of my control. Now, have you found anything else?'

'The sodger went up to the quarry, sir. In a shack they found about three hundredweight of powder.'

'Blasting powder, I presume?'

'Oh, no sir, fine grained stuff, suitable for muskets.'

'But at least it wasn't slow brown cocoa, so they can't accuse us of anything. We did fire off the main armament last quarter, didn't we?'

'Our log says we did, sir. By the way, the gunner says if we can get the last of our meal out of the lower deck by noon, he can have the main armament out of the hold and remounted at the end of the dog watch.'

'We are in for a complicated time.'

'Yes sir.' Collins tried to compose his face. 'And Captain Lidderdale's compliments, and the powder in the quarry was in casks with "HMS *Santorin*" branded into the lid.'

'Oh, dear. Perhaps we did not find it after all.'

'I will let Captain Lidderdale know that we did not find it, sir.'

'That would be very far-sighted of you, Mr Collins. And please, ask the sodger if it could be not-found in a series of small bangs, not in one big bang. I have a headache coming on, and I would be most grateful. Still, the powder might well have been stolen—'

'From the Yeomanry,' put in Talleyman.

'You ought to know,' said Only, tartly. 'But does this not mean that Delauny is implicated in that, too?'

'I am sure he is. But he is not here.'

'Without the powder,' and Pentstemon was looking through the scuttle again at the land 'we cannot prove it, and in fact all we can swear to is that he saved young Tal's life. And we do not know for sure what is happening ashore. I only know that we have taken enough arms for a brigade, and the ship has been here twice before. Do you think that this is the first load, or have they left two other cargoes here under our noses? Ten thousand muskets in the country and all in the hands of rebels—'

'A mob is not an army,' Only interrupted. 'You know how long it takes to make a recruit safe with weapons.'

'But have you thought of the organization to bring all those men down here on their little carts on the right day to take it all away before anyone noticed it, and then — where?' Pentstemon was still looking into the hills. 'If all this cargo had gone like the last lot of meal, we'd never trace it. Do you think that our own esteemed army could have managed anything like that?'

'I think this *is* the first load, sir.'

'Why, young Tal?'

'The muskets so packed are over five feet long. They could not be handled in small boats. The jetty, some jetty, was necessary. Certainly to get them all ashore in one day. *Cayuga*'s hatches are very small, too.'

'Very simple, and yet complicated,' Pentstemon turned his gaze back to his officers. 'Do you think the Young Irelanders, if it is them, planned all this from the beginning of the jetty?'

'They probably started from having the plan for the jetty fall into the hands of one of their leaders, as I suppose Delauny must be. Then they began to make their plans. Now once you have begun an organization, it is very difficult to bring yourself to change it, especially when you have to work by correspondence across the Atlantic. This reluctance to change is a besetting sin of first lieutenants. An obsession makes you rigid in everything. They would not change even when the navy came into the Tower. They probably thought that they had made Tom safe because of gratitude.'

'Or thought I was stupid,' said Talleyman.

'Oh, you're not stupid, young Tal,' Pentstemon tried to sound comforting. 'Stubborn, lazy, illiterate, incompetent, incoherent, but not stupid. At least, not very stupid. What does Langer say?'

'He told me it was his first offence, sir. But there, I was arresting him.'

'You believe him, Mr Only?'

'Oh, yes. He got very emotional when I spoke to him. I'm afraid I suggested that Tom should interrogate him, and he protested that this was a cruel and unusual form of punishment. He said the earlier runs were to throw us off the scent. The Relief Association, he thinks, is genuine, and paid for the food. The Young Irelanders got at the Captain and repacked the muskets. The pistols were his own idea, to make an extra profit.'

'The Relief Association paid for the food,' said Talleyman. 'They did not pay for the weapons.'

'Where did the money come from?' asked Pentstemon. 'Do we need to ask? The whole country is rich as Croesus, and the food runs out of it all the time. Rents don't get paid, but the exports are worth money to somebody. Ireland is paying for these weapons, and because of that the people starve. But however that may be, we have to tell somebody. I cannot leave the coast unguarded: be certain that the French will be out to take advantage of this. I will sail around to Baltimore, watching the coast, and put someone ashore to ride to Cork. I do not think that we will be very welcome in person to Admiral Napier. I still think it a pity that we annoyed him so by crossing his bows the first time we steamed into Cork, don't you, Only?'

'I was not responsible,' the first lieutenant defended himself icily, 'when we did it the second time in the hour.'

'How was I to know,' and Pentstemon was being very dignified, 'that he would change his tack at that very instant? But at least none of you had the honour to be told to go to the devil and the coastguard and not to come near the Experimental Squadron again. But if the Experimental Squadron is to fight the French when they come, we must keep them warned. And besides that we will have to inform the army.'

'The army, sir?' protested Collins. 'But isn't that rather … er … common?'

'Rebellion is a dirty business, and we cannot pick and choose our bedfellows. I am afraid that someone will have to go across country to General Hardinge at Kilkenny or wherever else he may have galloped to and explain the situation in simple terms.'

'Captain Lidderdale, I suppose, sir?' asked Talleyman.

'I propose to land Captain Lidderdale and his Marines to hold the Tower.'

'All of them, sir?' Only was disapproving.

'All of them, Mr Only. You don't want them cluttering up the decks if we have to fight, do you?'

'Of course not, sir.'

'Now I need you, first lieutenant, to sail the ship, and you, Mr Collins, will be needed if we do have a fight. And since I have to send an officer to talk to a general, and a mere mate will not do…'

'Mallow refuses to go into the interior again, sir. I had trouble getting him to take a landing party this morning.'

'Since they failed to drown him last time, they may well succeed in hanging him this. I see his point. Young Tal, you have been chosen after most full and careful consideration. At least you can look after yourself ashore.'

'But they nearly beat me to death,' Talleyman protested. 'I would much prefer—'

'Just think, you may catch the eye of a general, and consider what that may not do to your career — ruin it, probably, if you cannot hide it from the Admiralty. Take your chances while you can. You may travel in your frock coat, but take your full dress and your cocked hat, to wait on the General.'

'But, sir, I'll miss the battle. If the French come, I'll miss them.'

'Oh, there'll be more battles before you finish, lad.'

'Well, there hasn't been one since Navarino. That's twenty years.'

'And we're only just getting the medal for it. Have you applied for yours yet, Only? The navy is a place to learn patience in, young Tal.'

'Patience isn't all, sir. Forgiveness is just as important. If you really want me to wear full dress…'

'Well?'

'I lent my dress trousers to Mallow, when he went to that summer ball with the Fenit hunt. And they threw him into the fountain. You remember that, sir?'

'He's not stopped speaking about it since.'

'He was wearing my dress trousers. I'll have to borrow some. And only Mr Only is my size.'

There was a long silence. Then Pentstemon ruled, 'I will make it an order. The first lieutenant will learn forgiveness.'

PART IV: HARVEST

1

The urchins in the Cashel street watched Talleyman climb down from the Bianconi, stretching his legs after the long ride cramped on the side seat. They clustered round him, calling for a halfpenny, a ha'penny, only a ha'penny kind sir. The weather came in from the Atlantic, wet and chill for August, drizzling through the boat cloak as easily as through their shirts, chilling their fingers and faces, sailor and children alike.

It was the police and the Yeomanry in Kenmare, where Pentstemon had put Talleyman ashore in the dawn, who had insisted that he go on to Kilkenny by Bianconi. It goes nearly as fast as a ridden horse, they had told him, but it keeps up the speed much longer, and you gain on the time. And you find it more comfortable, and you arrive at your destination less tired. And it was plain, they did not want to have to send an escort to a sailor on horseback. The only good advice had come from Pentstemon: 'If the Moonlighters shoot at you, do not try to dodge, because then they may hit you.'

Now Talleyman was wet to the skin, from toe to knee, because the tarpaulin he had shared with a fat old lady on one side and a pedlar on the other had kept on blowing up with the speed of the journey, and it let in the rain. He clutched his valise and he sought a bed. The street was filthy, horse dung and waste rags and dead cats everywhere, beggars sheltering in every doorway, and the great church on the hill looking down at them through the dusk. The maid at the inn opposite the Palace saw him enter, and said to herself that there was no Englishman was going to have a night's rest there in no matter what unknown uniform if she could help it, to have herself and all the decent people murdered in their beds because there was going to be an army of loyal fellows pillaging the heart out of the town in the morning or perhaps the morning after. So before he could speak she flew at him shaking her duster in his face, and shouting, 'No rooms for you, no rooms, no rooms at all!'

The urchins in the street inspected Talleyman from a distance as he stood in the rain, the water running down his neck from the back of his round cap. They thought there might be a profit from anyone who would take the risk. The bravest of them approached Talleyman, murmured at him in his soft thick brogue. As last he made the lieutenant understand that he could be taken to a place to sleep — at a price. There were extra hands to carry the valise. The sailor followed them doubtfully, down a side street.

The landlord of the Huntsman's House opened the door to the knocking. 'Can you let me have a room for the night? I want to go to Kilkenny. The Bianconi driver will not go further.' The stranger's manner was half-apologetic, half-brusque, as if expecting to be turned away, yet determined not to be. The landlord laughed, a round warm laugh that concealed a despair, clouded the cold emptiness of the street.

'Indeed, and it's five rooms I can let you have.'

'Five?'

'And is it not the most improvident thing for a man to do, to open a hotel in the middle of a famine, and perhaps worse? Five rooms, and none of them ever slept in before in the way of business.'

Talleyman laughed aloud. 'Show me to just one of them. It will be enough.'

'Indeed, and I will that — here, you, go away now … oh, if your honour would give them a couple of ha'pence — no, no, not a whole threepenny, that was too much and will spoil the market for those who come after. Now, what would your honour be liking for dinner?'

'And what have you for dinner?'

'Indeed, and that was not the question at all, and what kind of answer is that either. For if there is any dish whatever in the whole gamut of the cookery of the civilized world that your honour would like, then for sure you shall have it, in as little time as it will take to cook. Irish cooking, English cooking, French cooking, Swiss cooking, Italian cooking, I am master of them all, and let you be naming the dish. Except only for anything that has potatoes in it, and that for two reasons. First that the potato is American and I did say the cooking of the civilized world, and second that there is not a potato to be had in the whole country, as perhaps your honour may have noticed.'

Talleyman sighed.

'I am very tired. I am wet. Because of that I am as cold as one may be in August. I cannot make decisions. What do you like cooking? Have you a chicken?'

'A chicken? A chicken, then, your honour shall have. Indeed, I can make a coq-au-vin. Or better still how would you like a chicken steamed in white wine, on a bed of rice? It will be all ready within the hour. Would your honour be wanting it down here, in the dining room, or in your honour's own room?'

'Oh, down here, down here. I am tired of eating where I sleep.'

'Then if your honour would be wanting a hot bath while you are waiting, then I can have the maid carry one up. Would you be wanting a bottle of wine with your chicken?'

'Wine? You mean real wine? Not whisky-and-water or porter?'

'Indeed, and wine I mean, whatever you may require, red wine, white wine, champagne, sherry, whatever your honour requires.'

'Well … have you a Sauterne?'

'Indeed, and a sweeter smoother Sauterne you never saw than the one I have here in my cellar, and the better it will be for drinking now than after it is broken in the rebellion.'

'You think there will be a rebellion?'

'And sure isn't there a rebellion already, all across the country from the one coast to the other and the whole county in flames and on the move together?'

'I came through Macroom and Mitchelstown, and I saw nothing untoward.'

'Then 'tis between here and Dublin that the people is all out in a terrible mood and burning all the fine houses and killing the police and there's no knowing what's the end of it to be but it's waiting they are for a hundred thousand muskets to come from America before they sweep the whole army and all the gentry and the English out of the country. You'll have heard of Mr William Smith Bronterre O'Brien, and isn't that a name to frighten armies with the very sound of?'

'I have heard of the gentleman.'

'Now, 'tis he has called out all the Young Irelanders, and their Committee has met in Carrick-on-Suir, and all the secret council that is too important to have their names said in the Committee are there, and the engineer has arrived that will build us a railway direct from Dublin to Paris, and sure was it not in this very town they were a night or two ago and not a man with the courage to arrest them? And soon it is that council will be ruling the country and an end then to honest men.'

'And to their hotels?'

'Indeed, yes, sir, and to their hotels. Now, the maid will show you to your room. And your honour…'

'Yes?' Talleyman paused on the stair.

'I have a friend who has an understanding with a water bailiff, and if your honour would be liking a nice trout…?'

The trout, sweet as the nuts that were not yet come, were the size of elderly herrings. The chicken, the landlord boasted with pride and truth, was the most splendid dish that any wandering Englishman had tasted in the island.

Talleyman asked, 'How do I compound for this sin? I have eaten a young angel.'

'Why, now, your honour, if you would—'

But another voice broke in.

'Talleyman, my boy, have you come to burn down another mansion?'

Captain Foster had not at first, from his deep corner of the dining room, believed that it could be Talleyman. But the voice reassured him.

'I'm trying to get to Kilkenny. The Bianconis won't go further. I'll try to hire a horse in the morning.'

'Then what are you going to be doing all the evening? This is not the liveliest of towns, not in normal times.'

'I don't know.'

'Then I'll tell you what you're doing. We've got all the Yeomanry from the county withdrawn from their outposts into the towns, like we are here, and the regular army is all together now, and it was at Kilkenny, but where now there's no knowing. The mess in the barracks is full, and there's some of us wherever we can find roofs for our heads.'

'What's all this about a rebellion?'

'Well, you know how it is, and when you English have any trouble with the workers you say "There's trouble at t'mill"?

Well, here in Ireland, we say "The peasants are gathering on Slievenamon," which is a mountain between here and Kilkenny, and that's just what's happening now and has been happening for the last week. But we're not to interfere, because if the French come, as well they may, and the regular army has to go back for a rebellion in England as your Chartists have been threatening, then we don't want to be all tangled up with hunting peasants that shoot from behind hedges. So, is it coming to the Ball you are?'

'Ball?'

'Oh, look now, 'tis not often we have a whole regiment of Yeomanry embodied, let alone three regiments all together in one place as we have here. So 'tis a grand ball we're giving in the assembly rooms, and all the beauty of the town will be there.'

'I have no invitation.'

'Look, lad, 'tis our ball, and isn't it the Queen's uniform you're wearing, and that's invitation enough.'

'And no partner.'

'Well, and there's all the girls for miles around come in to the music, as if half our officers weren't married already back in County Armagh and Downshire. But you have a partner, Tom Talleyman, you have the choice of two, if you'll only be coming with me in half an hour. Only one thing, have you ball dress or something like it, because it's very particular our Colonel is about proper dress for occasions?'

'I have my full dress. Will that do?'

'And isn't that an eye-catcher? I've ordered a brougham, and by the time you've changed, it ought to be here, for it's near five minutes past the time I told it I wouldn't be wanting it after.'

2

Jane Roding and Harriet Delauny were waiting for the brougham in the parlour of the Canonry. Jane was half sorry that she had let herself be persuaded into staying at the Canonry all the time that the vicar was in residence, through the best of the summer. It made things more complicated, for Mary Flannery was still at the vicarage, and there were no letters, only guesses. But her father had argued that if Jane would agree to go into the town, where it was safer, then her mother would also come with her; otherwise she would insist on staying with him. And on this evening, Mrs Roding would chaperone them, if any other chaperone was needed than that old woman Foster.

It's going to be a wonderful evening, thought Harriet, *with all these soldiers, well of course they're only Yeomanry, but they look just as good in ball dress. And with the rebels out already, wasn't it just like the ball before Waterloo?* There would be all these handsome young men and sure there must be some good-lookers among them although she hadn't seen any yet at church parades in their scarlet and gold and blue and white gloves and feathers, and tomorrow perhaps they'd all be lying dead on Slievenamon, after scattering the rebels, and all with the bullet holes through the middle of their foreheads where it wouldn't spoil their beauty. The brougham was coming, she could hear the wheels. She tried to compose herself for this tragic evening of comforting the brave warriors going out to die for her, she must be unselfish and make an attempt to enjoy the buffet and be bravely gay. Now there was Foster's voice in the hall talking with the canon. And what was that he was saying about bringing a sailor with him? And Jane had heard it too, and was pushing in front of her to the stairs.

It's Philip, it's Philip, Harriet thought, as she rustled into the hall in, thank God, the new flowered organdie she had at last persuaded her father to buy her. Let Jane push in front, she will never be able to keep up in the Ball, she'll — and then both girls saw it was only Talleyman.

Only Talleyman, thought Harriet, *only Talleyman. Well, if there's no one else there I'll keep him, but otherwise I'll let Jane have him. Or should I be generous and make sure that he spends the whole evening with her? It might be more tactful.*

But Jane, seeing him, almost stopped in her tracks, came down the stairs slowly, almost mechanically. *Oh, not now*, she thought, *not now. Why must he come now? If he speaks, if he touches my arm, it will be over, it will be at an end, all my promises will go.* She came slowly down the stairs, curtsied, and took Roding's right arm as he was putting her mother on his left. Harriet had little option but to accept Talleyman's arm, and go with him into the carriage.

3

It puzzled Harriet in the ballroom how Jane was so eager to fill her programme, put down so many dances to Foster, to take so much notice of these other northern Yeomanry officers, when one would swear that half of them were married too. It must be her last chance this season. How could she be so stupid? She herself had Talleyman down for the supper dance, but sure she wouldn't dance with any of these upstarts if they asked her too, even. Talleyman turned to Jane, at last was able to ask her, and she able to answer, 'I have no dances left, Mr Talleyman.'

'But your card surely cannot be—'

'I have no dances for you, Mr Talleyman. Please accept an answer. Look after Miss Delauny.'

Harriet had already decided that there was nothing better to offer. At least, alone of all the young ladies of the county, she had been brought by an eligible gentleman of her own. There were three Yeomanry regiments here, two of red Dragoons and one of blue Hussars. The colours of some tunics were faded, and others were no more than the best matches that local tailors could manage, so the whole room shimmered with the changing shades. Jane's vermilion and orange shot silk vanished into them. In all this colour, Talleyman stood out not only in height but in the stark simplicity of his blue and gold. Yes, Harriet thought, Talleyman was at least a respectable partner, and in the end she would see that Philip did something for him.

For she understood now, the rest of them were only make-believe soldiers in their shabby suits. But Talleyman, like Philip, was a real character, who had faced danger that was no sham. That broken nose, he must have done it in some desperate fight, loyally supporting her Philip. She must behave as if she were used to someone of breeding, like Philip, with such splendid manners, who had learnt to look after a lady at a ball. He was gentleman enough to steer her out of the press of the supper waltz after the first few bars and move her into the supper room before the crowd. He plied her with ham and cold beef, coaxed her to chicken and a pork pie. And when she was working her way into the second helping, which he had insisted so on getting for her, she realized that he was asking her, 'Where is your brother?'

'And is he not at Eyories?' She had not really been aware that Talleyman knew anything of her brother, other than that he was at Eyories.

'He is not. He has been keeping bad company. You know that?'

'Yes. That is why my father sent him away. Can you persuade him, Mr Talleyman, to give up this politics and come back to us?'

'I have tried. He will not be persuaded. Has he come to Cashel?'

'I have not seen him. Why? Has he left Eyories?'

'The country is out. He may be anywhere. If you know where he is, we may be able to persuade him to return to … not Eyories. Somewhere safe. He saved my life.'

'Do you think he is really in danger?'

'I will be frank. If he returns now, we may be able to help him, but if he goes further on his present course, he may be arrested for treason. He is wading in deep waters. How can you find him?'

'Oh, Mr Talleyman, I do not know. But *you* must find him. You must save him for me ... for us. My father is heartbroken over him, and weeps sometimes for him. He has ... he has even *prayed* for Lawrence.' Harriet tried to keep her composure. This was only a lieutenant, and when she was Lady Denain and an Admiral's wife this was the kind of errand she would give these deserving young officers, however low their social standing. 'You must find him. Tomorrow.'

'I am on duty, Miss Delauny. Tomorrow, somehow, I must find my way to General Hardinge. I thought that tonight, here, among these officers, I might hear something of him. Now, let me get you some salmon.'

And after the salmon, when Talleyman had done talking about a garden party his father had given at Fen Dilney Hall, and she enjoyed hearing of the dignitaries who had come and had not the experience to note who had not been mentioned, he went and got her the most heavenly raspberries and cream. When she looked up from the fruit, or rather from her empty plate, she found Talleyman facing away from her and talking to someone in a strange uniform, a dragoon tunic but with a great deal of yellow and blue shot-silk facings on the red, and a wide yellow sash about his waist. She supposed this must be the uniform of some regular regiment. And he was saying, in another strange English accent as unfamiliar as Talleyman's, '...so they detached a squadron to come down and let the Judge have trumpeters at next week's assizes. About halfway from here to Kilkenny, there's a village called Killenaule with a coal mine. You'd better miss that. The rebels have barricaded the street.'

'So the regulars cast round it?'

'Well, you'd better, old boy, but they didn't. Their captain, name of Longmore, did the coolest thing you ever heard of.

He just rode up to the barrier and sat his horse and explained that the army didn't deal with rebellions and they'd have to wait for the Constabulary. And d'ye know, they just pulled down their barricades and let the cavalry past, and then put them up again. Longmore had a good look.'

'How do you know about this?'

'Oh, saw it, old boy, saw it meself.'

'You were with the squadron?'

'Well, no … not really.'

'Sounds like old men talking about Navarino. How were you there?'

This one's a sight too keen, thought the regular officer. 'Oh, I just pop up and down, you know, up and down.'

'Like Mr Punch?'

The regular officer gave Talleyman a keen look, that even Harriet tried to fathom. He said, offhandedly, 'Yes, like Mr Punch. They're round to the south, mostly, old boy. You'd better cast north.' He drifted off into the ravening crowd fighting around the buffet. Talleyman returned his glance to Harriet.

'I'm sorry, I had to know. I must ride to Kilkenny tomorrow.'

'Oh, are you? Are you going with the army? Is that why they're having a ball?' She amended her vision of Slievenamon to include Talleyman, in full dress uniform, lying among the dead and herself telling Philip how brave he had been. But Talleyman laughed.

'I'm not going with this lot. I'm going *to* the army. The *army's* in Kilkenny. I will go round to the south.'

'But this man said to go to the north, because the rebels are in the south.'

'I want to find your brother. If he is anywhere here, he will be south of Killenaule.'

'How will you go?'

'I will ride. I have to find a horse.'

Harriet looked at him aghast. Surely with the peasants out in the way they were, like 'Ninety-eight, nobody could be so mad as to ride across country that way alone. Or, suddenly it came to her, so brave. This was as brave, almost, as anything Philip would have done. Sure, Philip would do that, ride across country infested with the enemy with … what was the word…? with despatches. She asked loudly, brightly, 'With despatches? Are you carrying despatches?'

Talleyman stood up, abruptly. 'Is it not time to return to the ballroom?'

He offered her his arm. Harriet regretted losing the chance of a second dish of raspberries, but there was a dense mob now at the buffet, and perhaps if this gown were not to go the way of the last long before it wore out she had better leave off such fattening things as fruit. She clung to Talleyman's arm as they pushed through the crowd of scarlet and blue, all due in her vision to be buried tomorrow in their spotless bright uniforms, the same they were dancing in, and she would be weeping for them.

But there, close to Foster and a major from his regiment, named she thought Cashman, and Jane and Mrs Roding in her green flowered silk, was actually a civilian, in an evening coat of the new fashioned brown, with his trousers a shade lighter. It was a fat back she was looking at, and the sandy hair, thinning a little, was sleeked back over the round head. His hands were clasped behind his back, and the rings on every finger caught her eye. He was a short man, head and shoulders below Talleyman. He turned to see them coming, showing a watch chain hung with seals, a cream waistcoat of a flowered texture, with six gleaming amethyst buttons. He had a round smooth moon face, light eyes, an automatic smile that remained there fixed and found nothing in the rest of the expression to match it. And it was Jane who was greeting them excitedly, almost shouting, 'Look Harriet, look who's here! How wonderful, see who it is!'

Harriet looked hard. There was something familiar here, indeed, something that reminded her of the past, touched off images half-seen that struggled to become explicit, and then the short fat smooth-faced dandy spoke, 'Why, it's little Harriet. Oh, how you've grown.'

And then she knew, it was Philip, her Philip, come for her, and she hadn't known him, nearly didn't recognize him, this fine sturdy man he had grown into, not a great tall beanpole like some. *Oh, how nearly unfaithful I've been to you my darling, and nearly didn't know you.* She stretched out both hands to him, and he took one and bowed to kiss it, very formally. And she realized, of course he couldn't show what he really thought here in this public place. Talleyman, behind her, asked over her head, 'Taking a holiday, Philip?'

'Oh, I came over to see what was going on, you know, and if all the tales were true. Some are pretty tall, I tell you.'

'Are you going down to Ballyfine?'

'And be shot at? Oh, no, this is near enough for me. I don't fancy affairs like that any more, and I like this kind of thing much better. I say, old Tal, those trousers don't fit very well, do they?'

'They're the first lieutenant's. My own were a casualty of Irish hospitality.'

Philip laughed. Harriet was blushing with fury that anyone should mention such things before ladies. She blushed as hard as she had the energy. She hoped that she were red enough to show, it must be possible to blush by willpower, she had practised it enough in front of the mirror and she was sure she could do it. But Jane did not seem at all put out, just laughed with the men, and sure but Philip would notice that and turn her off as only fit for talking with coarse sailors like Talleyman. And then, Harriet never understood how it happened, she was dancing with Foster, and Jane was with Philip somewhere off in the crowd.

'He's a bit of a show-off, our Hhhon Phil, isn't he,' Foster remarked cruelly.

'Indeed, and he is not. I have known him all my life—'

'And not seen him for the last five years, eh? You were a child then. Take some advice, Miss Harriet, and it's to forget what you were like as a child and don't put such store on him because it's a grown woman you are now, and not a child, and a handsome one at that, a fine handful and not a skinny whisp like Miss Roding there. It's a bit older than you I am, and a respectable married man when I'm not embodied, and I know it's a good-hearted girl you are and not one to make a fuss over a kiss more or less in good part. He's not worth it, and there's plenty in this room that are, and I'll show you that directly.'

But Harriet stopped her ears with her mind, and thought of the fine new life in England that would follow when Philip had swept her off there, as he had obviously come to do. But suddenly the dance was over and she and Foster were back to where Talleyman, Mrs Roding uncomprehending on his arm, was talking excitedly with a group of Yeomanry officers.

'All right, I agree with you,' he was saying to Cashman. 'A navy's for killing people with. If we have to. If there's no war, we're ready to fetch and carry what the Government tells us to. Like soldiers. And cornmeal. We're ready to fight the French.

But we aren't ready to be police. Half of you Irish want to fight the other half: half of you want to lord it over the others. If you want to fight among yourselves, do it. Don't ask the English to hold the ring. A plague on both your houses. Where's that wine?'

'Don't look at me, old boy,' said the regular officer. 'My name's Smith, from Brighton.'

'A likely story,' said Foster, loud, bellicose, filling Talleyman's glass and then every other in sight. 'And you'd rather be back there, I'll be bound.'

'I'd rather be in the Punjaub. The Sikhs are gentlemen.'

There was an uproar. Foster and Cashman took some time to pacify the group of Yeomanry cornets who wished to make it a gentlemanly question of fists. Then Foster waved his hand at Smith, as if to dismiss him.

'It's all the same to you and the sailor. You're just hired to fight, and it doesn't matter to you who or where. And us, we're fighting for our lives and our property in this island. But the ones we can't abide are those that are absentees, taking their rents and can't be bothered to stay and fight for them.'

There was a break in the flow as Foster drained his glass. Philip Suttle was standing alone at the back of the group, Jane on his arm. He observed, inconsequentially, 'Cool for the time of year, ain't it?'

Foster turned on him.

'There's some that come because they're told to and go home when they're told to, and those of us that stay here because this is our home and this we will maintain. Anyone who will not stay and help us is a coward.' He paused and looked around. 'Well, Hhhon Suttle, it's a coward I'm calling you, isn't it? And is there nothing you're going to do about it?'

'Hold hard, old fellow,' put in Smith. 'There's not much choice you're leaving him, you know.'

'And there's no choice I'm wanting to leave him, me that's been near enough blown up defending his father's property for him, and Lieutenant Talleyman the same and him suffer for us elsewhere as well, and me leaving my own house in a better county than this to be burnt over my head as soon as I'm out of it.'

'If you'd ever been after tiger,' Smith went on in the same soft slow voice, 'you'd know better than to press a dangerous beast too hard... Don't press this one.'

'I'll press him as I like. We'll see how a navy officer—'

'A *naval* officer,' Talleyman corrected him, in a mock pedantic tone. 'A *Royal* Naval Officer.' No one took any notice. Foster went on as if he had not spoken,

'We'll see how a navy officer takes to being called a coward, and being pressed on it. If you're not a coward, Hhhon Suttle, then you can come and show me, and whether you do it with your fists or with pistols or swords is all one to me. I'll match you now or when you like, and there's no time like the present, or as likeable as now.'

Harriet watched, entranced. Her Philip challenged to a duel? Surely, would he not now draw a sword and take on Foster and the major and anyone who spoke ill of him, or of the navy, all of them at once, anyone who wanted to join in, and make them all submit and own him the better man, the best man of them all? What if he were not as tall and slim as she ... well, as Talleyman, yet he was as brave, surely and as skilful, as any man. And clever.

Mrs Roding, abandoned on a settee, watched the silent show. There was a dispute, it seemed, but sure, when the gentlemen had the drink taken, wasn't there always a dispute. But she could see the strange officer, Smith, speaking: Harriet heard his interested tone.

'Oh, so you're a naval officer, are you. Half-pay? A commander, are you then, Mr Suttle? Or a lieutenant?'

'I left the service as a mate,' Suttle told him blandly. 'I had passed for lieutenant, but it's hardly worth the effort, and the discomfort, is it?'

'Oh, that's that, then,' Smith told Foster, ignoring Philip. Harriet could hardly believe what she was hearing. 'A mate's not an officer, you know, he doesn't hold a commission, not even from their Lordships of Admiralty, like a lieutenant. Doesn't mess in the wardroom. We couldn't have him in an officers' mess — can't think what he's doing here, in that case, but in Ireland…' He shrugged.

'He's Lord Denain's son—' Foster began to explain, almost apologizing for this breach of etiquette.

But Smith talked him down, dismissive. 'Doesn't matter a bit. If he's in the service and below commissioned rank, then he can't come in your mess, no matter what his station outside. So you can't fight him. Not your equal, my old friend. If you value your uniform, you won't want to demean it fightin' a warrant officer.'

'Well, no, if he's not an officer,' Foster agreed grudgingly. Suttle smiled all across his bland moon face.

'I didn't really think you'd want to fight me,' he told Foster, ignoring Smith. 'That's all settled, now.'

Harriet stared, incredulous. Was her Philip not insisting on fighting? Was he just standing there, with Jane, that brazen trollop, holding his arm, and not demanding satisfaction?

Thank God for that, thought Jane, *it would have been disaster*. She tugged at Philip's sleeve, whispered very soft in his ear 'Take me, take me, let us go at once, do not leave me here any longer.' What she could not say aloud was, *do not leave me here any more to speak to him, to see him around. I am afraid for myself, for us, that if he stays with me longer, if I must see him more, be thrown against him, I will be swept away myself, you will lose me, lose all the built-up longing of these years, the closeness of those letters, the plans. Take me from Talleyman, before he takes me from you.*

It isn't possible, thought Harriet, *that Philip should stand there still, and do nothing*. Then, from behind her shoulder, Talleyman spoke, and she had never before heard his voice so gay and light.

'I'll fight you, Captain Foster. You have insulted the *Royal* Navy.'

'Oh, play it down, old boy,' said Smith. 'Won't do you any good, you know. And you're drunk.'

'Probably. I'm a bottle of Sauterne ahead of the game before I started drinking with our warlike friend. I'll be court-martialled. My Captain's been court-martialled three times. Once for duelling. Once for pouring champagne over an ambassador. Once for losing his ship while he was dead drunk asleep. Guilty three times. All for the honour of the navy. And he's a captain now.'

Foster was aghast. This was not what he had bargained for. To show poor Harriet, that stupid mooning child, what a poltroon and a wet rag her Suttle was — well, he'd done that. But he had no intention at all of fighting a real duel, and certainly not with Talleyman. *Why*, he thought, *the man's a terror, he hasn't a ruth left, and if there's any way — but God help us, why is my own colonel taking against me like this?*

'A duel? Splendid! We haven't had a duel in this regiment since 'Forty-two, and then 'twas after a ball and not during one. Now Foster, my boy, who's going to act for your opponent, for it's myself will be your second, and Cashman will have to be master of ceremonies because was it not he who fought the last time, and soberer he is now than then, and he can't have Suttle because if it's not fit to fight he is then he's not fit to act—'

Foster was gazing at one last ray of hope, for if Talleyman could not get a second would he not have to call the fight off? But Smith was drawling, 'Well, as one professional gent to another, old lad, I'll see you through.'

Harriet stayed with the two regular officers as they moved back a little way to a table against the wall. Talleyman stripped off his coat, and hung it carefully over a chair.

'My best, can't afford to get it spoilt. Now, Harriet,' and this was, she realized, the first time he had addressed her directly by name, 'keep an eye on it. Feel this packet of papers in the pocket. If I am hurt, Captain Smith will take it to General Hardinge in the morning.'

'Oh, now, don't get hurt on purpose to miss the Big Boy,' Smith objected. 'But if you get killed, old campaigner, what d'you want me to do about him?' He nodded at Foster, on the other side of the ballroom.

'What d'ye do with tiger?'

'Tiger? Oh, follow up, of course, follow up. Can't let a man-eater loose.'

'In that case, you'd better follow up.'

The cluster of Yeomanry cornets standing nearby were much impressed and carried news of this exchange back to Foster. He was not encouraged. Smith added irrelevantly, 'I was at Ferrampore, you know, where the Sepoys ran away. So we ran, too. Bit messy, if you like that sort of thing. I suppose we're the injured party. Any choice of weapons? I'd take swords myself, you lookin' thicker in the arm than he does.'

'Oh, no, not swords. Take too long.'

'Pity. Well, you know your own lack of strength.'

Smith went off to confer with the Yeomanry colonel, pushing his way through the dancers. The band played louder than ever. Harriet found her teeth chattering. She looked round for Jane, for anyone to cling to, to assure her that nothing was really happening. The vermilion gown was nowhere to be seen, or the brown evening coat. But Talleyman was laughing down at her concerned look.

'Here, don't be nervous. Here, waiter, a glass of that brandy for the lady! Don't sip it. Drink it straight down. That's right. No, none for me. Makes my hand too steady for these games.'

Harriet could not understand it, but were his eyes not brighter, his voice shriller, his speech more disorganized than they had been? Talleyman took his watch from his waistcoat pocket and gave it to her. The music stopped between dances, and in the moment of silence, she could hear the rattle of wheels and hooves in the street outside. Talleyman told her, 'Midnight. Make sure I have a bottle of champagne at this table for a quarter past. You do that, now. It's time for you to be a lady and give orders. Right, Smithy, are we ready to go into the yard?'

'They're goin' to do it in here. Light's better.'

'Good God, they can't!'

'In Ireland, there's no can't. They'll stop the dancin' for us. I've tossed for ends. You're over there, and their man's under the chandelier, against that white curtain.'

'Do I need to ask who won? Are we ready?'

'Well, *we* are. They're still worryin'. I suggested loading with grape, but they didn't think it very funny. Foster is lookin' for a silver bullet. Ah, now someone's tryin' to clear the floor.'

Talleyman began to follow Smith away, then turned back and pressed Harriet's hand. Surprised, she watched him walk to his place. The band had not stopped, but everyone present was looking at the proceedings on the floor. Even the buffet was empty. She forced herself to catch at a waiter's arm, and demanded the bottle of champagne. The man hurried off, grumbling at having to miss the show.

Cashman came to Smith.

'Can we have your man move over a bit, because it's back to the band he is, and it's disturbing their man's aim.'

'My man,' replied Smith cheerfully, 'is perfectly comfortable where he is. Can we offer yours a pair of spectacles?'

'Then it's clearing the band we'll have to, because it's not more than one manslaughter we want to be charged with.'

'Oh, but that's no matter,' said Foster's colonel. 'It's not our band here at all; the other two regiments are supplying all the music.'

The other two Yeomanry colonels overheard and grasped the realities of the situation. The Hussar colonel ran to the band platform, shouting, 'Fall out the band! Fall out the band!'

'Cowardice in the face of fire?' snarled the Dragoon.

'Stand fast, you dogs and cowards, or it's shot you'll be under martial law.'

'You'll be shot if you stay!' yelled the Hussar. He was trying to pull the men, red or blue, from their seats by main force, while the Dragoon was pushing them back. The two colonels came to blows.

Cashman said, with an air of frustration, 'We'll be here half the night. Let's get on with it.'

He dropped his handkerchief, being tired of holding it at shoulder height. Harriet was biting her lip not to scream. She expected a double flash, a deafening bang, blood and bodies scattered everywhere on the floor. But both duellists were taken by surprise. Talleyman brought his arm up in a slow, smooth arc, fired — and the chandelier above Foster's head shattered into fragments, scattering candle snuff and grease and broken glass everywhere. Foster spluttered, brushed the burning snuff from his coat, and then remembered what he was doing. Harriet watched him taking careful aim, his arm stretched out rock steady. *Oh, no*, she thought, *he's going to kill him, why doesn't Tom run, why doesn't he* — she could not look, she closed her eyes, she couldn't even stand, she sat down plump and was glad that there was a chair behind her. The band had dissolved into an uproar of discord, as some men played and others fought without the benefit of a conductor to hold them together.

Then, above the music, came a shot, and a wave of shouts and bangs. She opened her eyes. There was no blood. Foster had held his aim, and fired, not into Talleyman but over his shoulder. The ball had ricocheted off the cymbals, which provided a convenient point of aim, and through the window into the street. The Hussar colonel, startled, fell against the Dragoon colonel, and both together into the kettle drums. Cashman was shouting out, 'Both parties, I understand, from their seconds, both parties I say, have expressed themselves satisfied in their honour.'

There was a burst of clapping and cheering. The band was persuaded to strike up again. Talleyman was in front of Harriet, demanding, 'You have not lost my watch? And my dress-coat. And my champagne. A glass for Smith. And for this fine fellow.'

'O, 'tis a fine fellow you are yourself,' Foster was enthusiastic, his ball-coat was hardly singed at all. 'You that stood up to fire as if you'd been used to it all your life.'

'Oh, it's the sea air, you know. More champagne? More champagne!'

'How long,' Foster asked, 'have you and your second known each other?'

'Oh, never met before this evening.' Talleyman peered closer at Smith's ornate uniform. 'Now, what regiment? I don't quite recognize it…'

'Oh, simple. Seventh Carnatic Irregular Light Horse.'

'A Company's regiment?'

'And a Company's commission.'

'Not the Queen's commission? So, strictly speaking, by your standards, you're not an officer either.'

'No, old boy. And these Yeomanry officers hold the Lord Lieutenant's commission, too.'

'Then why,' demanded Foster, 'did you tell me that I couldn't fight Suttle because he wasn't an officer?'

'Oh, got to save face, old boy. I could see that he wouldn't fight anybody, while Talleyman here would fight anybody — yes, anybody at all.'

'Thank you for your encouragement,' said Talleyman dryly.

4

The champagne went round. Then Talleyman asked, 'Where is Suttle, after all that?'

'He's over there … no he isn't.' Smith peered into the dancing crowd. 'Funny that, couldn't miss a shape like his in this hungry land. Odd, he doesn't seem to be here.'

'No more he is,' Talleyman agreed. 'Here, Mrs Roding, have a glass of champagne. And we should have one for Jane.'

'They've gone,' Mrs Roding enunciated. 'They've gone out of the door.' She gestured vaguely in the direction of the street.

'A happy couple strolling in the moonlight, after a reunion?' Smith laughed. Harriet felt a fury sweep over her, she almost flung her fan at him.

Foster corrected, 'Ashamed to show his face in here after all this to-do.'

'All the same,' Smith insisted, 'I think you ought to be magnanimous and bring him back in.'

'What, me?' asked Foster. 'He'll think I'm coming to kill him.'

'Here,' Talleyman solved the problem, 'we'll all go and take them some champagne.'

The street was empty in the moon. The rain had stopped, the sky was almost clear. There was no one to be seen but a groom in front of the livery stables up the street. Harriet supposed he was getting out the first of the horses for the end of the ball.

Talleyman asked him, 'Have you seen a lady and a gentleman? A gentleman in brown, and a lady in a reddish gown?'

'Oh, the ones that did order a brougham for twelve o'clock you mean, and were so intent it ought to be on time, and so it was. Oh, they've been gone this long long time.'

'What d'you mean, gone?'

'Why, 'tis down to Cork they've gone, and they were making a great joke about it and having slipped out of the ball with nobody seeing them go till someone did shoot a gun off at them through the window, and then they were shouting at the Jarvie to lash up and go so 'twas like the wind they went on the Cork road, for there is a packet they are to catch for France.'

'For France?' Harriet felt as faint as when she had watched the duel. 'And the lady too? For France?'

'That's right, Lady, they've gone off together to France, and it's a fine couple they make together, for all that he was an Englishman and she a Protestant.'

'For France?' Harriet asked again. 'They've gone to France?' She heard her own voice as if it were someone else's, she was able to marvel at the rising tone, the pitch that verged on a shriek. 'They've gone to France? Why? But why?'

'Oh, that's easy,' Smith had understood at once. 'They've eloped, that's all.'

'How old was Jane?' Talleyman asked, practical.

'She was … yes, she was twenty-one last Thursday,' and it was all clear to Harriet. 'And she wouldn't have a party or any fuss made of it.'

'Then 'twas *her* father they were afraid of as well as his,' Smith explained, 'to wait so long. They must have planned this over years. They have been meeting?'

'Oh, no…' and then Harriet remembered. 'Oh, Jane has been to Belfast three or four times in the last year. They have been meeting, she never told me, she was seeing Philip and never said a thing.'

'Well, she never told me either,' said Talleyman. 'So we've both been deceived. A pair of schemers, and may they do well with each other. But she was too good for him.'

'Oh, how can you say that?' Harriet leapt to defend her Philip.

'And too good for us all,' said Smith. 'Because little Miss Roding will be a Baroness in time, and not long either, because it'll kill the old man as soon as he hears about it.'

But it did not. It was another father who died. And not for a year or so.

5

'I don't know what my father will say,' Talleyman told Harriet. They were walking back through the dawn streets of Cashel. There was no rhyme or reason to this night any more, no thought of chaperone, no respectability at all. A bunch of Yeomanry cornets had ridden off down the Cork Road, hooting and screaming like a demented hunt, after the brougham, and come back an hour later, not having caught them but full of appetite for breakfast and sober enough to start the drinking again. Captain Foster had taken Mrs Roding home in the brougham, not at all certain if she had understood what had happened.

'My father,' Talleyman explained, 'and old Lord Denain were hoping to match up Philip with my sister Arabella.'

Oh, Harriet thought, *more deceit, all this was going on and never a word to her. And Jane must have known all about this, heard somehow, was ready this very night. And that agent Roding, must have known about it.*

'So,' Talleyman continued, 'that's why they had to keep this a secret. And wait till she was twenty-one. If they once blabbed to her father — he couldn't keep anything to himself, even sober.'

And she was, in spite of herself, a little horrified that someone of her own generation should be so scathing, in public, about a grown-up. She asked, 'But Arabella — what will she say?'

'What she was going to say all along. She wants to marry a *man*.'

And then it came to Harriet that her own plight was near to desperate, something she had never imagined in her golden dreams, all around Philip. If he would not rescue her from this dead dull boring island, if he were not to give her the brilliant glittering life that she had already built for herself, then who … who … one of those Yeomanry cornets? Some Ulster squireling, some half-baked curate… And she realized whose arm she was on. There was a way to start, she must ask, loud, with a hint of tears in her voice, and what matter if the tears were real, would spill over any moment, 'Oh, Mr Talleyman, Tom … please help me. I have no one else.'

'No one? Your father…'

'You know him. No one can talk to him, he lives in a different world from real people. If Lawrence is in trouble, he will be of no use. I have only you to depend on. Please help me. Promise not to leave me.'

6

At six o'clock, Talleyman was in the Yeomanry stables, haggling with Smith over a horse. They watched a groom trot it up and down. *A chestnut, nothing special, to make all this fuss about,* thought the groom, *and any rate if that's a sailor, then he won't know much about it. So why get me up at this hour? Wouldn't it have waited?* He yawned.

'I feel the same way,' said Talleyman. 'Long night, that.'

'Oh, yes, of course, in the navy you never work more than four hours at a time, do you? Full day must be dreadfully debilitatin'.'

'But you've got an easy day, waiting for trouble. Don't go out and look for it, do you?'

'Oh, but I've got to keep Punch and Judy goin',' and Smith laughed. 'Forty pound, and worth every penny of it. Four years old, and a goer.'

'Seven,' Talleyman contradicted him, looking into the teeth, 'and not fond of exercise. I'll offer you twenty.'

'Twenty for a fine piece of horseflesh like that, and to me who stood by you at the gate of death?'

'Who tried to push me through? If I buy a horse I'll still never be able to claim more than my fare on the Bianconi. Their Lordships are very close on money.'

'Sell her again.'

'I couldn't ask that much. Not with a straight face. I've not had much practice in lying.'

'Make it thirty-five, then?'

'Listen to this. You can have twenty pounds in sovereigns. Or thirty in a note of hand.'

'Cash and done,' said Smith with surprising promptness.

The groom approved. Who could hope to get a cheque cashed if they were signed by anyone fool enough to ride east alone. There was no certainty that General Hardinge was at Kilkenny any more. According to some of the bystanders at the barrack gates, men who had been moving about for their own reasons all the night, Kilkenny was already the capital of a new State, with Mr O'Brien President, or King, or Emperor of a free Ireland, answerable to itself alone, with a Parliament House already built under pretext of a parish hall, and ambassadors presenting their credentials from America and France and the Mandarin of Chinee himself.

Smith had heard all this. Nevertheless, there was nowhere else as yet that Talleyman could be advised to make for. So he and the groom watched the lieutenant ride out of the barrack gate. And then Smith went about his own business.

7

The children watched Talleyman ride up on his old mare. He dismounted at the farm gate, and called to them, 'Come and hold my horse. Here is a penny for you.'

They hesitated a moment. He was to them a terrifying figure in his blue coat with all its buttons like a constable. Besides, he did not speak like they did, and they could hardly understand him. They had a consultation among themselves as to what they should do, and agreed at last on appropriate action. One of them came forward and took the bridle, while the others went away to find a thorn, although they did not say so. Talleyman went into the house. They heard him asking the road, while they carried out their own business.

'I have been round and round again,' he told the old woman by the fireside. 'There is still a barricade at Killenaule. I have come across the fields. It is all these steep hills which are confusing. I cannot see what is ahead, or hear anything.'

'Straight on,' the old woman told him. She could only see the shape that blocked the doorway, shutting out what little light there was left for her dim eyes. But it was an official shape, there was no doubting that, and in the state things were with everybody who could walk gone to Killenaule to see the fun there was no point in annoying anything that had to do with Government. 'Straight on, and that's the road to Dublin. Straight to the Castle, where you belong, it leads, and never a turn off it.'

She waved a vague arm. She did not in the least care whether this stranger found his road or not, so long as he left her in peace and did not come back to worry her about it. He went away at last, and let the sun come back to her, so that she could return to her dreaming of the good days that had been, which was to her a more important thing and the main business of her life these days. Now her daughter was indeed gone to Killenaule and her man with her, and perhaps it was to find work they were bound, because things were tight here even in this fine corn land and around the coal mines. Oh, 'twas terrible bad they said it was in the west, where they had thousands dying in the streets every day, or so she heard, but if you believed everything you heard where would you be in the end — and there was not a bite of food in this house the now, and when was someone going to come to give her her dinner.

Talleyman came out into the light. The children, seeing him coming, scattered, giggling. He took the reins from the only boy brave enough to stay, and swung his leg over the saddle. He felt in his pocket, seemed unable to find a whole penny, and scattered three ha'pence on the ground for them. This the children remembered.

This was a country of small steep hills, sudden descents into valleys, into folds of land that hid the road ahead and behind, that muffled sounds. The sloping fields were thick with the ripening corn, and Talleyman passed here and there the gates of farms, with big gate pillars of stone. There was no life in this land, and no work done. The cabins were deserted except for the occasional child.

There was something wrong now with the gait of the horse. It began gradually, a halting and a stumbling, a favouring of the near hind foot. It was the kind of thing that breaks in gradually on a rider's consciousness, competing with his listening. Though there was no telling how far, or in what direction, there was shouting somewhere, a general wave of sound. But the limping of the horse was more real. Talleyman swore. He dismounted, and carefully lifted the leg. The horse made a little noise of protest but it stood quiet while he looked at the hoof.

The thorn had been slid in very carefully, and was hard to find. It was harder still to ease out. The tissues were inflamed and swollen, but not too bad. There was nothing that an hour's rest would not put right, now in the middle of the day. There was a farm gate ahead on the left. Talleyman led the horse up the hill, and turned in through the gate.

This was a house, not a cabin. It was a decent-looking place, much larger than the last place he had stopped. There was a curl of smoke from one of the two chimneys. It had two windows up and two down, with a door between them for all the world like the kind of house that children draw, with a face; it would not have been surprising to have found this house smoking a pipe, here where almost everyone, old or young, men or women, smoked.

There was a low garden wall close round the house, and a wicket gate. Talleyman turned his horse into the paddock, and went to the door to knock. He had no luggage except for his nightshirt and razor stuffed into his pea jacket pocket. His valise was at the Canonry. This was no time to risk one's full dress. There was a long silence. He knocked again. After a little while, although the door remained locked, a child appeared at the corner of the house. It was not clear whether it was a boy or a girl — there was no telling whether the coarse stuff about its waist was the remains of a skirt or the beginning of trousers. It was, of course, barefoot.

'What's your name?' Talleyman asked.

'The Constaaabulary went tha' way,' said the child, pointing in the general direction of Killenaule.

'Did they, now.'

The child looked solemnly at Talleyman. All uniforms looked like the Constabulary, and certainly that was the way the police had gone, ever so many of them, frightening to a morsel like this, who had never seen more than two together. And this uniformed man, just as frightening, asked again, 'What's your name?'

The child regarded him. At length it felt safe enough to answer, 'Patsy McCormack.' Thus leaving its sex still in doubt.

'Well, Patsy,' the uniform questioned further, 'where's your father?'

The child puzzled still more. This was surely a thing everybody knew. This was the first adult in Patsy's short experience who needed to ask such a question. But the demand was repeated. Wearily, seeing that there might be no end to the stupidity of this stranger, the child offered, 'Me da's dead.'

The stranger seemed abashed. The child was conscious of its younger brothers and sisters looking round the house corner, behind the stranger's back. It put its finger in its mouth, and looked fixedly at the man in blue. The man asked now, 'Where's your mother?'

'Me mither's gone away to Killenaule,' said Patsy, because this was something she did know, and worth boasting about, 'with Mr O'Brien.'

'Which Mr O'Brien?' asked the man in blue, standing there so terrible still and tall and the buttons on him shining like the sun itself. Patsy looked fixedly at him a little more, and then lost courage and fled to the back door. Talleyman followed, and found a farmyard. There was a wall along each side, waist high, and at the far end, closing it off completely about twenty yards from the house, a long barn, with a door and a window in it.

Talleyman asked, 'Please may I come in and rest? My horse is not very well, but she will be better presently, when she has had some nice grass.'

The children now all concentrated their doubtful looks on him. Then they broke and fled into the kitchen. Talleyman followed. At least this was not a filthy cabin, all lice and the smell of starvation. The famine had scarcely touched here; there was no more poverty than in England. True, the potato patch by the back door was all curled and shrivelled, but the corn crop was good this year, if only the rain held off a bit for it to ripen. Hard times here, perhaps, but not perilous times. Not like the west.

There was even an armchair by the fire. Talleyman sat down in it. This kitchen was a kind of outhouse, with a roof sloping up to the top ridge of the house proper, so that the only openings on this side facing the barn were the door and the window. There was another door that must go through into the parlour.

Talleyman, sitting, stretched out his feet and leaned back. The children stood round him and stared. They wondered what he was doing, sitting down there so bold and nobody in the house to offer him so much as a cup of tea. Patsy thought that something ought to be done, but the kettle was too heavy to lift. It did not cross Patsy's mind to tell the stranger to help himself; in the child's experience, it was always the mother who made tea in that house, and there was no conceiving of anyone else's doing it. Talleyman broke the spell. He took out his hip flask.

'Could you bring me a cup of water? Please?'

Patsy heard him, and understood at the third or fourth repetition, found an old tin cup, filled it from a bucket by the well, next the midden. Talleyman inspected the colour and gravely thanked Patsy. He poured a little brandy into it. The children had never seen anybody drink spirits like that before. When their relations could get whisky, and they knew well enough by the smell that that was what he was about, they drank it neat, the aim being anaesthesia rather than stimulation. They wondered how long it would be before he began to sing or lay down on his back on the floor.

But Talleyman did neither. He just sat in the chair, and closed his eyes. He dozed. And that he was doing when the men rushed in.

8

Delauny was hot and sweaty with shouting and running. He was almost out of breath. They had nearly taken the Constabulary there, down by the barricade, but Superintendent Trant had taken fright, the arrant coward that he was, and moved his men off. Perhaps it had been the silence that alarmed him. But as soon as he began to move away, all the boyos had come pouring out after him.

Delauny was not running directly after the police. He was making off at a slight tangent, trying to get in front of them, to head them off. But there were not enough men with him to do it. It was easier to stay close behind the police and pelt them with clods, because they were sure that the Peelers would never shoot at them. Not for clods. So clods it was, because the boyos were afraid of muskets.

This was going to be another fiasco, and for nothing but the lack of a little patience. There had been one already, Delauny knew, two days before at Ballingarry. There were five men marching into the Constabulary barracks, and the sergeant there shaving and one constable cooking breakfast and the rest in bed. Five men and they had them at their mercy and the magazine there full of muskets and cartridges. And what had happened?

'Oh, but Mr O'Brien, sir,' the sergeant had said, 'if it's having to tell Mr Trant I am that there was five of you with two little pistols that came in and held up the eight of us and captured the hundred muskets we have in the armoury and the three thousand rounds, then sure he'll have the stripes off my arm and there's an end it will be to my hopes of a pension. Now, be a kind gentleman and go away and find a good big crowd, so that I can tell the superintendent I had to surrender to overwhelming force, and give me and the lads a bit of time to get dressed and the place put tidy and eat the bit of bacon we've got, and come you back in about an hour.'

Mr O'Brien had insisted that they do just that, arguing that Young Ireland had come to create that trust in the people and weren't the Constabulary part of the people and all good Irishmen at heart and ready to join the cause if they were only treated right. So it had taken them an hour by Mr O'Brien's watch before they came back and a great crowd with them of five hundred men and it was pikes they had too and a couple of fowling pieces and the women and children with them, all to the barracks gates. And by then, of course, the barracks were empty and even the smell of the breakfast eaten. The magazine doors were left wide open, and the racks were empty and nothing left but the smell of the powder and clean oil. All the arms had gone off with the men in a couple of carts, galloping as fast as they could go to Kilkenny.

There had been that fuss over a hundred muskets, and now again over forty, and probably forty of the ones they had missed at Killenaule, and not worth it. For were there not five thousand muskets on the way now from the coast, and food for five thousand men for a whole campaign with it, and had he not told Mr O'Brien of it? And Macmanus had been preaching it all the week till his throat was raw and how else to hold all these men together with not a bite of food for them. And by the end of this night, they would be coming in, all of them, for there was no bringing the carts in by day when the Yeomanry were scouring all the country as he himself had nearly been run down by them last night on the Cork road, all galloping and firing off their pistols in all direction.

Yes, thought Delauny, *we will have arms for a regiment before tomorrow dawn, but even these forty will not be wasted, if they teach the men we have that they can defeat the Peelers with their bare hands. And not bare hands only. We have five pistols, and thirty-three fowling pieces and a couple of old muskets. And we have the great advantage: the police are unwilling to kill us, and we are willing to kill them.*

9

The children had watched Talleyman for what seemed a very long time. They were all very hungry. They wished their mother would come home. Still, unwavering attention to the stranger was better than absolute inactivity: it gave them a sense of ownership, of belonging, of looking after the house.

Slowly, their minds were being distracted by a growing noise outside, coming nearer. This was shouting, no more mistake. Shouting, and with it the sound of feet moving at a run, military boots in a hurry, the nails clashing on the stones of the road in the remnant of a step. It suddenly changed to the shuffling of gravel.

The children peeped out of the back door, aware that behind them Talleyman was stirring, standing up. The doorway was darkened, boots crashed too near small bare feet, the children ran squealing into the centre of the room. The kitchen was full of uniformed men, with brass buttons and big terrifying guns, panting and blowing and swearing and stamping and piling in through the narrow door as though the devil were after them, crowding into the parlour and up the stairs as if there were too many for the house to hold, till the walls seemed to bulge in and out with their breathing. The children saw Talleyman pushed back against the wall with a musket barrel held across his chest, pinning his arms.

And at the last, it was a dapper man, even the children could see that his uniform was of a different cut, of better smoother cloth, that came in. He did not carry a musket, only a little switch with which he urged the constables on as if they were so many cows. Talleyman called out, 'Mr Trant! Superintendent Trant! Don't you know me?'

'Oh, merciful God in heaven, and it was only this that we needed,' said Trant with some fervour. 'And what are you doing here?'

'I have naval dispatches for General Hardinge.'

'Then it's not today you'll be delivering them, and if it's my advice you're heeding, you'll do well to put them on the fire now before the whole world reads them. Were you not stopped in Killenaule?'

'I came a long way round. The pretty way.'

'Thank the Lord for that. We don't want anyone seeing you here in that uniform.' He saw the puzzled offence in Talleyman's eyes, and sought words to explain. 'For 'tis a revolution that Mr O'Brien is mounting, and a revolution that's put down by the wicked English soldiery is as good to him as a revolution that succeeds. And if we have to bring in the navy as well, than 'tis a brighter feather in his hat than any we have seen yet, and he can go down to history with Wolfe Tone and all the other blessed martyrs that wasted the country's time. But if I can be left to handle this with nothing but the Constabulary, then it's nothing but a riot it will be, indeed, and the laughing-stock of history that Mr O'Brien will become. So keep that coat hidden, whatever you do, but you can be of use here. I haven't here another — what you would call an officer, and you can be taking charge here in the back room if it comes to anything.'

'A plague on all your houses,' said Talleyman. 'I know what the army says — revolutions are a civil matter, and we are not concerned. And why have you brought your men into this house? You're all trapped.'

'Why, and would you be staying outside when there's ten thousand of them after you, and running faster than you are? And there's a rumour that any moment now they're going to have a musket apiece for every mother's son of them and powder and ball with it, though I can't be seeing here more than a dozen guns altogether. And to tell you the truth —' and he leaned closer to Talleyman, spoke lower '— it's only if I have these men inside, Lieutenant, that I can trust them to stay within four walls and not to go running all off each of them all at once in the same different directions.'

Trant pushed around, looking into the front room, and then upstairs, shouting, 'Don't be pointing any of those muskets out of the window, and remember, there's none of you to fire unless I give the word, and even then there's nobody but me to do it.'

He came back to Talleyman. 'Now, Lieutenant, if there's nothing else useful you can be made to do, then come and watch what I must do, and be ready to swear to it in a court if it needs that, because it's the fate of Ireland that I have in my hands today, and there's some that will make the most of any mistake.'

Talleyman and Trant, upstairs, twisted to look between the shoulders of the constables. 'There are certainly a great number here. I can see no guns. But I can see some spears.'

'Spears? No, that's not spears, that's pikes you're looking at, and a noble weapon indeed as you know from Shakespeare.'

'When I saw them in Africa, we called them spears. But whatever the name, they can kill. Partridge was speared.'

'Which partridge?'

'Never mind.'

'Now how many would you be making this mob, Lieutenant? Would you be saying five thousand? Or ten?'

'It's hard to count. There are certainly more than five hundred here. There are unlikely to be more than five thousand. Shall we say "of the order of five thousand"?'

'Now, there's a fine mathematical phrase I would never have thought of using myself.'

'They are standing well back from the garden wall.'

'I think there must be some lying behind it, where we can't see them and can't reach them. That's where the guns are, and they worry me. Now, Lieutenant, if there's nothing active I can make you do, go and stand in the back room and give a little stiffening, for they'll be needing it and none but you to give it.'

Talleyman stood in the sweaty crowd. The children were whimpering in the corner. The constables looked at the sailor in curiosity, and stared at him till they made him speak.

'How many are you?'

The man next to him wore a sergeant's badge, and answered,

'Well, it was forty-five we were when we come, and I haven't seen anybody that's dropped down dead of fright already, so I suppose it's forty-five we are in here now.'

The crowd seemed quiet. The superintendent called from the front, and Talleyman pushed back to him. Trant was still watching the dense crowd, all standing still and not coming within twenty yards of the low front wall. They were shouting and waving, but not otherwise engaged in anything the police could call violence.

'There's the man that's keeping them firm,' Trant told Talleyman. 'That one at the back, there, in the white coat. Would you ever be seeing him before now?'

'I'm not sure. Those white coats are getting very fashionable.'

'Now, he's the one the crowd are listening to, and it's as if he's waiting for something, or got them to wait. Perhaps he's waiting for those thousands of muskets we keep on hearing

267

about that are coming from France or the Americas or wherever.'

'There will be no muskets,' said Talleyman.

'Well, it's hoping we must be that you're right.'

'I know. There will be no muskets. That's why they're so keen on getting yours. What's happening now?'

There was a commotion in the crowd, a parting in it as if someone was pushing his way through it, and having as much difficulty in moving out there as Talleyman was having inside the house. The man in the white coat had turned his back on the Constabulary and their guns, was pulling men aside. There was a tall hat coming forward, and a face visible under it through the gaps in the mass of other faces. One of the constables said, in a voice of awe, 'Christ, 'tis Mr O'Brien himself, the great Mr O'Brien.'

Trant gave Talleyman what he hoped was a meaningful look.

'Now, Lieutenant, don't you be showing yourself too near the window, or it's a bloody revolution you'll be calling down on us. Do you keep an eye on the man in white, because it's round to the side of the place he's going now, where soon we won't be able to see him, and it's too good he is at making them do what he wants for my liking.'

Talleyman went to the kitchen again, and stood against the inside wall, under a picture, where he could see the barn and at the same time hear what Trant was saying, and even see a little. Mr O'Brien had come to the gate in the garden wall. He stood there a while, hesitant, and then suddenly rushed down the path to stand alongside the door, his back pressed against the wall.

'Now, now, Mr Trant,' called Mr O'Brien, 'what are you hiding in there for? What are you afraid of?'

Trant now opened the front door and leaned on the jamb, talking round the corner to O'Brien, loudly, hoping that his words would carry.

'Look here, now, Mr O'Brien, if you had a great crowd running after you with pikes and mattocks and scythes tied on poles and all kind of other dreadful things, wouldn't you be taking what shelter you could, and hard it would be to get you out of it. Be a good gentleman, now, and tell all these to go home before they get into trouble.'

'And where would you be having them go that is more home to them than here, because it is in Ireland they are and Ireland is their home.'

'Now, don't be making clever big speeches to me, Mr O'Brien, all about politics, because there's never a word I can understand about it. But this I do understand, that I have in my pocket at this moment of my life a warrant for your arrest for treason, and well you know it, so be a good decent man and surrender to it quietly now and there'll be no harm done.'

'I recognize no warrant of a foreign government.'

'Now, 'tis a decenter government the Queen will give us than ever we'll make out of your Committee of Three Hundred.'

'Are you trying to trick me into saying that I am connected with them?'

'And if you aren't, then who are you connected with? And isn't it the big men of them I can see around, Stephens and Meagher and a few of the other boys. Now, where's Doheny today? And there's a few around here I don't quite recognize, but I will again.'

And that's too much said, Trant thought. *Maybe I've signed my own death warrant. Well, it can't be helped.* 'Now, isn't it determined you all are to share out the land equally to every Tom, Dick and Harry? A Red Republic they're after and that's what *The Times* calls it, and in an Ireland like that there'll be no place for respectable people like you and me.'

'And so be it's Irish, what better can you offer your own people, Mr Trant? Come, lay down your muskets, and come out of there and we'll all be friends. There's not a thing you can do now to avoid our independence. Better, join us now while it's early in the day, and you shall have a fine time of it after.'

They must be desperate for these muskets, Trant thought. Perhaps the sailor was right, there'd be none coming, but I can't bank on that. They're fascinated now by these weapons they can see here, and they've forgotten what they're about. The longer I can keep them here, the better it will be, and if I can just talk on and on, there's the crowd at the back will think there's no fun at all, and just fade away out of boredom.

He sounded a protest, 'And if we come out without our arms, how are we to live in that mob? I've no wish to have my head scythed from my shoulders. If you have any control over these men with you, then you must tell them to march away, or at least let us march away in peace as we stand.'

'No, you must leave your muskets behind. If you do not put them down, the people will not trust you. The people will have no faith in an armed police.'

'And they will not obey an unarmed police, either.'

Trant found Talleyman at his elbow. He said, softly, 'The longer we keep him here trying for the guns, the better off we are. I've got half the county force in here, but there'll be the rest along after they've been found and got together and had their dinners and washed their hands and faces and kissed their mammies. I wish we'd brought our dinners too. But if we can keep him arguing, there'll be no blood shed the while. That's what we can't afford, Lieutenant, because a man killed cannot be hidden or made light of. Now, back to the kitchen with you, and keep an eye on that white coat for me. It's round the side of the house he's gone, out of my sight, and perhaps into yours.'

Trant returned to Bronterre O'Brien, who was still talking away, regardless of who inside the house could hear him, but making sure that his voice carried to the garden wall. The men behind that would need to hear him.

Trant told him, 'Let me have half an hour to consider that offer.'

'Half an hour you shall have, and not a moment more.'

'Go back, then, Mr O'Brien, and tell your people that.'

'What, and let you shoot me in the back as I go down the path? No, I'll stay here against the wall where you can't get at me.'

True, there the politician was in dead ground. And the white coat was somewhere under cover, too, perhaps against the garden wall outside, perhaps somewhere more threatening. Talleyman watched from the kitchen window, but saw nothing, till one of the constables said, 'Look there! What's that sticking over the barn windowsill?'

They all crowded to look. The sergeant assured them, 'Oh, that … 'tis nothing but the handle of a broom stuck out to frighten us.'

'Then it's iron brooms the Widow McCormack had, and hollow handles to them, and firm strong hands to hold them steady.'

Everybody now was crowding to look at the barn window, except Talleyman, who still looked to the front of the house. Was it a musket barrel? The constables argued about it. Then suddenly they noticed that the barn door was a little ajar, and had it been, or had it not, an hour before, and was there not something sticking out of the slit there, sure and couldn't they all see it? They could not quite agree. The sergeant produced a pack of cards, and tried to get enthusiasm going for a game of some kind on the floor, but he was too late, the men would not be distracted from the window.

The shouting outside, which had died down while Trant was talking to O'Brien, had started again. The constable who had first seen the musket barrel stirred nervously. He complained, 'Arra, and it's a poor lookout to be killed for thirty-two pounds a year, and do nothing about it at all.'

'Nobody's getting killed,' Talleyman told him sharply. Nevertheless, here and there a musket hammer was thumbed back, a percussion cap fitted on a nipple. Nobody was talking any more. Silence in the house contrasted with the growing noise outside. Then there was a thud as a stone hit the front of the house, not too far from Bronterre O'Brien. Trant leaned out of the window, and dodged a large stone that went near enough to part his hair. It made the back wall of the parlour vibrate with the impact: the men in the kitchen felt the shock, and the picture fell to the floor as the flimsy nail jerked out of the plaster.

'We want none of this,' snapped Trant. 'Push a few musket barrels out of the window to frighten them.'

There was a confused murmur of agreement, a rattle of straps and piling swivels, as the men rushed to obey. The crowd saw the guns, and shouted louder. Some of the words could be heard.

'They're shouting O'Brien for King, and Up the Committee,' Trant told Talleyman. 'But mostly they're daring us to shoot at them.'

'Sure, and chance would be a fine thing,' the sergeant in his turn told the sailor. 'It's all I'm waiting for. There's been enough of the Constabulary killed already, and never a thing done nor a word in the newspapers nor any of the moonlighters brought to trial, although we all know who they are. And there's no place for them as sits all the time in Dublin Castle to be coming down now and telling us to hold our fire.'

'Never mind about shooting back,' Talleyman told him. 'Knock the glass out of the windows or you'll all be cut to pieces with the splinters.'

The shower of stones was getting heavier, and even coming over the yard wall to the kitchen window. It was a long throw, across the diagonal, but there were some missiles reaching the house. Then men began to jump the wall and come closer to throw sizeable pieces of stone. One came through the kitchen window and hit a man on the arm. He rolled on the floor, clutching it and making a shrill moaning noise.

'Tell your people to stop, Mr O'Brien,' Trant shouted. 'The half-hour is barely started, let alone up.'

'When the people are roused, you must hold them back with soft words, not with musket balls,' the politician answered. 'And that is all I can try to do.'

'Look out,' shouted a constable from upstairs. 'The bleeder is waving a handkerchief!'

'None of your secret signals here,' growled Trant.

O'Brien protested, 'It's only a flag of truce.'

But the constable upstairs shouted again, 'He's calling on them to attack us, and us with the barrels of their muskets thrust in our very faces!'

There was another shower of stones, and another constable lay on the kitchen floor with a bloody face and his teeth scattered around him. The stone-throwers were vaulting over the wall of the yard into cover. And then, with no order given, an indescribable wave of noise rolled over the house, inside and outside, clouds of white smoke hid everything. Who had fired first, Constabulary or rebels, there was no telling, but once started the shooting rolled on like a tide. Men fired, pushing their musket barrels between their comrades' heads to gain window space, reloaded, fired again, not seeking targets, not aiming, just firing in front of them in a blind panic of fear. Talleyman watched them a moment.

Then he began to shout, 'Stop it! Stop! Cease fire!'

He knocked up musket barrels, pushed men aside, sent the sergeant tumbling into the corner.

'Don't fire! What are you thinking of? Those are your own people out there! You are here to protect them. Don't shoot! Don't shoot *them*!'

As the firing died away, Trant could be heard shouting in the front room. The shooting from upstairs went on a little longer. Then there was a silence, except for a confused sound of moaning and whimpering from outside.

'If anyone's killed,' said O'Brien, in a weak shaking voice, 'the blood is on your head, Mr Trant.'

'Mr O'Brien,' the superintendent answered, 'your hands are washed in blood and reeking still. You have had what you wanted, and turned a riot into a rebellion. More martyrs were you wanting, then, like Emmet, to die like dogs here and then be turned into heroes for ever after? Get you back to your friends, and we'll let you go. *You're* not worth the shooting. There'll be no statue to you!'

O'Brien scuttled like a crab up the path, bending low as if he feared being shot at by both sides at once. The white smoke was clearing now as he dived behind the garden wall. The crowd had not dispersed, it had merely moved away, out of range of the muskets. There were a number of bodies on the ground where the mob had stood, most of them wriggling or crawling.

'Aye, but what's behind the garden wall, Lieutenant?' asked Trant. Sure, and hadn't the sailor come through to the front to see the fun? Then fun he should have. 'There's good cover there, and maybe anything.' He deliberately put his head out of the window. There was a bang, a plume of smoke lifted near the gate, a bullet thudded into the window frame.

'Oh, so they have arms, then. I tell ye, lads, the next that fire without orders, I'll send him out naked into that lot, I will.'

'If it's collecting bullets you are, Superintendent,' shouted the voluble constable from upstairs, 'then it's half a dozen we have in the walls and one in a dead man up here.'

'If he's dead, there's no time to be worrying about him. Sergeant Mullins, will you be taking a count of the rounds fired, now?'

They waited in silence. Most of the constables were lying on the floor, protected by the thick stone walls. At last the sergeant reported, 'One man dead, sir, and seven hurt, and a hundred and fifty-three rounds fired.'

It seemed incredible. Few of the men could have fired more than three rounds, and some less. Yet they felt they had been locked in an interminable battle.

Trant cursed them collectively and by name, scathingly. 'You came out with ten rounds apiece, for extreme emergency. And it's a third of that you've wasted in a disgraceful state of terror, when perhaps a dozen rounds between us would have done as well, or better if they were aimed properly. So that's a hundred and forty rounds that you'll maybe feeling the want of before the day's out, and nothing to show for it. Now, there's nobody to fire except in answer to shots, and then only the ones I call out. And even then not unless I say so. Donovan … Murphy … Beirne … Franky Sullivan … Lieutenant, will you be taking charge in the back room here?'

'This is a police matter,' Talleyman protested. 'It is a quarrel between Irish and Irish. I came here to help the starving, and bring the Irish food. I did not come to kill them.'

'Then it's having your head scythed off you'll be, for all your benevolence, if they get in here. Maybe I am not a magistrate, but it's calling on you I am to give aid to the civil power, as formally as I can. Will you not heed that?'

Talleyman said nothing, retired to the kitchen. As he entered, there was a shot from the garden gate, and a bullet brought plaster down in the parlour. There was an instant reply from upstairs. The men in the back room watched Talleyman go to the kitchen window.

'Let's see what they're doing out there,' he said in a conversational tone. He leaned, like Trant, from the window. There was a flash from the barn, and a bang, and the bullet flattened itself on the inside wall. Talleyman sat down hurriedly on the floor, next to the man who had taken the stone in his face.

''Tis a bit late for ducking,' said the sergeant. 'For if you know you've been shot at, then 'tis missed you've been.'

'Have you been under fire?' Talleyman asked him.

'I was in a Company regiment in India for twenty year, but never so hot as this.'

Talleyman said nothing more. The constables watched him take his big revolver from his pocket, and weigh it in his hand. Then he thrust it into the waistband of his trousers, and took off his pea jacket, showing his white shirt. He picked up a musket from the floor, sniffed at the muzzle to see if it had been fired, blew down it to extinguish any burning dottle. He took a cartridge from the bleeding man's pouch, bit open the end, poured in the powder, rolled in the ball, stuffed the paper in for a wad, rammed each down hard. He put a percussion cap on the nipple, crawled to the back of the room, and stood up, his feet in the hearth. He brought the musket to his shoulder, and waited for a movement in the barn. There was a flicker of something passing the window. Talleyman fired. A constable stood up at once to see the damage. There was a flash from the barn door, a puff of smoke. Before the report had finished echoing between the barn wall and the house, the constable was still on the floor.

Talleyman called through to Trant, 'We have a dead man in here.'

'I told you, there's no playing in this game.'

Talleyman alone was on his feet. He gestured to the door between the kitchen and the parlour. 'Get that off its hinges, and bring it round over the window. Leave me a slit to shoot out of.'

'Sure, and that will never stop a bullet,' protested the sergeant.

'You know it, and so do I, but isn't it typical of people that they think what they cannot see through, a bullet cannot penetrate?' Even the sergeant noted that this was the longest sentence he had heard Talleyman utter. 'I could kill the man at the barn door. Through the wood. But it would put ideas into their heads.'

He moved sideways, and there was a little whining screech like a cat. He looked down. He was standing on Patsy's bare foot.

'Somebody,' he ordered, 'look after the children.'

He took no notice of them further. The sergeant plucked at his leg, passed him a loaded musket. Talleyman took it, and stood watching through his slit for a long time. Suddenly, there was a shot from the barn. He answered it.

10

Delauny crouched in the barn. He looked bitterly around him. Three muskets in here, and perhaps a dozen more by the gate, all that would fire out of the near enough forty they had been drilling with, and perhaps ten or twelve rounds left for each. No more. But in the house, almost within their grasp, fifty guns, and nothing to do but contain them till the carts came. He cursed O'Brien's fine ideas. That white handkerchief fluttering in the breeze, no wonder the police had taken it for a signal. Certainly some of the Irish had. No wonder the shooting had started, and no arguing now over who had begun; wasn't it to be an article of faith from now on that it was the cruel Peelers who had attacked this innocent crowd?

And this was a bad business. O'Shaughnessy there was groaning and bubbling out frothy blood on the hay. That was the last time anyone would stand up behind the windows. Perhaps someone could try a shot out of a window, but carefully and at an angle — there was at least one man in that house who could shoot, and more, had the imagination to keep aimed on the right place. There was not the least hope, now, of getting men to rush the house, for too many of them had seen what this marksman was like. It was one thing to be a general and calculate, it's worth so many men to take that position. It's quite another thing to be one of those men and count the risk to yourself. *Not the risk*, Delauny thought, *for himself, not after all he had done in the west, and his having to leave the jetty and the ship tied to it and the muskets in it, and rush off to this meeting of the Council, in case they'd have him off it, and it had been a near thing, but they'd not dared expel him in front of his face.* So, there was no rushing the house. But while Delauny was lying here by the door, nobody could get out of it that way.

There was no getting in there, Delauny thought, *without risk*. Tags of wisdom floated through his mind, half-measures are no measures … infirm of purpose thou shalt not excel … stone dead hath no fellow … who had said that to him? And it was Talleyman's voice he heard now in his ear, *the chances of hitting a man in battle are small. Especially if you aim at him. Out of every hundred rounds fired in war, only one is fired to kill. The rest are let off to keep the enemy's head down.*

How, then, do we keep the police heads down? They are under a handicap already, they dare not risk killing women or children. But we, who are going to take the whole island, can kill who we like and tell our own story after it and blame the police. Must we lie here, then for ever, on the hay, and take their fire, because O'Brien will not take the risk, and will not let the women rush forward? Fire…? Hay…?

11

The police were waiting too, in the house. Every once in a while, there was a chance of a shot, at a movement inside the barn or round the corner of the buildings. Talleyman took it every time. The sergeant loaded for him. The men in the barn had copied Talleyman, and no longer came close to the window to shoot, but hid well back in the shadows.

Every time Talleyman fired, the smoke filled the room, making the police cough. Two of the children were sick. Talleyman and the sergeant agreed that it was a pity they were all thirsty but there wasn't a drop of water in the house. What had seemed at first a ludicrous situation had become, so soon, desperate. One of the constables suddenly spoke, in an urgent way, 'Sir, it's in the stable I'm needing to be going now. Do you think they'd be letting me out for that, under a flag of truce?'

Talleyman looked at him, puzzled. Then he laughed.

'You'll have to piss in the corner,' he told the man to the amusement of his colleagues. But soon most of them were forced to follow his example, and the stench became sickening.

There were two more policemen wounded in the front of the house, but none killed. The crowd was still there, standing all round the house out of range, watching this strange battle. The atmosphere, said Talleyman, coming to the front upstairs window to see Trant for a moment, was like a country fair.

'There's cheapjacks selling what they've got, and a man with some poteen making a few ha'pence … and over there, see, it's a Punch and Judy show!'

'Oh, but the news travels fast, it does. Except for telling anyone who matters. Where the county police have gone to, who knows? But let me tell you, while we have Mr O'Brien penned here, it's short of revolutions the rest of Ireland is going to be.'

'And England?'

'Oh, that's another matter entirely.'

The sergeant saw Talleyman come back with some relief.

'I think they're trying to dig into us, sir.' There was indeed a strange noise outside, a scraping and a scuffling. Talleyman listened, gave a verdict, 'Not digging. Softer sounding than that.'

He took another musket, flattened himself against the wall by the side of the window. Suddenly there was a movement between the edge of the window and the corner of the house, a man struggling with a sheaf of hay. Talleyman tried a shot. The man dropped the hay and ran for cover.

Talleyman told the sergeant, 'They're trying to burn us out.'

'What about the children?' the sergeant asked. 'Will they try to burn them, too?'

'We'll see. Push that door out of the way.'

He waited till the window was unmasked, and then waved his white handkerchief gingerly over the sill. When he was not shot at, he felt down the face of the wall with his hand, trying not to expose his face. He told the sergeant, 'I was right. They've pushed hay all along the wall, under the window. If it burns, the house may not catch. We may not have to go out. But it will mask the windows. They can rush the door under the smoke. Pile all the furniture against the door. And hold a child up to the window.'

The sergeant picked up Patsy, showed it in the window. Then Talleyman shouted, 'The children! Let the children out! Let them out!'

Patsy screamed. A woman was helped over the wall, came running forward between the barn and the house, screaming something, they could not tell what.

'It's the old widow McCormack herself,' said one of the constables, standing by Talleyman. 'Not but that she's so old, but who'd be a widow here and not grow old before your time?'

A priest came after the woman and caught her, steadying her, pleading with her, pulling her by main force back towards the barn. The door opened a trifle to let them both in. The men in the house could just hear what was being shouted at them from the barn.

'You want the woman in too, as a hostage? Is it hiding behind her skirts you'd be, then?'

'For God's sake, can't we let the children out?' Talleyman shouted. The sergeant began to lower the child towards the hay bales. A bullet struck the wall above the window.

'They can shoot better than that,' Talleyman told the constables. 'They want the child to stay here. They're using the children to make us surrender.'

The sergeant brought the child in again. One of the constables nursed it. He could not stop it crying.

12

Aye, it's another fiasco, thought Delauny. *And now O'Brien won't let us fire the place because the children are still inside, and he won't let us bring the brats out because he hopes the police won't be able to stand seeing them around.* Nothing was happening now, only time-wasting, time going by, time that could never be replaced. Delauny wanted to do something. *Who would ever be taking notice of a rebellion in a cabbage patch? At the best, we could storm the house, lose a few men, seize the guns and move on again. At the worst we'd make them fire into the crowd, and have a bit better shooting at them. Then we'd have the Constabulary hated throughout the country, not seen as a joke like they are now. If it were the English soldiers we could get up a bit of a hate of them easy enough, just for being here, and as for the Yeomanry, 'tis hated enough they are already. But there's no hate yet against the Police because when all's said and done, what are they but a pack of poor frightened Irish lads doing it for the money and nothing more, and hiding in there like a pack of dead scared rabbits not wanting to do any more harm and likely weeping enough already over the damage they've done. But just to lie waiting like this — it would make anyone curse.*

Somebody called him. He moved cautiously, crouching well below the window level, but he must have let a shadow be seen because a shot went over his head. He got out through the end door of the barn, and now he could stand up with two walls between him and that cruel fire. At last he could breathe air that was not thick with powder smoke and death and blood, James O'Shaughnessy's blood. And here was a man waiting for him with a desperate face.

'And is it you, indeed then, Malachi?'

283

Oh, then, it was all saved. There'd have been trouble bringing the carts over the mountains, and doing it in the dark for fear of the soldiers. There'd be the Limerick men to satisfy, and the men from Kerry, and the guns for the men with the carts, but there ought to be a good three thousand of them near enough now, coming in with the dusk. It was all right, they could wait till the dusk and then leave the Peelers to rot in their house and keep their puny fifty muskets and no ammunition left by then.

'Indeed it is, Mr Delauny, and lucky to be here. Oh, 'tis an awful business, a terrible business. Would you be having a taste of the stuff about you, then, only a taste to bring the life back into a man?'

Delauny found a pocket flask. Doyle wheezed over the mouthful of poteen.

'There's the spirit it gives me, that haven't had a bite to eat or a drop of anything since yesterday.'

'Then drink up, drink well, drink to the new Republic that we shall have in Ireland.'

'Oh, but 'tis a bad business.'

'What is?'

'Why, the ship, for she's taken and lost entirely.'

'Lost? You're mad! I was in her, and you were there, too.'

'Oh, indeed, there she was and moored to the jetty, and all the boyos come down with their carts and all. And you talking to that long thin officer you were always so thick with, and going off and leaving him there, too. As soon as you'd gone, why 'twas exactly where to look that they knew, and you saying you'd pulled the wool over his eyes. Or was it telling him where to look you were?'

'What d'you mean, telling him?'

'Somebody must have told him, because it was him, that long thin man, that knew what to do. Waited he did till all the men were down to the waterside with their beasts and carts and you well out of the way, and it was from miles around they were and four counties away, but up he steps as bold as brass to the sacks with his naked sword in his hand and cuts them all open right and left, and the guns all on the ground. And then they were with the ship full of soldiers in a moment of time, and shooting and killing they were in all directions and I saw James Brennan with my own eyes shot down and drowned in the water, and that was the end of it, because there was entirely nothing we could do about it all now, was there?'

'And was there nothing you did?'

'Faith, and what was there we could do? Could we fight all those hundreds of soldiers in their red coats and the sailors with their swords and all them with their muskets and bayonets and cannon as big as Bianconi cars, and us with nothing in our hands?'

There was a moment's silence. Doyle looked from one to another of the men around him. He tried again to defend himself.

'But look how many ye are here, and it's all willing to stay they are. There wasn't a moment there before the muskets were on the ground and not a man left to watch, for they were all across the hillside like swallows in September. You know what it's like out there, and the lack of food that takes the spirit out of a man—'

'And you can see what it's like here, now, Malachi Doyle, where it's hot lead that takes the spirit out of a man, when it's yourself that has left the salvation of Ireland fall into English hands. How in God's name can you face any of us? I'll see your name read out in every parish in Ireland as a traitor—'

'In every Protestant parish, you mean? There's a Protestant hand behind this, I'll be bound.'

Delauny jerked his musket forward. The hammer was back, Doyle looked into Delauny's eyes, and did not like what he saw there. Besides, the men around him were strangers, and they had been in the barn with Delauny: and they had come from all over Ireland expecting the muskets that Doyle had not brought them.

He asked, apologetically, 'And what is it you're wanting me to do now?'

'It's yourself can go to Mr O'Brien, and tell him, because it's myself that's afraid to face him with a thing like this knowing the edge of his tongue is something to put the fear of God into a judge. Go you and tell him that there's no guns for us, and explain to him that 'tis because of this brave thing you did for Ireland the day you ran away.'

'I'll go if you'll come along with me.'

'Then get along in front of me and it's hoping I am that you'll be fool enough to raise your head above the wall and get it shot off.'

13

The day was going by. Talleyman stood, always with a fresh musket, in the hearth. He fired, the sergeant estimated, about once in four or five minutes. The other marksmen seemed to be keeping up the same rate. Twice O'Brien stood up near the gate, waving his white handkerchief. Each time, Trant sent a bullet near him, not at him, but close enough to be discouraging. The attempt to burn the house, Talleyman pointed out, had got no further.

The men in the kitchen now found it almost intolerable. Little air came in through the slit in the window through which Talleyman fired. The smoke hung heavy in the room, there were the smells of blood and faeces, urine and vomit, and little light to endure it by. Occasionally, Talleyman and Trant came together to talk.

'How long do you think this will go on, Superintendent?'

'Indeed, and it is a question I am asking, because it is a long dinner the Kilkenny Constabulary are having, or hard they are finding it to catch their horses after they were out all last night watching this very road and place in case this great host of rebels should come out and attack the army and take General Hardinge by surprise and destroy him utterly.'

'Can *we* hold out in the dark?'

'If it comes to that, then the whole country you could say to be in a bad way. If it's sitting here all the night we're coming to, then we *will* be having a revolution.'

'You do not call this a revolution?'

'Now look carefully, Lieutenant, and you will see that we have the King and leader of all these Young Irelanders, William

Smith Bronterre O'Brien, Esquire, Member of Parliament, barrister at law, lying down here on his face in a widow's cabbage patch for fear of the likes of you and me and not many of us. If there was enough sense on his side to make half a revolution then we'd have been dead before we got in here. But as long as we're in here and we can see him lying down there, then I don't recognize anything to worry about, Lieutenant, except on the personal level, and men of the rank of you and me aren't supposed to think of the personal level, now, are we. It's all right for privates and constables to think about their whole skins, and who's to blame them, but not us.'

'That makes it no easier. Two or three days ago, it might have been different. Now... I have engaged myself... I am obliged to return to Cashel, soon.'

'And so you shall, have no fear of that. I must say that for your first time under fire, you're standing up to it very well. I've seen men that were brave enough to talk about it, but would not stand for a second shot.'

Trant saw Talleyman frown, and was afraid that his patronage had been offensive. But the sailor's face cleared. He asked, 'Why should it be my first time under fire?'

'Surely, at your age...'

'I joined my first ship the day the old King died. I have done two whole commissions out on the Coast, chasing slavers. If I had a hot dinner for every shot that's been fired at me, I'd have enough food to end this famine. I killed my first man, to know it, when I was sixteen.'

Trant was abashed.

'Sorry, I'm sure.'

Talleyman went back into the kitchen.

'Anything new, Sergeant?'

'Nothing, sir, not a move.'

As if to mark his words, a bullet came in through the window, nicking the edge of the screening door. The sergeant looked at the path of the bullet from door to wall, and said, 'Not from the barn, sir. That one came over the wall.'

They waited a little more in silence. Then the sergeant observed, in a matter of fact way, 'If they rush us with those scythes, then there's not much of a chance we'll be having. We'll shoot a few in the yard and more in the door, but not enough to stop them.'

'Your bayonets?' Talleyman asked.

'I'm not fancying myself with one of those little prods against a big fella with one of them mattocks.'

'They're afraid to move,' Talleyman assured him. 'We've shot enough to stop them. Each man thinks he'll be the first to get hit.'

The constables on the floor murmured agreement. They did not really believe Talleyman: but they felt more comfortable where they were.

14

From his Punch and Judy stall, the man called Smith from Brighton watched the leaders crawl from where they lay under the garden wall round to the side of the house, out of view of the windows. He worked his way down towards them, merging with the crowd in his worn frieze. He was soon close enough to hear O'Brien say, 'We cannot remain here any longer, after this, because it will mean further bloodshed, and that we cannot allow.'

Delauny protested, 'There's no revolution without bloodshed, and if the guns had got through, you'd never have been so squeamish about using them.'

Someone, Smith thought it might have been Meagher, said, 'There's been enough blood shed here already. Let it be over and done with.'

'Three dead?' Delauny attacked him. 'That's only a sprinkling. There was a thousand dead in 'Ninety-Eight, and that was a failure. How many do you think we must lose for a success? The guns aren't here — well, then, we must go on, and resign ourselves to losing more. But the country is with us. We must fight.'

'And die yourself, then?' someone asked. Smith could not make out who this was. But whoever it was, Delauny turned on him in fury.

'And is it not in that barn I have laid all the afternoon and faced the fire, and for all I know I've killed for the cause already? And there was a good man there was shot when he had his hand on my arm—'

'Here's another Peeler!' came a shout from the crowd. The man was dragged forward, someone else bringing his horse, as proud as if it were a colour he had taken.

'Where d'you come from?' Delauny asked. The constable stared around him, then asked, stupidly, as if dazed, 'Can none of you gentlemen tell me where Mr Trant the superintendent is, if you please, because I am Constable Carrol and I have a message for him.'

'He's in there.' There was a spatter of shot from the house as someone by the gate raised his head too high.

'Then it's out here you'd better be calling him, because there'll never be room for the sixty of us inside unless it's bringing some of them out he is, to hold the horses.'

'Sixty?' asked O'Brien. 'Is that true?'

'Of course it's true, sixty of us on horses, and would I be lying to you, Mr Smith O'Brien, that's a respectable gentleman and high in the Queen's trust, or would you be in Parliament and taking the oath to her otherwise? Look, you can see the rest coming over the hill.'

It was true. The long column was a mile away, but coming. Everybody, silent, looked at O'Brien. He said in a dull voice, scarcely audible. 'No more bloodshed. We can have no more bloodshed. There was blood for nothing in 'Ninety-Eight. There will be no more killed for nothing this time. I did not know … we must go away.'

'Here!' there was a shout, 'get on his horse.' Constable Carrol's mount had a government saddle on it, and a government brand on its hide. Somehow they got O'Brien up on to it.

'Where will you be going then?'

'I … I do not know … home, I think. I think I will go home … to Limerick…'

'And there goes nothing worth following!' shouted Delauny. 'There's no kingdom was ever won by cowardice.'

The crowd near Smith was in a hubbub. A mob of men pressed around Delauny, someone threatening, some defending. Doyle was screaming at him.

'You're over-eager to accuse other people of cowardice. That's my man going off there, that knows when we must try another tack.'

'We are on the right tack here,' Delauny bawled back at him. 'Use fire, and those muskets will be in our hands in five minutes, and we will have the rest off their horses as soon as they come near.'

But two or three of the men who had been in the barn with Delauny took him by the arm and dragged him, protesting, to the rear of the house, behind the barn.

'There was this horse, you see,' one of them explained, almost apologetically, 'and we found it in the front field when we got here, so it was keeping it we were for you to ride at the head of us so proud into Kilkenny. But now, you must be a long way off before the Constabulary get here, for there's many of them must have got a good look at you.'

'Whose horse?' Delauny asked.

'Sure, and there's no knowing, but what's a matter of horse stealing after what we've done today? It's going you must be directly.'

'I'll not run away. I'm staying here to fight. Better to die here than to live anywhere else, and run to do that.'

'Then you'll stay here and die by yourself. There's hardly a man left here out of the Council that came up so confident. We'll have another go at it with you, Lawrence, somewhere, somehow, but it's away you must be now, to work it out for us. Get away, man, get away, and fight again. And for the love of

God, drop your coat and take another, because it's that white thing of yours they'll remember you by.'

'I'll not let you be taken for me!'

'Now, empty the pockets. I'll not be taken for you, but I know who will be. And have you seen yourself? The powder is grimed into your face and hands. There's not a Peeler in the county will see you but will know what you're at — a blind man will know by the smell of the powder on you. Keep out in the air, man, and grow your beard to hide it, because it'll be more than a week's work to wash it out.'

Another man came running from the debating group at the side of the house.

'It's all settled. The Council's to split up. Doheny is away up on Slievenamon already, and Meagher is to go to the Comeragh mountains. You're to go back to Eyories, and see what you can find there, and if there's to be any more muskets.'

'Here's the horse. Up on it, now.'

'But there's O'Shaughnessy—'

'We'll see to O'Shaughnessy. Off with you!'

Delauny let them push him on to the horse. The coat they gave him stank of something unpleasant; what it was he could not tell, but it was not powder. The mounted constables were getting near now, trotting down the road in pairs, well spread out. There was a rattle of firing from the back of the house. When it died away, the only noise was the Widow McCormack crying, with the priest still trying to comfort her and keep her from rushing into the house. The man who called himself Smith from Brighton watched Delauny and reflected that he had done well to get ready money for that horse. And he wondered no longer who had been the stiffening inside.

15

The sergeant pointed out that the crowd outside were not shouting any more. There was instead a continuous hubbub like an angry sea or the crowd at a fair. There had been no shot from the barn for twenty minutes. Talleyman took out his pistol. Slowly, deliberately, he fired six rounds at the barn wall, in different places, marking the impact of the shots. He reloaded the weapon, and put it into his waistband again. There was one answering shot, but the sergeant, spotting, told him, 'Not from anywhere in the barn, sir, but from over the garden wall at the side.'

It was near dusk. Then the noise outside again began to change its quality. There was more shouting, and something metallic behind it, a drumming noise. They could not believe what they heard. Suddenly Trant put his head in.

'When I blow my whistle, do you be making a sortie for the barn, if you can get into it.'

He went back into the parlour. Talleyman took a spare musket, loaded it, fixed the bayonet. The constables followed suit. Talleyman stood near the kitchen door, motioned the men to take away the furniture that blocked it. The shouting outside was overpowering now, a mixture of screams and wails. Then the whistle. Talleyman ran through the opened door, and across the yard, doubled up. He stood erect again against the wall of the barn, alongside the door. The constables noted with interest that he was not killed. There was a distinct sound now of horses, and therefore when he beckoned them, they came out and lined the walls of the yard. From here they could see that the mob was dissolving, running away into the fields.

Talleyman stood at one side of the barn door, the sergeant and a couple of constables on the other. Talleyman brought his weapon to the high port, and then screamed, 'Now! At them!!'

He was through the barn door like a cannonball, the sergeant told Trant later. 'But if there had been anybody inside to see him against the light, a dead man he'd have been. 'Twas only the dead man we found there, in his white coat.'

Talleyman stood over O'Shaughnessy, dead. The bright blood had bubbled over the barn floor. There was a bale of hay dragged to the window, and on it, resting on a spread handkerchief, at hip height and convenient to the hand, were a box of percussion caps and half a dozen cartridges.

The sergeant was rooting around the barn. Talleyman picked up the handkerchief from the hay, stood wiping his face with it, thrust it into his pocket. He strode across the barn to the outer door. There was nobody outside. There was a mass of litter as if there had been a fair, or a prize fight, or a sale. The ground was cut up into muddy furrows by hundreds of feet. But there was nobody there.

Trant was standing by the garden gate. Under the wall, sheltered from the house, lay a couple of muskets, two or three coats, a bundle of newspapers. There were two shapes decently wrapped now in Mrs McCormack's blankets. A constable was reporting, 'Two hundred and four rounds altogether, sir.'

'Not two pounds' worth, Lieutenant. Cheap, d'ye not think, for a kingdom?'

Talleyman gestured at the bodies.

'They have entered their kingdom. And two of ours in the house, and another man in the barn. Is it so cheap? For them?'

'There are some things that are cheap, if you have to spend your whole life to pay for them. If my fools had not panicked, if theirs had not thrown stones, it would have been cheaper still. There's no use recriminating. It's me that's responsible, and that's fair, and it's me that will take all the blame, and that's fair too. That's what I am a superintendent for, to take the blame and make men hold their fire. For the rest of it, they'll say—' and he looked sideways at Talleyman — 'how long d'ye think we were in there?'

'Oh, an hour and a half. Two hours perhaps.'

'Four and a half hours of continuous firing on a peaceful and unarmed crowd that never suffered to run away not all the day, that's what the papers will say, because that's how long we were in there. Well may you look at your watch now, and say "Good God!" because you should know by now how time goes in action.'

'And now, I suppose, the blooding starts?'

'That's not in my hands. But look at it, we've made a joke out of the wisest man alive in Ireland, and the best since O'Connell died. A battle in Sackville Street, or round Saint Stephen's Green, that would have been different. Or if the guns had come they thought was on the way from America. But a ridiculous comedy like this — who will make a martyr of a man who lies down in a cabbage patch?'

'There are no heroes,' said Talleyman.

'But, what of the man in the white coat? He was the dangerous one. Was it him you shot in the barn, then?'

'There is a dead man in the barn. I think it is my bullet in his chest. He has a white coat on. There is no bullet hole in the breast of the coat.' Talleyman looked around. It was the litter that was the most obvious. Rubbish everywhere, the odd inconsequential discards of a mob, unexpected things, shoes, shawls, a crutch even, the overturned Punch and Judy tent. And over the hills, as at Eyories, a litter of people, in little groups or singly, moving away. For the most part they were not even running, but just going home as they might have been going from a fair or a market or a wedding, or a funeral. The dead were just part of the litter.

'Is this,' asked Talleyman, 'how rebellions end?'

It was beginning to rain now, a fine light mist that would soak into everything, lay the dust on the roads, hide the hill tops. *Is this*, thought Delauny bitterly, *how rebellions end, in the rain and the dirt, with the leaders sneaking away separately, each one trying to find his own hole to hide in*. Nothing for Delauny to do now, but to find somewhere to hide.

'This isn't the end,' Trant told Talleyman. 'There'll never be an end to it. There's a curse on this land and 'tis beyond our power to lift it. All I know is that I am here to keep order and punish the wrongdoer, whatever I think in my heart. And what helps me is that as long as it stayed here, that crowd weren't going off to find worse — meet the Yeomanry and be chased over six counties, or meet the real English Dragoons and be cut to pieces.'

'I did not come here to fight,' said Talleyman. 'I came here to bring the people food. And this is the thanks I get..'

16

Delauny went west, keeping off the roads, over vast ruined deserts of blighted potatoes, skirting the woods and keeping near the hedges. It was getting dark. The horse was limping a little already when he mounted, and he did not dare hurry. When it was quite dark, he went into a little wood. He thought that here he could rest the mare, and in the morning he could make better speed. He had changed his coat, he could put on a deep Irish voice, he would fool a constable yet. He sat down with his back to a tree to watch to the dawn.

In spite of himself, Delauny fell asleep. When he woke, it was broad day. The horse had gone. He wasted some time trying to find it. At last he gave up and began to walk west, skirting the woods still for fear of getting lost. He avoided the roads. He did not go to any farmhouse or cabin.

Twice he saw cavalry on the road, Yeomanry he thought. At any rate they wore red coats and gay plumes in their hats, and that was a fine rigout to wear to hunt down poor men like himself, who had not a change of clothes to boast of and did not know where the next bite was to come from. And to hunt himself, above all, who was all wet through and hungry for he had not eaten since yesterday morning in Killenaule, when there had been a morsel of bread and cold meat and left that on the table in a hurry when the word came that the Constabulary was marching in their hundreds and thousands to pull down the barricades. And he was covered in mud, and cold with it this August day, and nowhere to shelter but the ditch.

It was that day the resolution began to dawn in him. It had nothing to do with Ireland, or the abstract idea of freedom, or whether O'Brien had been right and O'Connell wrong, or any other matter at all of religion or high politics. It was the injustice that was at the heart of it, that those fine well-fed men, in good clothes, riding on good horses and wanting for nothing that a poor country could be made to provide, should come out to hunt him and the other poor men down. It hurt, it did that, it hurt. The injustice of it, and the envy, entered into his soul, firm. He was being hurt, then, was he? So, and why was it not himself who would hurt them back?

Towards dark he began to know where he was, and to pick up a remembered rock or two, and a bearing on that peak up in the Shehy mountains. There was a wood he knew, and a place where the men came to dig turf, and here he hid among the turfstacks till it was dark and he could go to a cabin door and rattle on it, calling, 'Mrs O'Shaughnessy! Brigid O'Shaughnessy!'

The door opened at last. The glow of the turf fire spilled out on to the ground. The woman peered out at him, where he lurked against the house wall.

'Oh, merciful God, Mr Delauny, and is it yourself then, and alive? And have you no news of my James?'

'I have not. Not since yesterday, for 'twas then he was fighting alongside me, and wounded he was but only a scratch, and many there to look after him and see him safe. It's back to you he'll be in a few days, and never fear.'

What else could he say, even if the woman answered, 'Oh, but it's the Peelers may have got him by now. Oh, Mr Delauny, what are we going to do without him, what are we going to do now?'

Delauny had no answer. He sat down on the bed, the only piece of furniture in the cabin. The children looked at him curious, silent, wide-eyed. He avoided their eyes, they were more than he could bear. He asked, 'Have you nothing to eat?'

'I've nothing in the house at all, Mr Delauny, but a handful of broken crusts I did beg from a lady on a Bianconi, and that's the sacred truth, it is, now. But whatever there is you can have your share of, for James' sake.'

Delauny felt in his pockets. He still had his purse, and his pistol.

'I have a little money.'

That was not literally true. He knew that he had thirty-seven pounds in gold, besides silver, and that was more than a pair of O'Shaughnessys could earn in a year, and then they would have to pay the most of it back for rent for the bit of a cabin and a quarter acre of potato patch whether it had the blight or no. But it was not Delauny's money, though it had been paid him, a fair wage, for working on the jetty. It was Ireland's money, he reminded himself, paid him to fight a war with, paid him to kill soldiers with, those fat and well-fed Yeomanry on their fine horses in their warm coats. He could not let her have it, though she starve. Nor could he spend more on himself than was absolutely necessary. He asked, 'Can you buy me some food?'

She considered. 'I can, but it's not tonight for if it's going out that I am, then they'll be knowing that there's someone here with me, and there are those about here that would sell their own flesh and blood for bread and say it stuck in their throats while they still ate it. And I cannot be changing a big piece of money like that half-crown because they will all know about here what a state I am in. But there is someone I know who is of the Brotherhood and is a friend of James', and in the morning I will find a way to him and I will see if he is still to be trusted.'

With a dry crust in his belly and a drop of clean water with it, Delauny lay down on the floor by the fire. He hung his clothes up to dry in the hope that the peat smoke would drown out the smell of powder. One of the children woke him before light to take him back to the peat stack where he could hide and watch the road. The rain had stopped. He felt he could sleep to the end of the world, but he did not dare let himself drop off.

About mid-morning, with Brigid O'Shaughnessy long gone past with her half-crown, a man came by, the other way. He left the road, and came near the peat stacks, as if he were looking at the state of the diggings. Delauny took out his pistol, and made sure it was dry and the cap on the nipple. It might well be that by now 'twas death to have a pistol, but what he had done already was enough to bring hanging a hundred times over in any court in the world. He would hang with Mr O'Brien, and be happy with it, if it came to that, but wasn't that a waste it would be? The man came as far as the other side of the stack, and spoke aloud, 'Is it listening you are, Lawrence Delauny? Now be you hearing this. Stay up here today, and be ready to move tonight. We have enough friends to get you clear from here, but it's not safe to move in the day. The whole country is full of the Yeomanry looking for Mr O'Brien, but they'll snap up anything else they see. They haven't caught any of the Council yet. I'll leave ye something, and they will come for ye to the cabin when it's dark.'

He moved along the road. Delauny waited till he was well away, then came cautiously round the side of the stack. He found a twist of rag and in it a round of bread and a few pieces of boiled bacon. He gobbled the food in a few moments. He was beginning to feel the intense depression that comes with the first hunger. There was nothing to do now but to wait till dark. He found a trickle of water and drank of that. There were still a few drops of the stuff in his flask, and now he felt confident enough, in spite of all, to drain them, almost squeezing the flask to press out the last trace of the poteen. *At least*, he thought, *that had never paid a penny towards the soldiers.*

When it was dusk, but not full dark, he had not the patience to do anything but set off down the hill, persuading himself that if he stayed longer he risked losing his way or twisting his ankle. He let himself into the cabin without knocking. Brigid O'Shaughnessy gave him a bowl of maize stirabout, paupers' food, and a mug of weak tea without sugar. It was the first hot meal he had had in sixty hours. He began to recover his hopes. When he had finished, the woman burst out, 'He's dead, they tell me, James is dead, he's dead!'

'Oh, merciful God help us, no!'

What else could have been expected, the man shot through the chest like that and bleeding like a fountain? And yet it was the awful shock of it, that a man who had marched so cheerfully across the hills a couple of days ago should be dead, and all because I came here and called him out to join us, late in the day.

'What's to become of us? What's to become of us all?'

'What's to become of Ireland?' Delauny answered lamely. But she sneered at him.

'Ireland can look after herself, she's big enough. But who's to look after us?'

There was a rap on the door. Delauny crouched back in the corner, and took out his pistol again. But the woman slid open the door a crack, and the voice he had heard at the stack whispered, 'Are ye ready, then? We've a long way to go before the end of the road.'

He hesitated a moment. Should he not leave the woman at least a sovereign or two? But no, that was not his money to give away in private charity, it was Ireland's money and the means of waging war. He went out into the dark.

They walked twenty miles that night, before a place was found for him to shelter safe through the day and a boy to watch nearby so that he could sleep in peace. After dark it was quite different men who came to help him through fields and bogs and once across a river in a leaky boat. He never asked names. Whatever they were, Molly Maguires or Peep-o-Day boys, he took care not to know. And he dared not ask them what rankled — why they had not been out ten days before, with him and O'Shaughnessy and all the other brave fighters. Yet, they were the right boyos, he could swear it. These were the men who had lived through the famines and the evictions and they knew that there was nothing but bloody war would serve the Irish now. And war, he vowed, he would wage when he could. *I shall give them such a stroke*, he thought, *that they shall never know who kills them*, and he knew it was an echo of something read long ago; but he could not remember what.

The boyos could tell him about the siege of the house and the fight in the barn as they knew it, and the dreadful things they revealed to him pressed home the point.

'They're saying that they left the farmhouse in a dreadful state, them hundred Peelers you had caught inside it,' he heard. 'All the widow McCormack's furniture they broke up, every stick of it, and there was a picture of the Holy Family and Daniel O'Connell himself they pulled down from the wall and danced on, and they stole the blankets from her best bed. And all the filth — they made water and worse all over the floor of the kitchen, and left their vomit on the chairs and there's not a penny compensation she'll get from Government, and it's them that ought to pay well for it. Sure, 'tis dead drunk the Peelers must have been to do such things.'

'They were not drunk,' Delauny assured them. He remembered that nightmare in the barn, the enemy who saw the slightest sign of movement, and hit it sure, dead sure, dead sober sure. 'But they will pay.' He did not say, in money.

He asked, 'What news of Mr O'Brien?'

'Sure, there's nothing known of him now, save that he is gone off to the north. They do say that he is trying to reach Limerick, his own place, and there'll he be as safe as you are. There's nobody will inform on him there, if he hide down tight in the woods.'

But Delauny, cold and hungry and wet, shivering on the edge of a rainy wood on a moonless night, wondered if an O'Brien who had not the strength of will to press on with the attack on the farm could face life on the run.

17

'The news, I must tell you, is very bad.' Talleyman was with Harriet in the Canonry at Cashel.

'You have seen Lawrence?'

'No.'

'Then where is he?'

'Well may you ask. I hope he is far away. I will tell you this, he stole my horse.'

'Don't you dare call my brother a horse stealer!'

'He was welcome to it. That was the least of the affair. If others can keep quiet — there is nothing firm against him, only the tale of a white coat. But I have this.'

He laid the handkerchief on the table.

'That is Lawrence's.'

'You lent it to me. I gave it back to him. He left it where there could be no doubt — he has been engaged in a rebellion.'

Harriet was silent a moment. Then, 'Mr Talleyman, you must help.'

'There is nothing I can do. I cannot believe that his friends will keep silent. There will be a warrant out for his arrest at any moment. And for treason.'

'I mean, help me. My father — his father — must not know that there is any proof of this, and if I can stop him hearing of it at all, I will do that.'

'I don't see how that is possible. For a time, perhaps...'

'Then even a short time is worth gaining. His heart will break. Mine has already broken.' If it were possible to blush by trying, then it must also be possible to go pale. Tears were easy. Every girl knew how to hang on the edge of tears. *This that*

Lawrence has done makes it more important to get away, and here is the only way to do it. I must cry, thought Harriet, *I must weep buckets, and that will break him. My father doesn't care about Lawrence, only about himself and what such a scandal will do for his own reputation. Why should I be any different to those who have taught me?*

'Life, Mr Talleyman, will be very difficult for both of us here when all this comes out.'

That is not true, everyone knows about Lawrence already, they'll only wag their heads and say, sure and we knew he'd gone to the bad and this is the end of it. Now, I can hear the shuffle on the stair, that soft tread in the hall, different from the noises in the street and the clatter from the kitchen. This is the time to strike. 'Mr Talleyman, you must look after me, there is nobody else I can rely on.'

She was in his arms, crying, the tears soaking into the shoulder of his pea jacket, the acrid powder smoke making them run better than she had hoped. This, though she did not know it, was how Jane had clung to him the night the house had gone up. There was nothing better, though she did not know it, to bring back to him the vague confused emotions of that night, fear and excitement and desperation. He could only hold her to him, stroke her shoulder, say, 'Now, there, there. Do not cry. I will help you. You are not deserted.'

And it was at that precise moment, glory to God, that her father came in on them. And Harriet knew, not Denain Hall, but at least Fen Dilney Manor was safe.

18

After a week Delauny was in the wood he knew best. He could look down on the great house from where Talleyman had stood with Jane, and from there he could see the vicarage too. It was a long wait till the early evening, when Mary Flannery came wandering to the end of the path. He stepped out to her, and she was in his arms.

'Oh, in God's name, what have you been doing? And why have you come here? Don't you know there's been a warrant out against you by your own name, and that Captain Foster has been here to seek you?'

'My name? How is that? Who would betray it?'

'Look! I've brought you the latest paper.'

It was *The Times*, three days old, only come to the house that morning. He read his own name, he was wanted on a charge of high treason. But how had they got his name? He read further. There was a spirited account of the activities of the man in the white coat, and how the coat had been found but not the man. But there had been caught a man by the name of Doyle who could be proved to have been raising forces in the west a day or two before. After a long interrogation he had turned Queen's evidence and saved his skin, and blamed all on Lawrence Delauny. But there was not a word about the ship with the guns, not in Malachi's tale nor in the paper anywhere else. Oh, Government would never tell that tale: they would never admit that all those guns came so near to the hands of the Irish.

'But there's hope yet,' he told Mary, 'for Mr O'Brien is not yet taken. We must get to Limerick, and begin to form the Army again.'

'But that is an old paper. The tale was all round here yesterday. He went into Thurles and was arrested at the railway station. He was bold as brass, for he asked for a ticket for Dublin, and demanded it free because he was a Member of Parliament. So shouting his name he was, all over, and never any attempt to hide who he was, and it was arresting him they had to be, to stand his trial for treason. There's courage for you.'

'There's foolishness for you. They'll try him, and he'll be sentenced to transportation, and he can go with Mitchell and live in the Governor's house in Bermuda and have what food and visitors he likes and make all the money in the world out of writing his memoirs. There's others of us will never give up the fight while we're still free to move, like he's so quick to do. But, what's happening in the house? How is my father taking it? Can I come in here and hide, if only for a night?'

'There's no chance of that at all in the vicarage, for we've got Mr Roding living in the house, and a fine state he is in for fear Lord Denain will turn him out of his agentship because Philip Suttle went off with his daughter. If he sees you and he's sober enough, he will turn you over to the Constabulary as soon as look at you. Your father's in Cashel, and Harriet, and I suppose they're safe.'

'What am I to do?'

'There's nobody living in the mansion. It's safe you'll be there as long as you don't show a light. What it's like inside, I don't know, because the boyos have been around in it to see what they could have, and the Constabulary searched it three days ago, and they won't have left much for them to come back for. I'll bring you blankets up, and food.'

Delauny stayed in the echoing empty rooms of Ballyfine House for three more days, sleeping in blankets from his own boyhood bed on the floor of what had been Jane Roding's room, where there was an easy way out and down by the creeper. Or up? He wondered which way to go, for he knew the roofs well. He kept his pistol by him. On the second day, he almost used it but it was only one of the Clubmen who brought him news safer than the English papers.

'They're all for France. Stevens and Doheny are trying to get across the water from Dungarvan. There's been things said about them in the papers, and we can't hide them. Them reporters are more danger to us than the Peelers, because they search as though their hearts were in it, like hungry dogs, while the Constabulary will do no more than will earn their keep. But the crowds of reporters watching give the game away when a decent man does so much as change his coat. And 'tis lies they print about us.'

'You think I had better leave the country, too?'

'And what else is there to do? Do you not know that it's denounced you've been from every altar in Ireland by every priest there is, with the rest of the Council, because that Church has turned against us, that would have had the land to play with if we'd won, and taken it too. There's no hope for you here. If you stay, then sooner or later one of these good religious people will turn you over to the Peelers and what's to become of you then, or the people who have been hiding you? Think of them. No, 'tis clear away you must get. It's a figure of fun they may make of someone important like Mr O'Brien Member of Parliament, but the little men like you or me can look for the rope, or Australia for life.'

The next day, Mary came out to him again. He asked her, 'Bring me out some of my own clothes that are still in the house — a thick coat and breeches, and one of my best shirts that I left when I was off to Eyories that time. And a strong pair of my own boots: the brown highlows would be the best. Now, do I look like me?'

'That you do not, any more. You've not shaved for a week near enough, and there's a look about you — not starved, but like a hungry dog watching for things. Yes, like a wolf, although I've never seen a wolf, but what other word is there? I cannot remember you like this before: and I will not remember you like this.'

'I shall keep these rags on till I am safe. I think I am changed enough to pass, unless I meet someone who knows me well, and he is looking on purpose for me. But even then, not many would give me away, for those around here who don't like me being in these parts will be afraid of the Molly Maguires, since few of them like better being shot in the back.'

'Where will you go? To France? That's not far.'

'The ships to France will be too well watched. Think how few Irish go to France except to run from the Peelers. I must go to America. We have friends in Boston, who arranged the cargo, and there are so many of us going now.'

'And when will you return?'

'I do not know. When Ireland is free, perhaps. Perhaps never. Here, what are you crying for? Did I say more than that I would go? Did I say you must stay?'

She ignored it, not believing, for it was the kind of thing men said.

She asked, 'How will you live?'

'I am an engineer, a surveyor. They must have plenty of work in America, for 'tis roads and canals and railways they're building all across the country. There'll be plenty of work, you mark me. And as soon as I am right settled there, I will write to you and send the money and when I do you must leave all this and come straightaway. I shall be sending money for you to come comfortable. I will not have you travelling the way I will be travelling.'

'There is a ship at Castletown,' the Moonlighters had told him. 'They are asking five pounds for the passage, and there is a factor at Castletown will sell you meal for the journey for a sovereign, and a blanket for five shillings.'

19

Delauny came into Castletown, and bought his ticket from a man who sat at a desk in the corner of Clancy's front parlour. The ship looked small against *Santorin*, lying there between the town and the island, but it would do for this voyage. It would only be a short trip in September.

Delauny bought his meal. A blanket he already had, a good one taken off his father's bed. The people were waiting at the quayside in a long patient line. He had not thought a ship could hold so many, but almost immediately he had taken his place there was a man behind him for every man in front, and women too, and children of all ages, and not every one had a bag of meal.

They could not go on board yet. There was some trouble, the man from Clancy's was telling them, the Constabulary was there to look over all the emigrants, and till the special man was come that had wind of something, there was no letting them into the ship. Delauny reasoned that it might be him they were after, but with the Peelers on the ends of the quay there was no chance to run for it now. If he moved out of the line, they would have him.

There was talk around him, and he listened. Everyone was sure that there was one of the men from the cabbage patch trying to get on the boat. But there were so many single men in the line, going out in the hopes of making money quick to send home, they would have to look close at every one of them if the Constabulary were to find him.

But there were many families as well as the single men, husband and wife and children all together, clutching what little they had. And not many, for all that without the sack of meal and the blankets. As Delauny stood there and felt the fatigue slipping away and the hope coming back that even here he might be in luck, he began to distinguish faces and people again, to know who was who and what was happening. He looked to the family that stood behind him in the line, and he felt a chill.

'Noonan,' he asked, 'Patrick Noonan, is it you?'

'It is that, but there is no one will be greeting *you* by name, for there's no safety for any of us that way, and it's better we'd be liking it if there were somewhere else you would hide and not bring the Peelers on us at the last.'

'I have not seen so many of you since the jetty was building. But why are you — why are so many from Eyories leaving at last after all our labour? Is it the rebellion?'

'It is not the rebellion,' said the man in front of him.

'Hogan, is it not? Hogan, from Ballyfine?'

'There was no more in that rebellion than there is in the wind. What use was guns to men that wanted food? What use is freedom to a man who is starving? What can an Irish Parliament do for a man who has no land to live on?'

'And so, it is to the land of liberty you are going?' Delauny asked weakly.

'Another land of poverty it is, by all accounts,' said Hogan, 'and thousands dying in the streets of Canada and in the islands about it.'

'And it's not by our will we're going, for all that,' Noonan contradicted him, 'for would we be going if there was any hope that even a rebellion would let us stay? It's all Lord Denain's doing, curse on him and on his soul for ever.'

'What has he done?'

'He has started the evictions that he said he would, in his great speech in the Parliament. There's cabins he is pulling down on all his estates, and the people he is driving to the ports with the sodgers to see we gets here. And he is packing us all off with our tickets and a bag of meal and a blanket and five pounds in money for each family, and 'tis cheap he's getting the land to himself and no one to dispute it with him.'

The line began to move. Man by man, family by family, the Irish were going into the ship. The constables stood at the gangway, uniforms and muskets showing. Two men detached themselves from this group and began to walk down the line. One was a dapper man in a smart uniform, a superintendent. The other was in a different uniform, tall and thin, coarse-featured, stony brown eyes visible from far.

Delauny watched Talleyman come down the line, looking into each face. He forced himself to stay where he was, humping his bundle on his shoulder. He tried to hope that the beard and the dirt and the hungry look, the crazed look he had seen for himself in a mirror, the look of a man who had stood to his gun in the barn, would hide his name. But he knew it was a false hope, that this man had looked before now into his soul, and there was no hiding a soul under dirt.

The line moved slowly. Talleyman had stopped. He was watching the people move past. *You can hide a face*, thought Delauny, *you cannot hide a walk*. He looked at Talleyman and hated him, hated him for being well-fed and healthy and strong, for being free, the servant of a real government, with authority in his step and in his voice and in his face. Delauny hated this man who could walk away when he liked, who could go down the streets of any town and not look behind him, who could go into any inn and call for what food and drink he wanted and not fear the boy who slunk off to call the police to deal with him, who could buy what he wanted, read what he wanted, live in public and give his name to anybody loud and clear. And above all, now two weeks after the cabbage patch, he hated Talleyman for being so clean.

Delauny came closer and closer to Talleyman. This was the time, then. They had caught up on his track. There was one man on their side who knew him well enough not to be deceived. And he was here. Delauny drew level with the policeman. He tried to look down, but he could not lower himself to that. Talleyman caught his eye, held it. Delauny looked back at the man who could not be deceived. He sensed that he was not deceived. He looked steadily into those brown eyes, blank and smooth as a pool among the peat. Then someone was pushing into him from behind, so that he had to turn his head away, and stumble up the gangplank into the ship.

'No, superintendent,' he heard Talleyman say loud and clear behind him. 'I know Mr Delauny very well. I do not see him here.'

A NOTE TO THE READER

Dear Reader,

If you have enjoyed the novel enough to leave a review on **Amazon** and **Goodreads**, then we would be truly grateful.

Sapere Books is an exciting new publisher of brilliant fiction and popular history.

To find out more about our latest releases and our monthly bargain books visit our website: **saperebooks.com**

Printed in Great Britain
by Amazon

85459075R00180